ms MER

"Just d
you're in love with him."

"Don't be absurd," Gwen said.

"Ha. You *are*," Melody crowed. "Aaron must be great in bed, because you two are complete opposites."

"I haven't slept with him, for God's sake." Gwen stood, tugging her suit jacket into place. "And I am most certainly not in love with him."

Melody laughed. "Well, you're in something with him. But be careful. This would not be a good time to lose your job."

Gwen rolled her eyes at the other attorney. "I'm going now. And leaving our case in your hands. We have to get this right."

Still sitting at her desk, Melody became serious. "We'll do fine. Just promise me no more surprises like Aaron Zimmerman. Seriously, Gwen. Stay away from him until we get the hearing behind us."

Gwen left without explaining how hard staying away from Aaron was proving to be.

Dear Reader,

Opposites attract—except when they're lawyers. Put two opposing attorneys together and you've got mostly a war of words. At least until they begin to listen to their hearts. Yes, lawyers have hearts! And when they fall in love, they fall hard.

When I first set out to write about prosecutor Gwen and defense attorney Aaron, I had no idea where these two would take me. But they showed me the way, along a winding path, over a multitude of obstacles, and under each other's skin. It was an emotional journey to explore lawyers falling in love against their inclinations. It was also enlightening to delve deeply into their world, discover their hopes and dreams, and reveal how personal growth can evolve when least expected.

I invite you to join Gwen and Aaron on their journey. And I want to know what you think of their story. Please write to me through my website www.ElizabethAshtree.com. Or follow me on Twitter @eashtreebooks.

Elizabeth Ashtree

Reconcilable Differences

Elizabeth Ashtree

TORONTO NEW YORK LONDON
AMSTERDAM PARIS SYDNEY HAMBURG
STOCKHOLM ATHENS TOKYO MILAN MADRID
PRAGUE WARSAW BUDAPEST AUCKLAND

If you purchased this book without a cover you should be aware that this book is stolen property. It was reported as "unsold and destroyed" to the publisher, and neither the author nor the publisher has received any payment for this "stripped book."

Recycling programs
for this product may
not exist in your area.

ISBN-13: 978-0-373-78465-3

RECONCILABLE DIFFERENCES

Copyright © 2011 by Randi Elizabeth Dufresne

All rights reserved. Except for use in any review, the reproduction or utilization of this work in whole or in part in any form by any electronic, mechanical or other means, now known or hereafter invented, including xerography, photocopying and recording, or in any information storage or retrieval system, is forbidden without the written permission of the publisher, Harlequin Enterprises Limited, 225 Duncan Mill Road, Don Mills, Ontario, Canada M3B 3K9.

This is a work of fiction. Names, characters, places and incidents are either the product of the author's imagination or are used fictitiously, and any resemblance to actual persons, living or dead, business establishments, events or locales is entirely coincidental.

This edition published by arrangement with Harlequin Books S.A.

For questions and comments about the quality of this book please contact us at Customer_eCare@Harlequin.ca.

® and TM are trademarks of the publisher. Trademarks indicated with ® are registered in the United States Patent and Trademark Office, the Canadian Trade Marks Office and in other countries.

www.Harlequin.com

Printed in U.S.A.

To my son, Nathan, an aspiring author who writes better than I could ever hope to—may all his aspirations be realized.

And to my husband, who patiently listens to and consults on the motivations of my fictional characters.

ABOUT THE AUTHOR

Elizabeth Ashtree (or, more precisely, the person who uses this pseudonym) holds a B.A. in Anthropology and a J.D. from the College of William and Mary. She served as an officer in the U.S. Army Judge Advocate General's Corps and is currently an attorney for the Department of Defense. She lives in a log home on several acres in rural Pennsylvania farm country with her husband and little dogs. It's the perfect place for a writer.

Books by Elizabeth Ashtree

HARLEQUIN SUPERROMANCE

Don't miss any of our special offers. Write to us at the following address for information on our newest releases.

Harlequin Reader Service
U.S.: 3010 Walden Ave., P.O. Box 1325, Buffalo, NY 14269
Canadian: P.O. Box 609, Fort Erie, Ont. L2A 5X3

CHAPTER ONE

"YOUR HONOR, THE STATE strongly objects to the release of this convicted felon. Counsel from Release Initiative has produced inconclusive DNA results." Gwen looked at the defense table to her left. Her nemesis, defense attorney Aaron Zimmerman, wore a rumpled wool-tweed blazer despite the summer heat. In the years she'd known him, he'd rotated through several hideous jackets at court appearances. She didn't think he owned a suit, even though she'd recently made him laugh out loud by suggesting the name of a local tailor. She suppressed a sigh at what a cheerful mess he always seemed to be.

"Is defense counsel prepared to provide expert witness testimony on what these DNA tests mean?" Judge Tanner asked.

Aaron rose from his chair in that lazy, cat-like way he had. "I am, Your Honor. Our expert witness will testify to reasonable doubt in the culpability of James Edward Conner, given there's only a forty percent chance the DNA is his."

"Your Honor—" Gwen began, but the judge slashed his hand in the air. She'd been about to remind the court that eye witnesses in the original case had placed the convict at the scene.

"I'll hear your expert witness, Counselor, tomorrow morning at eight o'clock but this better not be a waste of time," Judge Tanner pronounced. Then he hammered his gavel to conclude the session.

Gwen's shoulders sagged ever so slightly as she gathered her files. She didn't need to add another appearance to her already overloaded schedule. And John Fry, Chief of Criminal Appeals for the Maryland Attorney General, would not be happy that she'd been unable to make this one go away. Her boss took a dim view of wasting time on the endless efforts of certain organizations to get ostensibly inno-cent criminals out of prison. She didn't like it much herself. Release Initiative, Inc., was one of their least favorite.

"Ms. Haverty, may I speak with you?" She looked up into the gray-green eyes of Aaron Zimmerman, counsel for that particular non-profit.

"We need to prepare for this afternoon's depositions." Her colleague Logan Brown was being protective, certain she wouldn't want to talk with Aaron. He was right.

"It's about another case," the defense attorney said. "If we could discuss a few details over coffee across the street, I'm hoping we can conclude at least one case quickly."

She eyed him, amused and wary at the same time. Was he seducing her into a private meeting with the promise of an easy conclusion or extorting the time out of her with the threat of another drawn-out court battle? This invitation was a first, so she couldn't be sure. Aaron had seemed direct and sincere when they'd worked against each other in the past, but she'd been fooled by men—particularly male attorneys— before. Her experiences forced her to suspect he was manipulating her in some hidden way.

"If you have hard evidence of a wrongful conviction, the State Attorney's Office will cooperate in the release of the incarcerated individual," she recited coolly. "Produce the evidence and there won't be a drawn-out court battle. We don't need to chat over coffee to make that happen."

He smiled at her, which seemed as inappropriate as his attire. "C'mon. Please? It won't take long and you'll see why we need to talk when you hear the situation. And everyone needs a coffee break now and then."

She almost laughed. But then he looked past her as Logan opened his mouth to protest again. "I promise I'll have her back in time for the deposition," Aaron said.

He made it seem as though she required Logan's permission to have coffee. She couldn't let her young and sometimes overly protective colleague believe he had anything to say about her activities. As manipulations went, Aaron's ploy was stunning. And effective. She had to admire that.

To Logan she said, "You can get started on the prep. I'll only be a few minutes with Mr. Zimmerman. I'll meet you back at the office." She touched Logan's sleeve to indicate her appreciation and to assure him she'd be okay with the Release Initiative attorney. Logan went all hurt-puppy on her anyway, but then he nodded and resumed packing his briefcase.

To Zimmerman she said, "I'll meet you at the Starbucks in five minutes and then I'll give you ten. If you need more than that, you'll have to schedule a meeting."

He put his hand theatrically over his heart and vowed that he'd be eternally grateful. He backed away, holding her gaze with his ever-amused eyes. At the door, he saluted jauntily and disappeared. This time, a small grin escaped her, despite her best efforts.

"He's such an asshole," Logan said. "You don't have to listen to whatever he wants to say."

"Actually, I do," she said. "Once in a while his organization finds someone deserving of the help they offer. Prosecutors are all about fairness and justice, right? We don't want people in prison if they shouldn't be there."

"Ha! Tell that to the boss," he said. "And you know as well as I do that ninety-nine percent of Release Initiative's clients are hardened criminals. They're all supposed to be in prison."

She looked at Logan, sorry he was already jaded. "You haven't been at this job long enough to be quite so cynical."

He grinned. "I've had a good teacher, so I caught on quicker than most."

She sighed at the truth of that. She'd certainly been an excellent role model in cynicism. There was no denying she shared her supervisor's belief that the clients of Aaron's nonprofit legal-aid organization were mostly guilty of something.

"Nevertheless," she said, "the public needs to have confidence in our impartiality on each individual case. So I'll listen to what he has

to say at the coffee shop. If it's his usual non-
sense, I'll soon be back helping you with the
preparations."

"Waste of time, if you ask me, but we have
to go through the motions, I suppose." He
picked up his briefcase and headed for the
door.

Gwen watched him go. Alone in the courtroom now, she glanced around the space. She'd
always loved the sense of impending truth that
permeated an empty hall of justice. Too bad a
populated courtroom lost that noble ambience
courtesy of the human propensity to lie. She
sighed again and wondered how Zimmerman
managed to stay so positive. Maybe it was because his job was to get people out of prison
while hers was to put them in. And keep them
there.

She picked up her purse and briefcase and
headed into the stream of people in the hallway outside the courtroom. She would give
Zimmerman a few minutes of her time and
maybe, just maybe, he'd have some reliable
evidence that would allow her the rare pleasure of helping to return an innocent person
to freedom.

As she left the building, the Baltimore
summer enveloped her in humid heat. In
seconds, the blouse beneath her suit jacket

became damp with sweat. But she didn't take it off. It was important to be professional at all times, and wearing a well-made suit—the uniform of a state's attorney—was part of that, especially when going to meet opposing counsel. Besides, the Starbucks was within sight. The air-conditioning inside would seem frigid by comparison.

Sure enough, the place was downright chilly once she crossed the threshold. Zimmerman had secured a table and waved when he saw her. He waited while she got a latte from the barista. She hadn't had lunch and eyed the cookies and scones, but decided she didn't want to be eating in front of Zimmerman while they talked business. Taking her drink, she sat across from him.

"The clock is ticking," she said as she took her BlackBerry from her purse and placed it on the table where she could see the time.

He raised an eyebrow, withdrew his identical unit from an interior pocket and set it across from hers. It was as if they'd laid down their respective six-shooters as a sign of truce. She almost laughed, but sobered when she realized he'd intended to amuse her.

"Talk," she commanded.

"Are you always so tense?" he asked without any hint that he might be making fun of her.

"I know your job is stressful, but I hope you can let yourself relax now and then."

She squinted at him. "Is this what you wanted to discuss?"

He quickly suppressed a smile. "So there's this young man, Omar Kingston. He was convicted of armed bank robbery, but he didn't do it."

She resisted the urge to roll her eyes. "You say that about all your clients. You and the other lawyers at Release Initiative have devoted your lives to getting people out of prison on the premise that they didn't do it. Too bad it's seldom true."

His gaze took on an intensity she'd rarely seen in him before. "It's true this time. One of the witnesses is recanting her testimony—the eye-witness testimony that got him convicted."

"That doesn't mean he didn't do it." She delivered this truth as gently as she could. Zimmerman worked hard for his clients and it wasn't his fault most of them didn't deserve his help.

He sat back in his chair. "I didn't have you pegged as one of those prosecutors who figure that even if someone has been wrongly convicted, they surely must have committed some crime or other, so they ought to be in prison anyway and we can let 'em rot."

It was her turn to lift an eyebrow. "I'm not. I don't think that." Or at least she told herself she shouldn't think that way. "The justice system wouldn't work very well if we got to put criminals away on the easiest charge to prove to a jury, regardless of the actual crime," she added. But she also recalled Logan's cynicism and her role in making him that way. And then there was her boss, John Fry, who believed with all his heart that public safety required them to keep all convicted criminals behind bars without the right to endless appeals at taxpayer expense.

Aaron's shoulders relaxed. "Okay. That's good. My faith in your fairness is restored. So I'm hoping you'll come hear what the witness has to say and join me in a motion to release. She's dying in a hospice center."

"You know I don't have the authority to make that decision on the spot."

He nodded. "But you could work your awesome skills of persuasion to get Counselor Fry to agree."

She couldn't detect any note of sarcasm laced through the compliment, but she suspected it was there. While she had no doubt that her skills were awesome, she couldn't imagine her opponent sincerely agreeing with that assessment. "Send me the details and I'll get back to you. But we may have to let the judge decide this." She reached for her Black-Berry, but he put his hand over it.

"Give yourself permission to drink your latte," he said softly. "I swear it won't ruin your career to be seen talking to me."

Gwen couldn't keep herself from stiffen-ing and he immediately withdrew his hand. She sat still for a moment, considering her reaction. Maybe any suggestion to relax for a few minutes sounded like a wicked tempta-tion after all the years of pushing herself to excel. On the other hand, it seemed vaguely ridiculous to dash out without taking so much as a sip of her drink.

She lifted the cup to her lips, and his gaze seemed to linger on her mouth. The heat of a blush spread over her cheeks as she wondered what he was thinking—or wanting. Her own focus drifted once more to note the changeable color of his eyes, sometimes green, sometimes gray.

She needed to say something distracting and found herself speaking before she knew what would come out. "As a nonprofit, Release Initiative can't possibly pay you enough. Yet you work very hard for people who are rarely innocent. Why do you do it?"

"So you *do* think my clients are the scum

of the earth," he countered. "I'll have you know that our recidivism rate is the best in the nation—very few of our released clients commit new crimes."

She took another sip from her paper cup. "You believe they're decent, hardworking and upstanding citizens who were caught up in a corrupt justice system?"

He laughed. "No. They're usually pretty unproductive members of society. But every now and then, the ones who really deserve our help make my job worth every hour I put into it." He grinned. "Despite the paltry wage they pay me."

"You could come over from the dark side and join us in putting the bad guys out of business."

"Ha! You don't get paid all that well yourself, working for the State." He looked like he was about to say more, but his attention shifted past her.

"Hello, Gwendolyn," she heard. Suppressing a groan, she looked up to see her ex-husband standing behind her.

"What do you want?" she asked, pleased with her tone. Pointed but calm.

He ignored her and turned to Aaron. "J. Clayton Haverty, estate planning," he said as he held out his hand.

"You're Gwen's husband?" Aaron asked after introducing himself.

"Not anymore," Gwen muttered as she got to her feet so she could herd her ex away. She couldn't help but notice Clayton was wearing one of his power suits, probably Armani. Nothing but the best for Clay.

"Ex-husband now," Clayton said pleasantly, stepping back to give Gwen room. He switched his attention to Gwen and his voice took on a familiar chill, meaning he was annoyed with her. "I wanted to let you know I'll be taking Joshua to New York with me this weekend."

"No!" Gwen couldn't be calm about this. She clenched her fists at her sides. "Josh and I have tickets to see the Blue Man Group. He's waited a long time to go. You changed your visitation schedule so you could have him next weekend and we planned around that."

Clayton shrugged and smiled at Aaron like a conspirator. "Sorry to hear that, but it's my weekend to have Josh. I haven't seen him in two weeks. Now that I got my work trip postponed, a weekend in New York with his father needs to trump the Blue Man Group. Change your tickets to another night."

"That's not possible. It's sold out. We got

lucky with these tickets. I'm not going to let you do this, Clay."

The man's false smile evaporated. The cool, calculating look in his eyes didn't scare her anymore, but she knew the conversation would be going downhill from here. Lately, he'd become more aggressive regarding his rights to see his son, even outside of the court-scheduled times. Gwen wouldn't think of limiting his visitations, but she couldn't let him shift plans around randomly. Clay had been increasingly less cooperative and this was beginning to worry her. She didn't trust the man.

"You don't have a choice, Gwendolyn," he said coldly.

Sadly, that was true. This weekend was scheduled for Clay to have visitation with Josh. Even if she wanted to fight him on this, she wouldn't get a judge to decide the issue in time. But she couldn't let him create havoc. And she knew she couldn't let this wait for a more private moment. Squaring her shoulders, in a subdued voice, she did her best to persuade Clay. For Josh.

AARON LOOKED ON AS THE two adults quietly bickered over their son. Mesmerized by the pair, he also wished he could escape. What they were doing to each other was so foreign to him. Didn't they realize that either one of them could die in a heartbeat? Were they unable to see that the son they were arguing about could be left without one of his parents in the blink of an eye?

Backed by the wall, Aaron couldn't easily get up from his chair. So he stirred his coffee and listened. He thought of Ben, the nine-year-old son he'd raised alone these last three-and-a-half years. The boy had been only five when Beth had died. Ben's memories of his mother were hazy at best. But Aaron thought of Beth every day. He missed her still.

He took a sip from his cup, trying to make himself invisible. He and Beth hadn't even had time to say goodbye. One second she was humming in the bathroom, pinning her hair into a twist so it wouldn't interfere with her nursing job at the hospital. The next second she was on the floor, gone. Aneurysms were like that—sudden and catastrophic. No pain, they'd told him. For that he'd been grateful. But he still wished he'd had the chance to tell her how much he loved her, to say he'd be a good father to Ben, to assure her she would always be in his heart. There had been no time for words.

Gwen and Clayton Haverty clearly had time for words. They snarled them at each other.

Gwen, Aaron noted, was clearly able to hold her own, even in an emotional argument about her son. She zeroed in quickly on inconsistencies and weaknesses in Haverty's arguments. But after a while, the exasperated woman pleaded, "Clay, please stop disrupting our lives every chance you get. It's not good for our son."

"I know what's good for my son, Gwen. You're not the only one with his interests at heart. Josh will finally get some quality time with me, his father. I've got lots of great things planned. Hopefully he'll feel relaxed enough to bring up any—" he looked at Aaron and then back at her "—man-to-man questions he may have."

"We're divorced," she interjected. "It's over. I got sole custody of Joshua and you got visiting rights. Those rights don't include taking him with you whenever you feel like it regardless of my plans with him."

Aaron wished he could say something to help her—an unusual response given their opposition to each other in court.

"He's my child, too," Haverty said. "And I'll take him to New York if I want to. Do you think this chance comes up every day? I don't get much time off from work, Gwen. You're being unreasonable."

Gwen rubbed her temple with trembling fingers. "I'm trying to be reasonable. But he's wanted to go to this show for a long time. You just want to spoil it for us, or drive a wedge between us. Why would you do that?"

J. Clayton Haverty squinted at her. "I'm doing no such thing. You're being overcontrolling, as usual. And overprotective. A boy Joshua's age needs to experience new things without the coddling of his mother. He needs to spend time with his father. In fact, I've been thinking about revisiting the whole custody issue."

Aaron winced. Those were fightin' words. Gwen's whole body tensed. He wished he could say something to defuse the moment.

"Um…" Aaron pushed the small table far enough that he could get to his feet. "Maybe you should take this discu—"

Gwen spoke right over his effort to suggest sanity, glaring at her ex-husband. "Don't you dare threaten me about Joshua's custody," she said through clenched teeth.

Haverty squared his shoulders defiantly. "Or what? What will you do?"

Gwen gasped and stepped back as if she'd been slapped. Aaron reached out to steady her, but she regained her balance before he touched her. "You know I'd fight you," she said. "And

I'd win. He's better off with me. You said so yourself the day you left us both to go live with your girlfriend."

Haverty's gaze didn't waver. "That was a stressful time. I may need to reconsider what's best for Josh. Is he happy with you, Gwen? Because all I see is him plodding halfheartedly through public school and then plugging into video games."

Aaron sensed that anger drove the man now, making him want to hurt Gwen. Her ex had certainly picked the best possible way. Threatening to take her child would pierce any mother's heart.

Suddenly, Clay turned on Aaron. "Can you believe she's making such a big deal out of one weekend?" he asked, aiming to draw support from the closest fellow male.

"Whoa!" Aaron raised his hands, palms out. He wanted no part of Haverty's calculated camaraderie. He'd only gotten to his feet in an effort to help Gwen.

She took a breath as if readying for a shouting match. But Aaron touched her sleeve gently. "Gwen," he said. She looked into his eyes, not really seeing him at first, but then focusing and regaining her composure, as he'd hoped she would.

She let out the breath on a sigh and relaxed

her shoulders before turning back to her ex. "I don't want to fight," she said with strained civility. "Please. Let's just remember what's best for Josh. If you want him for a weekend in New York, then take him with you. But please tell me you're not serious about vying for custody."

Haverty shrugged. Gwen's shoulders relaxed slightly as if she'd taken this gesture to indicate it had been an idle threat. Aaron wasn't so certain. A shrug could mean anything. Or nothing. But Gwen was in no position to insist on a better answer.

Aaron jumped in while he could and faced Gwen's ex. "Good to meet you," he said, before the fragile truce could be broken and they started at each other again. He held out his hand once more. "Gwen and I are going to get back to our meeting," he said, trying hard to make the point casually, but firmly.

Haverty shook his hand ever so briefly. "I'll pick Joshua up on Friday at six." Then he turned and strode away.

Aaron and Gwen were left standing there, staring at each other across the café table. A moment passed and Aaron said, "Let's sit a minute longer."

She sat, saying nothing, simply staring into space.

"I have a son, too," he offered. "Benjamin. He's nine. How old is Josh?"

"Ten," she whispered. Then her gaze refocused on him. "Just turned ten," she said in her normal voice. "Did it sound to you like Clay meant what he said about custody? Or was he just being hateful?"

"Maybe both." He didn't want to lie to her, but he was sorry to see her tension ratchet up another notch when he gave his opinion. "But you can work it out, I'm sure. You used to be married to each other. Maybe you could tap some of what you once loved about each other and find a way to compromise."

She chuffed dismissively. "We'll never work anything out. That's why we're divorced. And I'm not sure we ever actually loved each other. Clay has always been mostly in love with himself. His mother is the opposite of nurturing—something I didn't realize before we married—and Clay learned to take care of himself at the expense of everyone around him. Although I suppose he loves Josh—in his own way."

Aaron leaned back in his chair and gaped at her. "Why did you marry someone you didn't love?" he asked, though he had no right to pry.

"Youth? Stupidity? Lust? Who knows." She took a drink of her coffee. "Are you and your wife one of those perfect couples who always get along?"

"We were before she died," he said simply.

It was Gwen's turn to gape. "I…I'm so sorry. I didn't realize."

"It happened a few years ago. I have Ben. My mother-in-law helps me with him. We're fine." But he had to stifle a sigh, as he often did when he thought of Beth. Was it normal to be grieving for his wife this long?

"You know what?" she said. "You and Ben can have our tickets to the Blue Man Group Friday night." She rummaged in her briefcase and took them out.

"Are you sure you don't want to use them yourself, with your boyfriend maybe?" As soon as the words were out of his mouth, he wished he could recall them. It sounded way too much like he was fishing for info. She would have no way of knowing he couldn't bring himself to betray Beth's memory by dating anyone, not even someone as attractive as Gwen Haverty.

"There's no boyfriend," she said in a disgusted tone that told him she'd written off all men. She held the tickets up. "This show was something Josh wanted after he saw a Discovery Channel episode about them. I was so happy about going with him. It wouldn't be the same to go alone. You take them. Unless you have other plans for Friday."

"No plans," he said, bemused by the inexplicable whisper of relief that had passed through him when she'd said "no boyfriend."

She handed the tickets across the table. He took them, but reached to his back pocket for his wallet at the same time. "What did they cost? I'll pay you for them."

She waved her hand, dismissing the offer. "No, I don't want you to do that. Really. You weren't planning to go, so you shouldn't have to pay. I just don't want them to go to waste." Amusement suddenly lit her lovely brown eyes. "You can just owe me a favor."

CHAPTER TWO

AARON SAT FOR A WHILE longer after Gwen left the coffee shop. The idea of owing her a favor both amused and intrigued him. He liked seeing her lighten up enough to strike the bargain, but he knew she could be a formidable adversary. There was no telling what Gwen Haverty might ask of him.

He thought about mailing the tickets back to her and claiming that Release Initiative had ethics rules that prevented him from accepting the gift. But that would be a lie and he knew she'd be insulted. He tapped the pair of tickets on the table in front of him. That's when he noticed the BlackBerry sitting by itself on the left side of the table.

Hadn't he set his on the opposite side? How had it gotten over there? Unless...

He picked up the device and hit a key to wake it up. Sure enough, the BlackBerry wasn't his. No photo of a smiling boy greeted him. There was no personalization at all. Clearly, this BlackBerry belonged to Maryland District Attorney Gwendolyn Haverty. She must have taken his by accident.

He grinned. "At least I'm guaranteed another chance to talk to her about Omar," he said to himself as he contemplated the prospect of exchanging phones. Maybe she'd need hers badly enough to invite him to her home this evening. He admitted to some serious curiosity about the woman who so frequently thwarted his professional efforts in court. It would be helpful if he could figure out what made her tick. And he wouldn't mind seeing her relaxed and dressed in something other than tailored suits.

He nudged the BlackBerry into a spin on the surface of the table and watched it as he thought about Gwen—her troubles with her ex, the son who was nearly the same age as his own, her glossy brown hair.

Her what? Wait. He slapped his hand over the spinning phone as his brain tripped over a horrifying possibility. Was he attracted to the woman?

That couldn't be right. He still loved Beth. And Gwen was the polar opposite of Beth. Gwen had a serious nature, Beth had loved to laugh. Gwen made a point of maintaining a perfect external image, Beth only ever cared about what was on the inside. An attraction to

Gwen would make no sense. And asking her on a date out of curiosity would be an insult to Beth's memory. Gwen would not welcome it anyway. She would never reciprocate his interest. If he *had* any interest. Which he most certainly did not.

Frustrated with the drift of his thoughts, he picked up the BlackBerry and dialed his own number. He'd tell her they'd mixed up the phones and arrange to trade. And that would be the end of that.

No answer. She had depositions this afternoon and may have silenced the phone for the duration. He'd try again later.

For now, he'd do things to remind himself of what he'd had with Beth. Even after three years, it still felt imperative that he remain faithful to her. Otherwise, what had their love really meant? He pocketed the BlackBerry and headed for home, taking the bus out to the suburbs because he couldn't call himself an environmentalist if he drove his car everywhere.

At home, chaos reigned, as was so often the case.

"What?" he asked his mother-in-law as soon as he saw the scowl on Phyllis's face.

"That boy," she said.

"And?" he encouraged. But he knew Benjamin's propensity for adventure often led him into trouble.

"He turned my entire load of laundry blue."

"How?"

"I don't know, but it's definitely blue and it was definitely Ben's fault."

Aaron sighed. "Ben!" he shouted up the stairway of the house they'd only just moved into. "I need to talk to you!"

Ben came without hesitation, clattering down the stairs all elbows and knees, and rushed into Aaron's arms for a hug. "What's up?" he asked cheerfully.

Aaron hugged him back, glad for the warmth he and his son shared, but then stepped away so he could be more parental. He looked Ben squarely in the eyes. "What's with the blue laundry?"

Ben looked puzzled, then he caught sight of the soggy clothing his grandmother held in her hands. The formerly white T-shirt was now splotched with blue. "Wow, I didn't know it would turn anything a different color. Cool!"

Aaron tried to retain his scowl, but it was hard when Ben was so irrepressible. "Why were you messing with the washing machine?"

"I needed a centro-fridge."

"A centrifuge?" Aaron asked. "What for?"

"Experiments. I saw it on the Discovery

Channel. It didn't work, though. And I guess some of the stuff got out of the jar during the spin cycle. Sorry."

"You ruined all the clothes, Benjamin," admonished Phyllis.

"Not on purpose," he responded, unfazed. "And I don't mind if my stuff is blue. It's kinda cool."

Phyllis growled. "It's everyone's laundry, Ben, not just yours. The adults in this family may not want all of their white things to be blue."

"Okay," Ben said. He turned his remorseful gaze toward his grandmother. "I'm sorry I accidentally turned some of your clothes blue. Can I go back to my room? I was in the middle of a major Wii tournament."

Aaron had a hard time seeing why the laundry issue was so important in the big scheme of things. What did it matter if a few clothes turned blue? The kid had apologized, the damage was minimal, the reason was youthful experimentation. It all seemed like normal boy stuff to Aaron. "Sure," he said to Ben.

"Aaron!" Phyllis exclaimed as Ben thumped back up the stairs to resume his game. "That boy will never learn to respect others if you let him get away with this kind of behavior."

"He's respectful," Aaron protested, stung by

the accusation. "He's a good kid, just exuberant."

She tossed the sodden T-shirt at him and he reflexively caught it. Drops of water splashed the front of his shirt. "That boy needs some discipline and consistency. He doesn't listen to me and you're not staying on top of him. Do you want him to have the same problems in his new school as he had in the last?"

Aaron didn't agree that children should be controlled, necessarily, but she had a point about Ben getting into trouble at his last school. They'd recently moved to this house so Phyllis could have a couple of rooms for herself, and there was a yard for Ben, but the move also meant a new beginning for Ben in a different school where people didn't know about his mischievous nature.

With a sigh, Aaron drew his mother-in-law into a one-armed hug, careful not to get the wet shirt near her. "You're right. Discipline and consistency. I'll talk to him again before bed. And if you set the blue laundry aside, I'll teach him about bleach and have him rewash the load to see if we can get the color out."

Phyllis hugged him back. That was something Aaron loved about his family—none of them could resist the healing properties of a warm hug. "Just make sure you watch him with the bleach and impress upon him that it's dangerous stuff, not to be played with." She took the T-shirt from his hands.

"Dangerous. Okay. Got it." Then he made a strategic retreat to the sanctuary of his bedroom on the second floor.

"I'M LATE," GWEN SAID to no one in particular as soon as they wrapped up the final deposition.

Logan nodded. "Aren't you pretty much late every night?"

"Pretty much," she agreed. "Fortunately, Clayton's child support helps cover the extra cost of the babysitter. She gets twenty bucks for every half hour past six."

Logan looked at his watch and whistled appreciatively. "Misha will be buying a new car very soon."

Gwen nodded. Misha Gooding, the young woman who picked up Josh from summer camp and stayed at the house with him, certainly had a good thing going with her part-time job for the Haverty family. "Still, I better call and let her know I'm on my way." She took out her BlackBerry and pushed the power button even as she continued to stack documents with her other hand. When she heard the tune indicating the phone had powered up, she hit the button on the side so she could give a voice command. "Call Misha," she told it.

A computer voice chirped back, "Did you say call Mitsubishi?"

"Who?" she said, as if she could have an actual conversation with the phone.

"Did you say 'call Hunan Manor?'" the voice asked in the same chirpy tone.

"Hunan Manor?" she said aloud, puzzled.

"Calling," said the phone.

"No!" Gwen powered the thing off with her thumb to prevent it from placing a call to Hunan Manor, a Chinese restaurant near her home. It freaked her out that she couldn't remember programming that number into the BlackBerry in the first place.

The whole exchange took about ten seconds, but once she'd turned the device off, she had a moment to think. Then she looked at it more closely.

"Is something wrong?" Logan asked.

"No," Gwen said. She didn't want to tell him what she suspected. "The battery might be dying," she hedged.

Not really a lie, but certainly not the truth, and she felt guilty for the deception. She quickly scooped up her things and headed for the door. "I gotta run. Thanks for your help with the depositions, Logan."

Once she was alone in the privacy of her Camry, she pulled out the misbehaving Black-Berry once more. She knew right away that this unit belonged to Aaron Zimmerman. A photo of a little boy appeared on the faceplate.

"Benjamin Zimmerman, I presume," she said aloud. "And I'm still talking at the phone," she added with a sigh. Resolving to stop treating her BlackBerry like a human assistant, she prodded the key pad to ring her own cell phone. Her voice mail answered. As tired as she was, she almost left Aaron a message, but realized just in time that doing so was silly. The man couldn't listen to her voice messages without her numeric code and everything else was locked behind passwords.

As she thumbed the end key, she wondered if Aaron had the information on his own phone protected. Or did he just trust people to do the right thing and not try to access the private information on his personal digital assistant. Curiosity compelled her to depress the menu button. Sure enough, all his contacts and text messages were listed and she could have read any of them without trying any of the obvious passwords he might have used. "Beth" was the first one that came to mind. "Ben" or "Ben-jamin" would have been the next possibility. After that, maybe his wedding anniversary.

She could get it from public records. It would be interesting to know if she'd sized up Aaron Zimmerman with any accuracy.

But there was no need for passwords. His text messages were hers for the taking with the click of a button. She didn't have enough of the killer instinct to snoop into the information on Aaron's phone. The fact that he trusted strangers to be decent about his personal data made her want to be worthy of that trust. She clicked the phone off and tossed it back into her briefcase, vowing to try calling him again later.

First, she needed to get home, relieve Misha of her duties—and pay her an extra forty dollars unless the traffic cooperated—then tell Josh the bad news about the Blue Man Group. The prospect made her wonder if she could pay Misha a thousand dollars to spend the night with Josh so she could put off telling him he'd be with his father for the weekend instead of attending the show. That information would not go over well with her child, she felt certain.

"You promised!" Joshua accused as soon as she told him.

"I know, and I'm sorry."

"We can exchange the tickets, right?"

Gwen sighed. "No, Josh. The shows are

sold out. If we can't use our tickets, we're not going to be able to go until the Blue Man Group comes back to Baltimore, maybe next year." But she knew it wasn't likely to be that soon. By the time the group performed nearby again, Josh would be too old to want to go. She grieved for the lost opportunity to make this childhood wish come true before he outgrew it.

"Are you kidding?" he shouted. "Sold out! That's not fair!"

"You're right. It's not fair." Then a thought occurred to her. "Hey, maybe your dad will take you to see a Broadway show in New York City." She tried to sound enthusiastic, implying with her tone that a show in New York would be a thousand times better.

"Ha. That's what *you* know. Dad doesn't have time for that kind of stuff."

"He takes you places when you're with him, right? And this is New York City, Josh. It's a very cool place to visit."

"We went to the museum in D.C. once and he spent the whole time on the phone to clients. And he just wants me around to impress his girlfriend. She says she likes kids. But I hate her." He was working himself up into a tantrum that he was far too old for. "And I hate Dad. You, too, Mom. You always give in to him. Whatever he wants, whenever he wants to show me off to that girl, Brenda." He said her name in a sneering singsong that Gwen would have appreciated if he weren't also spewing venom about his own parents.

"Joshua, stop this right now," she said, but she was struck numb by his accusation that she never stood up to his father.

"You don't care what *I* want. You just do whatever *he* wants, no matter what your own son needs. It sucks!"

"A lot of kids would be thrilled to have a father who wants to spend time with them," she said, but it came out sounding petulant. The divorce a year and a half ago had been hard on Josh and she knew she should cut him some slack.

"Oh, great!" he barked back. "Like this is all *my* fault. It's *your* fault. You still let my ex-father run our lives."

"He may be my ex-husband, but he'll never be your ex-anything. He's the only father you'll ever have," she retorted. But there was some truth in Joshua's words, and that stung her. Her ex-husband did seem to end up running her life, even now. She'd have to work on that. But not today.

"He sucks!" Joshua declared, then he spun

toward the stairs and began to stomp up toward his bedroom.

"Joshua Marcus Haverty, you stop this behavior right this instant."

He halted halfway up and turned, resentment in his eyes. So like his father, she thought. She was responsible for how he was turning out. Yet, what hope was there of raising a decent young man when his father was such a selfish jerk?

She found herself blinking back sudden tears. This was her son, her beloved child, her baby. How could she compare him to Clayton or think for a single moment that he'd turn out badly? She loved him too much for that. "Josh," she began. But her voice caught on those tears she wouldn't allow to fall. She had to try again. "Let's not fight. We need to get some dinner, talk about this calmly."

"I'm not hungry," he said. "May I please go to my room?"

Unspoken was the obvious sentiment that he couldn't stand to be with her for another second. And she couldn't blame him. She'd let him down. How had she allowed Clay to win the battle over the coming weekend?

"Yes, go ahead for now," she said. "I'll call you when dinner is ready, but no more drama from you, young man." It crossed her mind that she sounded exactly like Clayton's mother, Charlotte Clayton Haverty. Same tone, nearly the same words about no drama. Her own mother would have baked cookies and said children need space for their natural emotions. Gwen had never been able to embrace her mother's easygoing approach to parenting, secretly fearing that her son would run wild, the way she'd done behind her mother's back when she was young.

Gwen made her way to the kitchen, forcing herself through the motions required of her as a parent and the only person who cooked. And she told herself she'd only resorted to parroting her mother-in-law because she felt helpless when it came to Joshua. It was not because her mother-in-law was a font of wisdom— quite the opposite. Charlotte was too cold and self-centered to be of any help to Gwen. She'd raised Clayton as a single mother, and look how that had turned out. As for Gwen's own mother, she might be kind and sweet, but she'd enjoyed such a happy marriage she'd left Gwen without a single hint about all the things that could go wrong between spouses. Gwen felt an abiding resentment for that lack of preparation.

Pulling leftover chicken out of the refrigerator, she wondered if she should try to find a decent male influence for Josh—someone who would show him there were other ways to behave besides those exhibited by his father. Immediately, Aaron's smiling face came to mind.

She shuddered at the thought of involving herself with any man, especially Aaron. But of all the men she knew, Aaron was likely the safest. He would never have any romantic interest in her. For one thing, he undoubtedly had a girlfriend by now. Although she'd learned the hard way that when a man had a woman in his life, it didn't necessarily mean he'd be faithful, she somehow believed Aaron would be the exception. Plus, their opposition to each other in the courtroom would add to her comfort level. He wouldn't likely leap to the conclusion that she had a hidden personal agenda if she wanted to make a playdate for their two sons.

Dinner wasn't pleasant. Joshua refused to speak to her, but he did sit at the table and consume the simple meal she'd prepared. Not much affected her growing boy's appetite.

By the time the dishes were cleared, Gwen's fatigue had eclipsed her will to work things out with her son. She let him return to his bedroom full of electronic amusements, despairing that her attempt to be both a mother and a full-time prosecutor would lead to her doing both jobs half as well as she should. With her self-esteem plummeting to a new low, she took herself into her bathroom for a long soak in the large tub. She even lit some candles.

When the tub brimmed with steaming water and bath salts, and the fragrance of lavender filled the humid air, she recalled that she needed to review some documents before a meeting she'd be attending in the morning. Sighing at the injustice of it, she retrieved her briefcase and set it next to the tub so she could read while she soaked. It was better than giving up the bath completely or staying up late to read.

But once she got into the soothing water, she couldn't bring herself to pull the files out of the briefcase. Instead, she drowsed lazily and let her mind go blank, hoping that even a ten-minute mental vacation would restore her energy so she could once again face her two daunting jobs as mother and attorney.

"Puff the Magic Dragon" began playing in the bell-like tones that only a cell phone can manage. Gwen laughed out loud. She dried her hands and fished Aaron's BlackBerry from her briefcase, thinking it had to be the defense attorney himself, looking to get his phone back.

"Hello?" she said, still smiling at the implications of a free spirit like Aaron having "Puff the Magic Dragon" as his ring tone.

"Where's Aaron?" a woman demanded.

CHAPTER THREE

"OH," GWEN SAID INTO the phone. She guessed this was Aaron's girlfriend, the one she'd hoped he'd have so she could safely get him to spend time with her son. But for some reason, the delight she'd felt over the ring tone dissipated at the sound of this woman's voice.

"Is Mr. Zimmerman available?" the woman asked.

That seemed odd. Why would Aaron's girlfriend refer to him so formally? "Aaron's not here," she said. "We mixed up our phones. He has mine. I have his. By accident. We work together. Well, actually we're usually working against each other. But we had a meeting. Our phones are identical BlackBerries." Shut up, she told herself. Just stop babbling.

"Yeah, right. Whatever. Can you give him a message for me?"

"Uh, sure."

"Tell him to call Opal Kingston as soon as possible. It's about my brother. It's important. He has my number."

"Okay. I'll tell him." Gwen realized this must be Omar Kingston's sister. Which meant she was talking to a close relative of Aaron's client—the same client he'd spoken about at the coffee shop. Even though it wasn't her fault, Gwen felt uneasy about intruding into Aaron's professional world without his knowledge. She wanted to end the conversation quickly and then try calling Aaron again.

"Are you his secretary?" Opal asked. She didn't wait for an answer. "Can you tell him Omar got hurt in a fight at the prison. We need to hurry up and get my brother out of there before worse things happen."

Gwen did not want to hear more. The desperation in this woman's voice could end up affecting her ability to be impartial about Omar's case. She couldn't afford to let emotions enter into her work. "I'll tell him. Thanks for calling." And she thumbed off the phone before Opal could interject another word.

The water hadn't even cooled, but she lathered her skin, determined to finish her bath quickly. Keeping Aaron's phone felt like a betrayal somehow. She might be his opposition in court, but she wanted to be an honorable enemy.

She'd begun to swipe the soapy washcloth over her legs when "Puff the Magic Dragon" began to play once more. Startled, she dropped the cloth and sat upright so suddenly, water splashed onto the BlackBerry. It kept on chiming the happy tune, so she gave two fast wipes of her hand on a nearby towel and picked the thing up again. The number on the caller ID was her own.

"Why didn't you answer when I called you before?" she asked without preamble. "I need my phone back. And you need yours."

After an infinitesimal pause, Aaron said, "Wow. You like to get right to the point."

"Sorry." The warm water swirled around her body, making her very aware that she was talking to Aaron Zimmerman while naked. "I just don't like the idea of you having my phone."

"Hey, I'm the one who should be worried, not you. Your PDA has all the information carefully password protected. Mine, on the other hand, is available for you to sift through at will."

"I didn't look," she assured him. "I wouldn't go through the stuff on your phone, but you should consider better security." She sat up straighter as a thought came to her. "Hey, wait a minute. Did you try to get into my stored data? How else would you know everything is password-protected? Where is your honor?"

He laughed. "To tell the truth, I just assumed you had everything locked up carefully inside your electronic little black book. Nice to know I guessed correctly."

Was he implying she was uptight and prudish? "It's a matter of protecting client confidentiality," she said. Then she was annoyed he'd made her defensive. She reacted as any lawyer would by going on the offensive. "Why didn't you answer before when it was early enough to make a quick exchange of PDAs? I got my own voice mail when I tried to reach you."

He sighed. "Sorry. I called as soon as I realized the mix-up, but you were doing those depositions and must have had the ringer silenced. Then I was distracted at home by my son's antics."

"Antics?" she asked, wondering how she could be interested in the answer at a time like this. The bubbles were disappearing and the water was cooling around her. Silly, but she found herself wrapping her free arm across her chest, partially hiding her breasts from a man who couldn't see her.

"Yeah. He turned the laundry blue by accident. My mother-in-law lives with us now that we've moved to this bigger place in Columbia, and she's taking care of some of the chores I used to need a housekeeper to do. You can imagine how upset she was when all the white clothes came out blue."

"How did he manage that? Food coloring?" Stop asking about his household drama, she told herself. The only thing that mattered was setting a time to switch phones.

"Hmm, I forgot to ask. I suspect it was something from his chemistry set. Maybe I should confiscate it."

"Ya think?" she said with a laugh. She couldn't help it. Hearing Aaron Zimmerman as frazzled father was entertaining. "But listen, as much as I'd like to hear more about the blue laundry, we need to make arrangements to switch our PDAs."

"Right. I guess it's too late for me to come over to your place tonight," he said.

Inexplicably, Gwen felt her nipples harden. "Not a good idea. How about first thing in the morning at the—"

"Hold on," he interrupted. "There's another call coming in. Do you want me to answer it?"

"Okay," she said, and she heard their connection go silent as he picked up the other call. Too late, she realized she'd given him the go-ahead to answer her own line. Who would be calling her so late? And how tricky would it be to explain why the defense attorney for

Release Initiative was answering her phone? "Shit," she muttered. But at least this interlude would give her the chance to get out of the bath and into her robe.

She had risen partway out of the tub, dripping water and suds, when Aaron's voice suddenly came back to the phone.

"Sorry about tha—"

Reflexively, she dropped back into the water, splashing loudly. He can't see you, she reminded herself.

But he could hear her. "Was that water splashing?" he asked.

She didn't speak.

"Sounded like maybe too much water for a sink, so I'm guessing bathtub."

"Um…I plead the fifth." It was all she could think to say, even as heat rose to her cheeks. Then her training kicked in again. "We need to stick to figuring out a time and place to do the phones."

A pause made Gwen wonder what he was thinking.

"Sure," he said. "But you probably want to know it was your ex-husband on the phone just now. And I'm not going to keep talking to you while you're… Well, just call me back after you get settled and…just call me back. Bye."

Gwen heard the connection go dead before she could respond. But she didn't think she could have come up with any words anyway, she was so embarrassed. Aaron was a man, after all, and any man would now be picturing her bare, dripping body.

Then she remembered she'd forgotten to tell him about the call from his client's sister. Should she phone him back right away? No. She should get out of the tub first and try not to think about Aaron Zimmerman in the context of her own nakedness.

AARON TOSSED GWEN'S PDA onto his bed as if it had caught on fire. Staring at it, he ran his fingers through his hair and then held on to his head as if the gesture could erase the erotic pictures that danced through his brain. It wasn't that he thought sexual fantasies were a bad thing, but fantasies featuring Gwen seemed very wrong.

Now he had to cope with a new woman invading his most intimate thoughts. Gwen hadn't meant to put the images into his head, but they were there. Again and again, he heard the splash of the bathwater, and from that one sound came visions of his courtroom opponent rising from her tub and walking toward him through clouds of steam—wet, warm, naked.

"Damn," he whispered as his body began to respond. In desperation, he started humming the national anthem and pacing back and forth past the foot of his wide bed in the hope of evicting Mrs. Gwen Haverty from his mind. He managed to achieve a measure of control. But when the BlackBerry began to ring, his blood ran hot all over again.

He gave himself a moment to breathe deeply before answering. Affecting the composed tone he used in the courtroom, he said, "Hello, Gwen."

"Sorry," she said. "Awkward as hell to have to call you back right now." She sounded nearly as flustered as he felt. That made everything a little more tolerable. At least he wasn't alone in his discomfort. "I need to—"

"Don't worry. I explained to him that our phones got switched." He'd figured out she'd be deeply concerned about how bad it looked to have defense counsel in possession of the D.A.'s phone.

"Good. Clay's always looking for an excuse to make things difficult for me. If he's serious about suing for custody—even just for spite— he might twist the fact you have my phone into something else. He's a master at making people see the world through his own reality.

He—" She stopped midsentence and didn't continue.

Filling the silence, he said, "He let you have custody when you first split up. Why would he sue for sole custody now?"

"I'm pretty sure he just doesn't like not getting his way. And I think he believes he's lost some control over Joshua's life, which he's not happy about. Or maybe he just wants to impress his girlfriend. Josh tells me she likes kids, even though she doesn't have any of her own."

"She'll like kids right up until one of them turns her laundry blue."

Gwen laughed and he felt his tension ease. It pleased him—in a completely nonsexual way, he told himself—that he could make her laugh.

"Why does your phone play 'Puff the Magic Dragon'?" she asked, apropos of nothing.

"Because it's funny."

"I don't get the joke."

"I'm a big proponent of legalizing marijuana. I do pro bono work on the medicinal weed legislation we've been trying to get passed in Maryland."

"Why am I so not surprised," she said. "You really are a hippie."

He chuckled. "Well, that's true, but another reason for my interest is my mother-in-law's glaucoma. She moved here from California where she'd been prescribed the stuff."

"That's not legal here," Gwen pointed out.

"But it helps her. So I'm not taking it away from her."

"You're an officer of the court," she reminded him.

"I'll take my chances. Hey, on a much more important subject, Clay asked me to tell you that he wouldn't be taking Josh to New York this weekend after all," Aaron told her, deftly changing the subject from marijuana use—an issue that would once again underscore the differences between him and the prosecutor on the other end of the line. "He said he had a change of heart."

"What? Are you serious? Josh and I have already had a big fight about him missing the Blue Man Group."

"Well, you can have the tickets back," he offered. Then he wondered if Ben would be as disappointed as Josh. He'd told his son about going to the show when he'd tucked him into bed for the night and Ben had been excited.

"Only if you haven't told Ben yet," she said. "If you've already told him, then I'm not taking the tickets back."

Aaron hesitated. He wanted to lie so she'd agree to take her own son to the show. But lying didn't come easily to him, and before he could come up with the words, she knew the truth.

"You already told him, didn't you." She said it as a statement of fact. "Ben was happy about going, right? So, I can't accept the tickets back. I'll figure it out with Josh. Don't worry about it."

He could hear the tension in her voice. "Are you going to be okay? Is there anything I can do to help?"

"I'm fine. But, hey, a call came in on your phone earlier." She told him about Opal Kingston and the brother who'd been hurt in prison.

"I need to call her back." Though he felt frustrated about ending the conversation with Gwen—as if they had unfinished business— he said goodbye and closed the phone.

"CALM DOWN, OPAL. WE won't do your brother any good if we're freaked-out," he said to his client's sister. "I'll go to the prison right now and see what I can do for him."

"He needs to be outta that hellhole," she shouted. "He's getting beaten up because he don't belong there."

"I know. I'm doing everything I can. Trust me." But then he thought of his conversations with opposing counsel and he wondered if he deserved Opal's trust. He hadn't even persuaded Gwen to talk to the recanting witness in Omar's case.

He thought about that all the way to the prison in the nearby town of Jessup where Omar was incarcerated. Even if he couldn't get him freed as quickly as he'd hoped, he'd at least see his client in person, regardless of the late hour, and make sure he hadn't sustained any serious injuries. He had to listen to some grumbling from the guards, but eventually Aaron settled into an interview room and waited for Omar while trying hard not to think too much about Gwen in the bathtub.

The gray metal door swung open and a guard stood aside to allow the prisoner access. A shuffle of awkward footsteps preceded Omar's appearance. A second before he saw the young man, Aaron's stomach knotted with dread. Opal's fears were justified.

Omar's bruises were less noticeable against his dark skin, but the cuts on his lips and the swollen eye couldn't be missed.

"Why weren't you admitted to the infirmary?" Aaron asked.

"I told 'em I'm fine. No sense showing weakness in a place like this."

"Where else are you hurt?"

The stoic expression Omar had been maintaining wavered slightly then quickly returned. "I'm awright," he said.

"You don't need to be tough with me, Omar. In fact, it's important that you tell me about every cut or bruise." He looked steadily into those dark brown eyes, hoping to see some remnant of the boy he'd been before prison. But Omar had learned to keep his thoughts hidden, much as he'd learned to bury the gentle nature his sister spoke of so often. At six foot four and with a rock-solid two hundred and fifty pounds, Omar looked like the kind of man who would be able to hold his own while incarcerated. But his teddy-bear temperament was his undoing. It hadn't taken the inmates long to discover the sport that could be made of tormenting a big guy with a soft heart.

"I said I'm awright," he insisted, but this time Aaron heard the lisp in his speech that hadn't been there the last time they'd met.

"Did you lose some teeth?" he asked.

"Yeah, a couple. So what?" Playing the tough guy, even in the privacy of the interview room.

"What else?" Omar said nothing, so Aaron tried a new tactic. "Your sister is worried sick, Omar. That's why I'm here at this hour of the night. I need to be able to tell her honestly that you're okay."

"I didn't start nothin'," he said, sounding a bit more like the kid he'd been before prison had aged him. "They just got into it and I had to defend myself, but then there were four, maybe five others joined in, and it was a brawl on my ass." Abruptly, he lifted up his shirt and showed a hematoma the size of a dinner plate across several ribs.

Aaron stifled an expletive. "Did a doctor take a look at this?"

"Didn't look this bad when I went. And I figured it'd go bad if I complained."

"Well, I'm getting you transferred to the infirmary for the next few days, at least until you're healed."

Omar's expression softened. "You serious? I could stay there awhile?"

"Maybe longer, if you have broken ribs. Does it hurt to take a breath?"

"Shit yeah!"

"Can I see the back of you?"

Omar stood up slowly, careful not to jar any part of his abused body. He turned. This time Aaron couldn't stifle the gasp. The broad muscled shoulders and torso were a mass of straight dark purple lines, as if he'd been beaten relentlessly with a pipe. Aaron didn't hesitate another moment. He took out his cell phone and rapidly took photos from every angle. To avoid any possible loss of evidence, he sent the pictures to his email account at Release Initiative. He pocketed the phone and urged Omar to sit down again, then went to the door and pounded until the guard opened up.

Aaron made his demands for medical treatment for Omar in no uncertain terms. He waited until the prison's clinic sent a medic and a stretcher to take Omar to the infirmary. Once his client had been taken into custody by the health officials, Aaron filled out dozens of official forms demanding copies of the dental treatment plan, X-rays of skull and ribs, and reports of any other tests done. At the very least, this ensured that all concerned knew Omar's attorney would be keeping a close eye on how the prisoner was treated.

Driving home at two in the morning, he plotted various ways he would get justice for Omar, none of them very practical. And the half-baked speeches were all, inevitably, aimed at a certain district attorney who had ever so recently been talking to him by phone while she was in her bathtub. As he drove and his rage about Omar's situation settled down under the weight of his inability to do anything more, he found his mind drifting to the same erotic thoughts as earlier in the evening—Gwen in the bathtub, stepping out of it, moving toward him. He tried to thwart those visions, but they kept reappearing.

By the time he got into bed, his fantasies about Gwen had extended far beyond the bathtub incident. The vulnerability that he'd heard in her voice when she'd talked about her son and ex-husband had stirred his imagination. He couldn't help but be unsettled by this other side of Gwen so unexpectedly revealed to him. As a single parent himself, he could empathize. And the protective side of him, which had always been a strong part of his personality, wanted to help her. If he could do that while making love to her—or so his fantasies went—all the better.

But he knew it would be his undoing to dwell too long on either the protection or the lovemaking. Gwen was, for all practical purposes, his professional enemy. If he began to feel any personal connection to her, it would be very hard for him to manipulate her for the benefit of his clients.

With that realization, he recalled that they'd never planned a time and place to exchange their PDAs. Given the late hour, he tapped out a text message to her: Need to figure out how we can exchange phones ASAP.

Before he could set the BlackBerry down, a reply appeared. Y r u up @ 3 am? Crzy.

He chuckled and wrote: I just got back from the prison. Feel sorry for me?

Mere seconds after he'd hit the send button, her response lit up his screen. No. 2 bzy feeling sry for me.

He couldn't resist: Why is that, counselor?

Evl x & custody probs.

That took him a few seconds to decipher. Evil ex-husband and custody problems. That sucked. Tell me what's happened since we last talked.

2 much 4 text.

So he gave up on texting and called his own phone number.

"I shouldn't be talking to you about this," she said instead of *hello*.

"I'm awake and not likely to sleep anytime soon. So if you want to vent, I'm willing to listen."

CHAPTER FOUR

DEEP INTO THEIR CONVERSATION, Gwen confided, "Sometimes I think Clayton is fighting over Josh's custody only because he's obsessed with winning." She could hardly believe she'd spilled her story to Aaron Zimmerman, of all people. But he'd offered to listen at the exact moment she'd desperately needed someone to talk to. She'd been talking and he'd been listening for nearly an hour.

"Maybe he just misses his son and wishes he could spend more time with him," Aaron suggested. "He may be dealing with his loss badly."

"Ha. Not Clay," she insisted.

"He reconsidered his New York trip—doesn't that show he wants what's best for you and Joshua?"

"Are you taking his side in this? Men sticking together or something? Trust me—Clay had some personal reason to jerk me around about our weekend plans. Don't be so naive as to think he was being altruistic."

Instead of taking offense, Aaron laughed, and the sound sent an unexpected flash of delight through her. At the same time, she was irritated he'd try to defend Clay. Knowing the danger of enjoying Aaron's easy laugh—or anything else about him, she clung to her irritation and was silent.

"I guess I just can't believe Clay could be so one-dimensional," Aaron said. "He must love his son, right? And he sounded contrite when he gave me the message that he'd leave Josh with you for the weekend. He couldn't have had any way of knowing you'd given away the tickets so quickly."

"You don't *know* him. Clayton Haverty is a narcisstic ass, Aaron. He only wants what's best for himself." And why, she wondered, did she feel the need to defend her image of Clay to Aaron? She shouldn't care how Aaron perceived her ex, or at least she knew she shouldn't care.

"I'm not trying to annoy you," he said. "I just think there may be another way to look at things."

Even if he was right, Gwen didn't want to hear it. It angered her that she'd spilled her guts to this man—the worst person on earth for her to confide in—and now he was taking

Clayton's side. "Wow, it's so late. I chewed your ear off and I'm sorry for that."

"No problem. I'm a single parent, too. Except I don't have to cope with still having the other parent…around."

Gwen heard the hitch in his speech. At times she might wish that Clayton would just disappear off the face of the earth, but losing a well-loved spouse would be a whole different thing.

The undertone of their late-night conversation turned awkward. At last she said, "I can't even remember why you called me in the first place."

"Right. I just realized we still hadn't made arrangements to trade our phones. And I need mine back. Name a time and place to make the trade."

"I have court in the morning. Can we meet before that at the coffee shop, say around eight o'clock?"

"Sounds perfect," he said. "See you then. Sleep well, Gwen."

His words came across the phone in a soft, sensual whisper, though she told herself he couldn't have meant them to stir her the way they did.

Gwen stared at the dormant PDA as if it had suddenly caught fire. She cringed over the intimacy of the conversation she'd had with Aaron. Knowing she needed to put some distance between them, she came up with an alternate plan to exchange phones, one that didn't involve actually seeing each other.

HE DREAMED OF BETH. BUT not the smiling, sweet woman he'd been married to. This Beth was sullen and accusing. She kept demanding to know why he was glad she was dead, asking him why he didn't love her anymore, threatening to take Ben away from him. He startled awake from the nightmare, shaken and sweaty. He looked at Beth's photo on the nightstand.

"What the hell was that?" he asked the image. But he thought he knew why his subconscious had gone in such a horrible direction.

He was developing a fondness for Gwen Haverty. And last night, he'd talked to her about how hard being a single parent must be when the other parent was still around to meddle. Right after he'd said it, he'd wanted to explain that he hadn't meant he was glad his wife was dead. But he hadn't found the opportunity to correct the error, and his dreams had tormented him as a result.

"I still love you," he whispered to Beth's picture. "I will always love you." Yet, in a corner of his mind, he knew he needed to begin living more fully.

Fortunately, the responsibilities of getting Ben ready for another day at summer camp took his mind off the unnerving paths his thoughts seemed to be taking lately. In fact, a very chatty Ben demanded so much of his attention while they were in the car that Aaron didn't hear the PDA ring. It wasn't until he'd gotten all the way to the coffee shop and inside to order a latte that he realized Gwen had called him.

He dialed her back. "I'm here. Where are you?"

"Oh...I...well, I have to prepare for court. And I need to leave in about two minutes. So I thought it would be better if you just come to my office and drop off my phone and I'll leave yours here for you to pick up." Her voice was cool and her words clipped.

"Uh, no, sorry, that won't work, Counselor. It's bad enough you've had my phone all this time—at least you're trustworthy. But I don't want my phone hanging around the State Attorney's Office, thank you very much. Don't let it out of your sight—it could fall into the wrong hands."

A split second later, she laughed. "I don't know of anyone whose hands could be more wrong than mine, from your perspective. But thanks for the vote of confidence about my trustworthiness."

He wanted to put her at ease, if he could. "Hey, we forged a bond as single parents last night. You can't be mean to me so soon after talking about our sons."

"That sounds about right," she agreed.

"So meet me for lunch at Lexington Market and I'll treat. But only after you give me my phone back."

"Um, I really have to get to court—"

"So twelve-thirty right out front at the main doors. It's a date." And he thumbed off the phone.

NATURALLY, THE STUBBORN man had thwarted her alternate plan. He was always thwarting her. It seemed to be his favorite pastime. And now she apparently had a lunch date with him. She could call him back and declare that she would not be meeting him today or any other day, but she couldn't think of how to justify taking such a hard stand. It's not as though he'd been hitting on her. Quite the contrary, he'd behaved more like a best friend, a buddy, a kindred soul in the tar pits of single parenthood.

When the hour to meet him finally arrived,

Gwen didn't want to go. She had no clear understanding of why she wanted to stand him up, but there it was. The closer she got to the area of town where her GPS guided her, the more anxiety she felt. She'd never been to Lexington Market, though she'd heard of it. Her parents hadn't taken her into Baltimore when she'd grown up in the nearby suburbs, because D.C. was nearly as close and the activities there were mostly free of charge. This part of the city was unfamiliar to her. She told herself that this was what was making her anxious.

Even when she found parking, she couldn't relax and enjoy the unseasonably cool August day. As she walked across the lot to the main doors of the large building, she wondered what she'd gotten herself into. And she asked herself why this meeting wasn't similar to all the others she'd had with different attorneys, many far more intimidating or handsome or difficult than Aaron Zimmerman.

Then she saw him standing there. She stopped dead in her tracks, wondering why he made her so uncomfortable. Aaron caught sight of her from across the open space. He smiled broadly and gave a welcoming wave. Gwen had her answer then. Despite his rolled-up shirtsleeves, too-wide tie with loosened knot, and pants that would have been appropriate at a barbecue, the awful truth was that she was susceptible to Aaron's charm—and especially that smile.

Wrong, wrong, wrong! She couldn't be attracted to the enemy. Or any man, for that matter. She'd learned her lesson with Clayton. She would keep this meeting professional.

She lifted her hand to acknowledge him but forced her smile to remain tepid. "May I have my phone, please?"

"Only if you give me mine," he said. When she rolled her eyes and reached into her purse for the PDA, he added, "Maybe we should hand them over at the same time, make sure neither of us does a double cross."

She had a hard time tamping down a grin. Facial expression under rigid control, she proffered the phone to him. He held out the identical one to her.

Slowly, he inched her BlackBerry closer to her, then jerked it back a little. "How do I know that's mine? Maybe it's a decoy so you can get yours and still keep mine."

The laughter in his eyes was hard to resist. "Stop it." She grabbed her PDA and tossed his the three inches into his hand. He captured it against his chest, then thumbed it to life.

"Okay, unless you had the cleverness to put

Ben's photo on a bogus phone, this one must be mine. So that's settled. Now let's go eat."

"To be honest, I'm not very hungry." Which was a lie. She hadn't gotten breakfast and she was famished. "Now that we have our own phones, let's just go our separate ways."

He looked crestfallen for a moment. "But then I'll have to eat alone and I hate that. Besides, you don't want people to think you're avoiding me and denying my clients justice. C'mon. I'm buyin'." Then he flashed her that smile again.

She hesitated, but hunger forced the decision. "Fine. Then let's get on with it."

"Today, we're going on a Baltimore food adventure. Follow me."

AARON KNEW HE SHOULD have accepted her suggestion to go their separate ways, but he hadn't been able to do that. All morning, as he waded through a stack of letters and case files that had come into Release Initiative from inmates asking for help, he'd thought about taking her through the famous public market with its specialty food booths. He'd known she'd be in a crisp suit and heels, and he hadn't been disappointed—and delighted—at the prospect of taking her around such an informal place to sample the phenomenal tastes

Baltimore had to offer. Maybe he wanted to loosen up the district attorney for a few minutes, expose her softer side. Then he might more easily extract a promise from her to talk to Omar's witness.

Yeah, that was it, he told himself. He'd think about whether there were any other reasons later on when he had time to deal with the resulting guilt he was sure to feel.

He led her to a food booth.

"How ya doin', Aaron?" said the guy behind the glass case of the Mary Mervis Deli.

"Doin' just fine, Pete." He eyed the offerings. "What's good today?"

"Got our world-famous shrimp salad, but we also got this crab salad here." He pointed to a bowl in the display case. "I could fix you up some nice subs with that." Pete glanced toward Gwen, who stood with a bewildered look on her face. "This your lady friend? Miss, you got yourself a real nice man here." He turned again to Aaron. "Guess what?"

Aaron chuckled. "What?"

"Paul is gonna graduate college next May!" Pete said.

"That's great!" Aaron knew Pete's brother had struggled through college. It was good to hear he'd finally made it.

"Yeah, he's doing something with computers at U of M, Baltimore Campus." Pete pronounced Baltimore like a native—saying *Ball*-more. "So, what can I get you two."

Aaron ordered both seafood salads, then led Gwen to the Harbor City Bake Shop for fresh bread.

"Everyone knows you," Gwen observed after he chatted with the shopgirl and they headed toward Lexington Fried Chicken.

"I like coming here when I find the time. Some of these shops date back decades."

"It's not just that," she said. "You're a hero to these people."

He shrugged, uncomfortable taking credit. "They equate me with Release Initiative. My employer is the last hope for some Baltimore families. And naturally I'm only taking you to the spots where people like me."

"Aaron!" the manager at the chicken place called out. "How 'bout them O's?" Dave was referring to the Baltimore Orioles baseball team but he didn't wait for an answer. "Who's your lovely lady, here?"

Aaron made introductions, but perversely failed to make the correction that Gwen was not *his* lovely lady.

"Aaron and I are colleagues," she said as she shook hands.

"Colleagues, huh?" Dave leaned forward

as if he was about to tell Gwen a secret, then said, "Take my advice, miss. Keep it that way. I knew him back in high school and he was a real stoner. A nice lady like you can do better."

Gwen looked so perplexed, Aaron laughed out loud. "I asked you to keep that information to yourself, man! I'm an officer of the court now."

Dave winked at Gwen and she smiled, then laughed. "Good to know," she said.

There was hope for Gwen, Aaron thought. He quickly ordered and led them away before any more of his secrets were revealed. "Dessert's next."

Gwen smiled. "Okay, I admit I'm starting to enjoy this. I can hardly believe I've lived near Baltimore all my life but never came here. Funny how that works—you live near a major tourist attraction and never go yourself."

At Konstant's Candy, he bought freshly made fudge. Finally, they picked up Southern Sweet Tea made with honey instead of sugar at Mother's Deli.

"We have too much food here," Gwen observed.

"Maybe," he agreed. He found them a table and they set their bundles down. "You should come in May when they have the Preakness Crab Derby. Hilarious. We could bring Ben and Josh." The instant he said this, he regretted it. She would close down now, he predicted.

But she smiled. "That would be fun. But don't think for a minute my professional judgment can be swayed by the taste of Maryland crab."

He laughed. "Maybe if I withhold the fudge."

"You wouldn't dare," she exclaimed in mock horror. "Josh loves fudge."

"You can take him whatever's leftover from our feast today."

"And he'll be bouncing off the walls from the sugar high. That kind of thing has to be planned far in advance to insure the least craziness afterward." She smiled at him. But then she looked away, giving him the impression that she was uncomfortable about something.

"So, try this first," he urged as he held out one of the tubs of salad.

"Um, no, that's okay. I'm not a big fan of shrimp."

"Okay, we'll save that one until I get you warmed up. This one, then." He opened the lid of crabmeat salad and stabbed a morsel onto a plastic fork, then passed it to her. With a second utensil, he took a bite for himself and savored it. "Mmm."

"Seriously? It's just crab salad."

"But it's the first bite of a meal that includes local crab, world-famous shrimp, the best fried chicken ever and concludes with freshly made fudge. You gotta think about the flavors, the tang and the sweet and the texture. Go ahead and try it. But think about what you're eating."

She put the crabmeat into her mouth. Nodded. "Okay, it's good. But I'm really hungry, so anything would be good right now."

"Hmm, not long ago, you said you weren't hungry. But that's okay. Maybe it came on suddenly. Try this." He shoved the bag of fried chicken toward her.

He even got her to taste the shrimp and admit it was the best she'd ever had. It was impossible not to watch her lips close around the food. Impossible not to notice the fullness and the slight upturn at the corners of her lips. Impossible not to imagine those lips on his own.

"It's all so good!" she said as she let herself truly enjoy what she was eating.

Her exclamation broke the spell. He was able to look away. When he dared to glance at her again, she was just Gwen Haverty, district attorney. He wanted her to stay that way. Because if he let his image of her change too much, his world would turn upside down.

"So about Omar Kingston," he said. "I hope

you'll read the file I sent you and then go with me to hear the witness." He handed her a package of fudge and she nibbled on a small piece.

"I've already read the file you sent over," she said. "And I have to depose the witness with you or risk accusations from your organization. But I don't think it'll matter. Kingston is a danger to society and needs to stay where he is."

And with that declaration, Gwen reminded him of all the reasons the two of them couldn't really be friends. They were opposites on the job, in temperament, and in beliefs about justice. Too bad she was the first and only woman to make him feel this alive since Beth's death.

He looked at her and disappointment suffused him even though he knew he shouldn't have been surprised. "And your judgment of Omar is based on what, exactly? Could it be his background as a troubled foster kid? Or was it that car he stole five years prior to the murder he was wrongly blamed for?" He waved his hand, not really wanting her to answer. "He was beaten up last night by thugs in lockup who know he wouldn't hurt a fly, even as big as he is. He doesn't belong there and we need to get him out before he's hurt worse."

She stared at him without a shred of sympathy in her eyes.

"Never mind," he said. "Just tell me a date and time to go out to the hospice in Frederick to see the witness and I'll make the arrangements."

She sighed and began to collect the remains of their meal. "If you can't get the woman to the court, it could be a while before I can clear enough time on my schedule."

"She's dying. I explained that already. She doesn't have 'a while.' Neither does Omar." He helped her divide the food into two bags.

"Look, get an affidavit and I'll see what I can do with that." Gwen accepted one of the bags of leftovers and stood.

"Gwen, we both know your boss isn't going to approve springing a man convicted of murder based on the affidavit of a dead woman. I need you to hear her yourself." He stood, too, and tossed their trash into a receptacle. When he looked at her again, he could see the coldness seeping back over her.

She was hardening her heart, as he knew she often had to do to be successful at her job. "I'll get back to you."

"I'll be waiting," he said gravely. She wouldn't make eye contact with him, and he turned to go.

"Thank you for lunch," she called to his back. Aaron waved his hand farewell without turning to face her again. Now that he knew her softer side, the ice-princess facade she wore like armor just broke his heart.

CHAPTER FIVE

GWEN WASN'T SURE WHAT she was feeling as she watched Aaron walk away. She coolly noted he needed a haircut and an iron for his shirt, but she felt a small regret that she'd disappointed him.

She was saved from further introspection by the familiar ring of her own phone. She thumbed it to life. "Gwen."

"Where are you?" Logan demanded. "There was a staff meeting and you missed it."

"Damn," she muttered as she looked at her watch. Where had the afternoon gone? "I need to meet with that Internal Affairs guy— Gerard something—in a half hour."

"Gerard Bainbridge. I don't know where you are right now, but you probably need to head over there now."

"On my way," she said as she eyed the bag of leftovers Aaron had made for her. She couldn't leave it sitting in her car to bake in the late summer sun. As she thumbed off her phone, she sighed and tossed the food in the trash. All except the fudge. She tucked the small package into her purse. It was chocolate, after all.

But after she hit the end button, she saw an odd icon lit up on the face of the Black-Berry. She'd never noticed it before. It took her a minute, standing there next to the garbage can, to figure out what it meant. In another couple of seconds, she was able to bring the mysterious photographs onto the tiny screen. Every one was a different angle of a young man who had been beaten badly. The bruising and swelling were horrible, but she looked at them all.

These were photos of Omar Kingston. Aaron had taken the pictures with her phone the night before and clearly forgotten to delete them. Or perhaps he'd intentionally left them for her to see. Maybe he hoped to garner some sympathy. If so, the ploy was working. No one could look at such pictures and not feel sorry for the victim. The ones of his bruised face were particularly compelling. Omar was young. It wouldn't be very long before her own son was his age.

After she'd seen each photo, she redialed Logan. "I need you to arrange for me to in-terview a witness at a hospice in Frederick as soon as possible. Call Aaron Zimmerman and he'll make it happen. I'll need a court reporter, too."

"Seriously? You're gonna cave to that guy?"

"Justice, Logan. Remember? Our job is to mete out justice. And that means making very sure we've put the right person behind bars."

"Whatever you say, Counselor."

"Text me with the details," she said. And yet during the whole drive to police headquarters where she would be meeting with an Internal Affairs rep, she seethed with annoyance that Aaron had gotten his way by tugging on her heart in such a sneaky, underhanded manner. Leaving those photos on her phone was pretty low. But she shouldn't be surprised.

Still, she was tired of men taking advantage of her caretaker side. First Clay, now Aaron. No matter how hard she tried to repress that softer aspect of herself, men were able to exploit it anyway.

GWEN'S ATTITUDE TOWARD the men in her life didn't improve much the next day.

"I'm telling you, Gwen," said John Fry, Chief of Criminal Appeals and her boss. "I've reviewed the file. This guy has gotten his sister, and God knows who else, to turn the witness somehow. He's behind bars and it's where he needs to stay."

"With all due respect, John," she said, looking across his desk at him, "I have to hear what the witness has to say and give her new story fair consideration. If Kingston belongs in prison, you know I'll do my best to keep him there."

"You could have stalled until the witness died," he said coldly.

Gwen stared at him for a moment, let the shock pass through her without reacting to it, then searched his eyes for some hint on how best to respond. His expression remained implacable.

"That's *not* what I do," she said evenly. "You know that. I do whatever it takes to make sure the public sees this office as just and fair. That's why you hired me in the first place. You needed to repair the image of the office with someone who actually cares. Right?"

John finally dropped his gaze. He pulled a stack of files across the surface of his desk. "You've done a great job with public perceptions. Just make sure you don't put any actual criminals back on the streets." He picked up a file and opened it, still avoiding eye contact.

"You know I always do my best." She left his office feeling a bit shaken. John had never before come down so hard about keeping anyone in prison. What could his motivation be? she wondered.

The organization in the office being what it was—barely existent—it took Gwen an hour to find the two files that made up the history of Omar Kingston's prosecution. But she didn't have time to do a thorough review. As she turned a page, Logan popped into her office.

"Gwen, Judge Merkle just agreed to hear an emergency motion filed by Release Initiative," he told her. With a smirk, he added, "It's on that Kingston guy."

Her first reaction was to close her eyes and sigh deeply. Why, oh, why couldn't Aaron have just waited. Her second reaction—

"You didn't call Aaron's office yesterday about scheduling the meeting with the witness, did you." It wasn't a question.

"It was on my list of things to do today," he said with no hint of remorse.

Gwen shot him her very best glare and he sobered and took a step back. "This is your fault," she muttered as she grabbed her purse and briefcase, "therefore, you're coming with me. And so help me, you better have every document I need, when I need it, while we're there."

"But—"

She put up her hand, palm out. Logan stopped himself from whining.

Instead, he said, "I've got the file from Release Initiative on my desk. Is there anything else you need me to bring?"

"Yeah." She pointed to the two wide folders holding the prosecution history for the Kingston case. Maybe she'd get a chance to read more while she waited for Aaron's motion to be heard. If not, it gave her some satisfaction to make Logan carry them.

AARON COULD FEEL THE heat of Gwen's anger as he sat beside her in Judge Merkle's courtroom waiting for his motion to be heard. Odd that he could read her so much better after just one lunch together. She was furious. Her legs were crossed, giving him a nice view of one calf. Her arms were crossed, making him note the sliver of exposed skin at her throat above the lapels of her suit and blouse collar. Her hair was tucked behind the ear nearest to him, but a few strands had come loose and he wished he dared move them back into place. She would likely bite off his hand if he tried.

Her anger didn't matter, he told himself. All that mattered was getting Omar out of prison as soon as possible. Gwen hadn't appeared cooperative enough so he'd taken the necessary steps to force the issue.

"You could have waited," she whispered to him.

"But Omar can't."

"I asked Logan to set up a time to go talk to your witness."

"Then the motion to make you do that ought to only take a minute of your time."

"Uh, sorry. My office doesn't like being the subject of a court mandate. I have to oppose."

He looked at her, confused. "Even though you were going to do it anyway?"

"There's a principle involved."

His eyebrows shot up. "And you're going to protect that principle even though you know you should hear my witness?"

"We've never been sure whether your witness is freely recanting or being pressured to do it. I was only going to cooperate because of the photos."

"What photos?"

Logan leaned forward and turned to glare at the two of them. "Shh," he admonished, even though they'd been whispering.

Without saying more, Gwen pulled out her PDA and brought the first photo up on the screen.

Aaron muttered a curse. He'd forgotten to

delete them after he'd sent them to his email account. Not wanting to be shushed by the likes of Logan again, he texted her a message. I meant to erase those. Sorry.

He watched her work the keys on her phone, then felt his vibrate in his hand. U wnt me to blv? Lol

He looked over at her BlackBerry as she went through the pictures again. He'd forgotten how bad they looked—worse than Omar had seemed face-to-face. Aaron wondered if he'd get a chance to use the snaps to win his motion today and called them up from his own email account.

Dnt evn thnk abt using tday, she texted him as he flipped through the pictures on his own phone.

I'll do whatever I have to do for Omar, he wrote back. Then he watched her recross her legs in the other direction, away from him. Her shoulder shifted, too, so that her body language shut him out.

You'd do the same, he tried.

I wldnt hv ur jb! Evr!

No time to respond. His motion was called and he and Gwen went to their respective tables.

Judge Merkle silently reread the motion, then looked over the top of his reading glasses at Aaron. "Seriously, Counselor? This is an emergency?"

Aaron stood. "Your Honor, I have indications that there are inmates in the Jessup Correctional Institution who've made it their goal to murder my client, Omar Kingston. These inmates have already done him serious bodily harm. He's currently being held out of their reach in the prison infirmary, but he won't remain there for much longer."

Merkle nodded. "Yes, fine, it's an emergency. Make your case."

Aaron almost regretted winning this part of the argument so easily—it meant he'd have no excuse to show the photographs. A perverse side of him wanted to use them here today, just because Gwen had demanded he not do it.

"A witness in Mr. Kingston's case has recanted, Your Honor. Prosecution has resisted hearing her testimony. On behalf of my client, I request you enjoin the government to schedule a disposition hearing immediately. My hope is that we will not need to retry his case to overturn his conviction, but rather we will be able to come to agreement based on the new testimony." He glanced pleasantly toward Gwen to indicate his willingness to cooperate.

She got to her feet, but held herself in check until the judge turned to her. "Ms. Haverty?" Merkle inquired.

"The State would be more than happy to hear Mr. Zimmerman's witness in a courtroom as soon as a hearing can be arranged. We were working on that just prior to being called here today."

"This cannot wait for a hearing in court, Your Honor," Aaron said. "The witness is already in hospice. It's critical for prosecution to conduct depositions immediately and at her bedside."

Merkle looked once more toward Gwen, his eyebrows raised as if to ask why in the world the prosecutor's office would resist doing this.

"You Honor, there is every likelihood that this witness is recanting under pressure or because of some promise made to her by the convicted prisoner or his people. In addition, this witness was not the only evidence of the prisoner's culpability at trial. The importance of her testimony should not be overblown. Nor is it possible to accommodate this request without pushing back other work on behalf of Maryland taxpayers."

She would have said more, but Merkle stopped her. "Go take the dying woman's deposition, Ms. Haverty. And do it within the next few days." He banged his gavel, passed the file to his clerk, and immediately called for the next problem on his docket.

Gwen packed up her things and exited the courtroom quickly, Logan struggling to keep up with his stack of unneeded files. She didn't look to see what Aaron was doing. She just wanted to get out of there.

He caught up to her anyway. "Gwen!" he called.

She stopped in her tracks, sure that she needed to be professionally polite but wishing she could either storm away from him or turn and confront him with her anger. Toggling between the two extremes, she did nothing.

"You don't have to talk to him right this minute," Logan advised quietly. He shifted a file that threatened to slip from his grasp. "We can just go."

"You go," she said. "I can't refuse to talk to him just because he's annoyed me. Again. You go ahead. I'll catch up with you."

She watched Logan depart, then turned to face Aaron. She did her best to keep her expression impassive.

"I have a surprise for you," he said with the engaging smile he used to defeat his opponents.

She took a small step back. "I don't want

anything from you," she snapped. "Just contact my office for times to depose your witness and—" She hesitated a fraction of a second, then lowered her voice to a whisper. "Otherwise, leave me alone."

His smile disappeared, his eyes wide. "It's really a surprise for Josh."

From the inside pocket of the blazer that didn't quite match his slacks he pulled out an envelope.

"Tickets to the Blue Man Group," he said.

"I told you to keep them. I won't have you disappointing Ben."

"These aren't the ones you gave me. I called in a favor and got two more."

Stunned, she said nothing for a beat. Then, "It's been sold out for a long time."

A smaller version of his smile came back and he winked. "Pays to be nice to people," he said. "Especially those with season's tickets."

She was stumped for an appropriate reply. "I don't get it."

"You don't get what?"

"Why go to the trouble of calling in a favor for me and my son even as you prepared an emergency motion, making me look bad, calling John Fry's attention to the case, forcing me to oppose you in court?"

He shrugged and held up the tickets. "This

is about two parents trying to make their kids happy." Nodding his head toward the court-room, he added, "That's just work."

"Just work? Are you joking? You made me look like an idiot back there." She wanted to shout the accusation but resisted somehow. She refused to give him the satisfaction of break-ing her composure.

"I did that?" he asked, and his amused ex-pression implied his belief that she'd done it without any help from him.

The element of truth in that implication brought her anger up another notch, but she said nothing and simply turned to go.

He put his hand gently on her arm to keep her from storming off. "Take the tickets, Gwen. For Joshua's sake. Take him to the show. It's for the same night as the ones you gave me. Our boys could meet. Maybe they'll hit if off. Ben doesn't have any friends in our new neighborhood yet. Maybe Josh could be a good influence on him."

She stared at him a moment, then found her-self admitting, "I only opposed your motion today because Fry insisted." Why did she feel the need to defend herself? Why did she want him to understand she had no choice?

"That sucks. Maybe you should find another job."

The way he said it elicited a chuckle from her. "Maybe so, but now's not a good time to be job hunting, what with Clayton threatening to sue for custody."

"Maybe when you work things out with him you can give job satisfaction more thought." He offered the two tickets to her again. After another hesitation, Gwen accepted them. She wanted Josh to be happy. Aaron grinned when she took them.

"Thank you. But I don't think our kids should meet."

He sobered. "They should be able to be friends, despite our opposing jobs. *We* should be able to be friends, too."

"I'm not trying to offend you. It's just that I have to be careful right now. About everything. Clay is willing to twist my actions, even innocent things, so he can use them against me. He's very convincing. I will not underestimate him ever again. He could make a friendship between us seem like the worst judgment on my part and play that into major problems for me if he files a custody petition. And I can't risk making my boss any angrier at me than he already is. He may be an ass, but I need my job to support my family."

Aaron's expression softened and it was this side of him that Gwen found so difficult to resist. Whenever he became sympathetic to her custody woes, or understanding about her parenting challenges, or especially kind when few others were willing to listen to her worries—she longed to spill her guts to the man.

"Let me know if there's anything I can do to help if he actually files a petition. You have a good attorney, right?"

"Melody Michaels. She's one of the best family practice attorneys I know."

"Good choice. There's no way she'll let Clay end up with custody."

Moved by his support, Gwen nodded and rushed out into the heat and then to the oven of her car. She headed for the safety of her office, where deep emotions dared not enter.

CHAPTER SIX

"I REVIEWED LOGAN'S notes," John said. "Didn't seem like you tried all that hard at the hearing today." His voice was calm but cold. He didn't take a seat, instead standing before her desk with hands on hips.

Gwen had no patience for him. She rose and picked up the stack of files Logan had replaced on her desk, then offered them to her boss. "You want to take over the Kingston case? Be my guest."

John's eyes went slightly wider as she all but shoved the files into his hands. She was so insistent he finally took them from her, then immediately put them back down. "You bring impartiality to the case and—"

She cut him off. "But you'd rather I just show an *appearance* of impartiality, is that it, John? You don't want me to actually *be* impartial. Is that how you're running things these days? You tell me what to do and I perform like a marionette?" She glared at him. But then it registered that she'd shocked him.

Had she gone too far? She felt deeply that she hadn't gone anywhere near far enough. But this man was her boss. And while government work was usually very secure, he could fire her for no reason at all.

In frustration—and maybe to hide her anger—she retreated to the window and looked out, giving the chief her back, allowing herself a moment to collect herself. She rubbed her temples where a headache was taking root. "I apologize. I shouldn't have spoken to you that way."

"Rough day?" he asked. It was the kindest thing she'd ever heard him say.

She turned to him again. "Actually, it's been a rough week. But I've managed worse." She went back to her desk chair and sat down heavily. "We could all use some serious vacation time."

Placated, he nodded his agreement. "You know you're a valued member of my team, right? Not a marionette."

She forced a smile. "You know I'd just tangle all the strings if you tried to make me into one."

"That's for sure," he agreed. "Just try not to let that weasel Zimmerman undo the hard work this office went through to put Kingston in prison. Okay?"

"I will do my best," she promised. The office phone saved her from listening to John speak any more uncharacteristic kindnesses, which made her feel worse instead of better. She gave him an inquiring look and he indicated she could answer because he was leaving.

She waited until he'd gone before she picked up. The receptionist said it was Melody Michaels on the phone. The bottom seemed to drop out of Gwen's stomach. Why would her custody lawyer be calling her?

"Gwen Haverty speaking," she said after she'd switched to the proper line.

"Hi, Gwen. Sorry to bother you at work. But I thought you'd want to know right away. Your instincts were right. Clayton filed the petition for full custody today."

AARON WENT HOME EARLY, for once. He'd prepped for the following day and taken home some files to review from the comfort of his bed later on. Before that, he wanted to spend a little time with his son. There were days when he felt he'd hardly seen Benjamin for weeks. Today the weather was nice outside. Not too hot. Maybe the two of them could go throw some balls at the park near the lake.

As soon as he walked through the door, he

was struck by a heavenly mixture of aromas both savory and sweet. Phyllis was a great cook. He headed back toward the kitchen to see what she'd started for dinner.

"I'm home," he called out, not wanting to startle anyone. He heard the thudding of Ben's feet racing from the family room to greet him. That brought joy into Aaron's heart. Even when Ben crashed into him and drew an involuntary "ooph," Aaron grinned. Until he realized Ben was clinging to him.

"What's up, buddy?" Aaron asked his son.

"Nothing." But his voice lacked its usual enthusiasm. "This is just one of those days, you know?"

Aaron thought about that a moment. "School okay?"

"Yeah," But he continued to cling.

"That's good," Aaron said, not sure what could have made this day "one of those" for his nine-year-old. Then Ben let go and led the way to the kitchen, where Phyllis could be heard puttering with cookware.

"Something smells really good," he said to her.

She turned and looked at him and he could see her eyes were red-rimmed. She'd been crying. "You know I always make her favorite on this day."

Aaron went very still. He didn't speak, didn't move, didn't even breathe. Inside, a hot mixture of dread and sorrow and guilt swirled around, knotting his stomach. The world tilted for a moment.

He'd forgotten.

Not once through the whole day had it crossed his mind that today would have been Beth's birthday—her thirty-fifth. His wife, his beautiful, loving wife had been gone only three years, and he'd forgotten her birthday.

"You forgot," Phyllis said without recrimination. "That's okay. It's hard for men to remember these things. And it's been three years now." But her voice broke on the last two words and she turned away, sniffing. The meatballs and sauce would be seasoned with tears, as they were every year.

Ben stood nearby, staring at him wide-eyed. He didn't seem upset, but he watched closely, waiting to see what would happen next.

Aaron had no words. But breathing returned to him, as nature dictated. And with the resumption of lung activity came a surprising flash of rebellion. It had been three years. He'd mourned his beloved for three years. Wasn't it time to let go and move on? Didn't he deserve to get on with living instead of just pacing through time?

But on the heels of those unexpected thoughts came a surprising burn to his eyes. He thought he'd run out of tears. Thought his grief was abating. But here it was again, as if she'd died only yesterday. And yet…

He glanced at his son. Ben was waiting to see what his father would do or say. Ben deserved a life that didn't revolve around his dead mother, didn't he?

"Your mom would have been all over those meatballs by now." He forced a smile. "She would have been sneaking tastes, not caring that they were too hot. I can see her dancing on her tiptoes, waving her hand across her mouth as if that would cool things down faster. She would laugh at herself, but she'd do it again in an hour. She loved your grandmother's meatballs and sauce."

A light seemed to seep into Ben's eyes and he smiled, first hesitantly, then more fully. "Why didn't she just wait for dinner?"

Aaron was suffused with a need to celebrate who Beth had been and to share that with the son she'd blessed him with. This time, his smile was genuine. "Because the smell of them cooking was too much for her. Or so she said."

"Because she liked to drive me crazy," Phyllis added with her back still to them. She kept on stirring the sauce, but her voice was not as tremulous. "She just couldn't wait. Your mother always knew what she wanted and went after it. You're a lot like her, Ben."

"I am?"

Ben hadn't asked many questions about his mother. Perhaps he'd sensed that it would cause his father and grandmother pain. Aaron hadn't thought to give him stories about Beth. Until today.

"You are," Aaron confirmed. "Isn't that your favorite cake I smell baking in the oven? You have the same eye color, the same spirit of adventure." He found himself speaking past a lump in his throat, but he smiled to let Ben know this subject was not forbidden. At least not from now on. Why had it been taboo these past years? Aaron didn't know.

"You're smart like she was, too. You're so curious all the time, just like your mom." He ruffled Ben's hair. "Maybe someday soon, we can get out the old photographs and I can tell you more."

"That'd be cool," Ben said.

"Right now, help your grandmother set the table for this great meal she's made for us in honor of your mom's birthday." He looked over at his mother-in-law and saw the wistful expression in her eyes. But she wasn't weeping anymore and that was a good sign.

Aaron left the kitchen and headed up to his bedroom to change out of his work clothes. As he climbed the steps, the weight of guilt descended back onto his shoulders. How could he have forgotten the significance of this day? Beth's birthday, of all days?

The question he knew he would have to wrestle with now was whether to forgive himself and begin to move on with his life, or continue to live in grief and regret and guilt? The choice seemed obvious. He even knew a particular woman he'd like to date. Then why was it so damn difficult to make himself let go of the memory of Beth and allow himself to get to know the living, breathing Gwen Haverty?

WITH THE NEWS OF CLAYTON'S petition for custody weighing on her, Gwen left work earlier than usual. She let Misha go home and then went in search of Joshua, who had not come running to greet her as he used to when he was small. She couldn't remember the last time that had happened and she mourned those days when her relationship with her son had been simpler. The fact that he no longer so much as acknowledged her arrival made her worry that Clayton would, or perhaps already had, put ideas into Josh's head about how much better things would be living with Dad. Thoughts of losing her son were like shards of glass cutting through her. She couldn't bear it.

She found him in his bedroom, earbuds plugged in, eyes glued to his TV, game controller clutched in his hands, thumbs actively working the buttons. He didn't even look up at her when she made her way into his room.

"Hi, Josh," she said.

He glanced ever so briefly in her direction, but instantly returned his concentration to his game.

"I have a surprise for you."

He grunted something that sounded like *What?* but his thumbs never paused in their frenetic movement.

"I'll wait until you're finished with your game," she said. The last thing she wanted right now was to end up in a fight with him about spending so much time gaming. Normally, she'd have made him turn the thing off as soon as she walked in the house, but not tonight. Feeling drained and yet also electrified by worry, she headed out of his room.

At the threshold, she turned back and caught his gaze upon her and his fingers still. But the meaning of his intense focus was indecipherable. He shifted his eyes back to the screen so quickly she wondered if she'd imagined the moment.

"I'm making dinner tonight. Mac and cheese, minifranks, corn and peas in butter sauce." This was his favorite meal and she hoped it would help to win a smile from him. He only spared her a slight nod. "I'll call when it's ready," she said.

Feeling frustrated and confused and scared, she went to her bedroom and changed out of her suit into her pajamas, even though it was early still. Daylight streamed through her bedroom window, an unusual sight for her on a weekday. She rarely came home before dark. She'd dash around the kitchen still in her suit, putting some semblance of a meal together. She'd eat with Josh, usually in silence, then retreat to her bedroom. She owned a pair of jeans, but wasn't sure where they were. She lived in her suits.

Shoving her feet into slippers, she noticed how soft and cuddly they felt. How long had it been since she'd last put them on? She couldn't remember, which seemed very, very wrong. She should come home at this hour more often, spend more time with her son, put on her jeans or maybe even a sweat suit and relax.

Another thought struck her. Would it reflect badly on her in court that she worked so many hours, or would a judge see her as a good provider?

Staring at her slippers, she felt the sting of tears, then saw one fall onto the fuzzy fabric. Without conscious thought, she slid slowly down the doorjamb where she'd been leaning, until she ended up sitting on the floor of her closet, wrapped in a fog of misery.

Stop crying, she told herself. If Josh saw her like this, he'd be upset. She didn't think he'd ever seen her cry. She'd always been strong for him. Even when she'd found the hotel receipt in Clayton's pocket when he'd said he was at work. Even when she'd discovered he'd had more than one affair. Even when his latest cheat had found the audacity to call him at home. She'd been strong. She hadn't shed a tear. At least not in front of Josh.

But the tears came now.

Pull yourself together. Get up and go make the dinner you promised your son. But she sat there and remembered all the times Clay had persuaded her she was imagining things, all the lies he'd told so convincingly that she'd begun to question what she'd seen and heard. Then there were Clay's pleas for mercy, his tears, his promises to reform. He loved her, he'd said. He loved Joshua. He wanted to be a family. Sometimes she believed him. Even now, he could still be kind to her. He'd changed his mind about taking Josh to New York. She wanted to believe he had some evil motivation, but she knew her ex may have simply decided to be decent. And yet, for Gwen, Clayton remained the monster. His manipulations of her, his anger and his unfaithfulness had stolen so much of who she'd once been. How had she let that happen? Then a door seemed to unlock inside her brain and she could see him standing in front of her, anger etching his face and his fist raised above her, ready to come crashing down upon her.

Abruptly, she shut that memory off and covered her face with her hands. "Stop," she said aloud. "Enough." And she rubbed her eyes as if she could physically push the tears back to where they'd come from.

"I thought you were making dinner?" Josh said from the hallway as he looked into her room and across to where she sat in her closet doorway.

His chilly, self-centered comment prodded her out of inertia, but she didn't immediately rise. "I'm not having a very good day," she said.

"Why not?" This time he sounded a little warmer, as if it might be possible he held a shred of caring in his cold little ten-year-old heart.

The debate inside her head seemed to go on for an eternity, but only seconds passed. In the end, she decided to tell her son the truth. While she hated to worry him, he'd find out eventually.

"Because your father filed papers in court to try to get sole custody of you. And I don't want that." Her voice broke on the last word, but she kept herself from openly weeping in front of him.

He looked at her steadily without any expression. Then he said, "That would suck worse than living here."

Despite everything, Gwen cracked up. She laughed even harder as she repeated his matter-of-fact words between gasps for air. After a while, she saw Josh was laughing, too, though he clearly wasn't sure what could be so funny. "Suck…worse…than here," Gwen said again, and she had to hold her stomach as she tried to stop laughing.

Working to regain control of herself, she motioned for Josh to come over. When he got within reach, she grabbed his shirt and pulled him to her. He resisted, so she tickled his ribs and wrestled him to the floor. The raucous laughter started all over again. But after a while, she just hugged him as their silliness ebbed. And her son hugged her back.

"I'm sorry living here with me has sucked for you, Josh. I promise I'll try to make things better."

"You've said that before," he noted without emotion, but his small arms squeezed a little tighter around her shoulders, making Gwen recall how close they'd been when her son was younger.

When had things changed? When had they begun to drift apart? Certainly before Clayton had moved out.

She'd mistakenly let Clay stay too long in their lives because she wanted Josh to have a father. But then Josh had grown to be so much like his father—insensitive, often selfish. Why couldn't her boy have grown up with a man more like Aaron—kind and sensitive? She set aside that disturbing thought and responded to Josh.

"That's true," she admitted. "I've said that before." She eased her grasp on him and he shifted back so she could look into his eyes. "I guess I'll just have to try making things better with actions instead of words. For one thing, I'm taking you to see the Blue Man Group, after all."

"How is that going to happen?" he asked.

"Your dad changed his mind about taking you to New York, and even though I'd given our tickets away, a friend got me two more. That was the surprise I had for you tonight."

"Well, that's a good start at making things suck less." His small grin warmed her heart.

"Sometimes making things suck less is a two-person job. Will you help?"

He sobered, looking skeptical. "How?"

"Let's start with you helping me make dinner tonight."

He rolled his eyes. "It's always about me not getting to play my games."

"Tonight, it's just about getting dinner on the table at a decent hour, okay?" She got to her feet and so did he. She looked down at her son. When had he grown so tall? "I love you, Josh." She resisted the urge to touch him, sensing he was feeling confused and wouldn't welcome it.

He shrugged. "Am I going to end up living with Dad?" he asked. He tried hard to keep his voice even, as if he didn't care. But she could hear the edge in his voice.

"You said that would be worse than living here, right?"

He looked up at her and there was anger in his youthful eyes. "When does it ever matter what I want? No one ever asks me what I want."

"I'm asking you now," she said softly.

Another shrug. Oh, how it strained her nerves to see that frequent gesture.

"Well, I'll go with 'it would suck worse' until you tell me otherwise. Right now, I'm starving and I'm going to go cook. If you want to help, that would be great. If not, well, I'll be a little sad about that, but I'll get over it after a while." With that, Gwen made herself walk away.

She padded in her seldom-worn slippers down the stairs and into the kitchen, while her longing for her son's love stretched like a rubber band until it seemed it would have to snap.

But as she pulled pans out from cupboards, she realized she wasn't alone in the room. Her heart turned over as she glimpsed Joshua lurking on the threshold of the kitchen. He was watching her. Should she invite him in? Give him a job? Tell him what to do?

Or was this one of those moments when she had to quash her motherly instincts and let her son find his own way?

"I already told you. Living with Dad would suck worse than here."

"Okay. That's good to know." She continued

to get out ingredients for a slapdash meal. "I'll do my very best to make sure you stay with me." But then she knew she had to say something to help her son cope with the conflict his parents were about to step into. "Josh, he's still your father. You need to spend time with him, do things together. He's trying, I think, to be a good father to you. He loves you."

Josh shrugged, but some of the tension seemed to ease out of his shoulders. "We should make double so we have leftovers," he said as he got out another box of macaroni and cheese.

"Good idea. So I'll need a bigger pot."

When he opened a cupboard himself to get it out, Gwen's heart leaped with disproportionate pleasure. It was the little things, right? This small gesture from Josh just made her want to sing.

"Measuring cup?" she added, wondering if he'd cook the stuff while she focused on the franks.

"I'm on it. I'm not a baby anymore, Mom. I know how to do this."

"Great! I'll work on the rest. Do you want peas and carrots or a salad?"

"Peas, please," he said with a goofy grin.

And the light mood, so different from the rest of her day, went on like that all the way through cooking and eating the meal. Josh actually participated in a conversation, telling her some things about his three-day-a-week summer camp, asking if she'd donated money for the recent earthquake victims. He even remembered that he had some camp papers for her to sign.

"Go ahead and get your backpack and pull out the papers," she said. "I'll get these dishes into the dishwasher."

Next time she looked up, she saw him holding a single bright green sheet of paper in his hands as if reading it for the first time.

"What's that?" she asked, wanting to know what would hold his rapt attention.

"It's some stuff about a karate class once school starts. It's an after-school program, but it's right there in the gym. It's just two days a week." He finished reading and looked off into space for a moment. "Can I go?"

"To the karate class?"

"Yeah. It'd be cool. And better than sitting around here after school with Marsha."

"Her name is Misha, as you well know." He'd been calling his babysitter Marsha for months because she looked like Marsha Brady from the *Brady Bunch* TV show. Gwen cursed cable TV for airing those old shows—as if they hadn't been silly enough the first time.

Josh dropped the paper onto the table. "I figured you wouldn't let me go. You can't pick me up, or something. It's always something." He began to walk away, heading out of the kitchen.

"Wait!" she said. "I didn't say that. Can I have a second to look at the information, please?"

He paused in the doorway and she could see he toggled between hope and his certainty that he would be denied. She read the paper and her eyes went straight to the time of day the karate classes got out. Five o'clock, Tuesdays and Thursdays. Late enough for some parents to be off work, but not late enough for Gwen's job.

She wished Misha didn't have such a bad driving record. For a fee, she might have agreed to pick him up from the class, but Gwen couldn't trust her driving. Too bad Misha was the only sitter flexible enough to accommodate her crazy work schedule. Would she ever be able to find someone who could pick up Josh when she absolutely couldn't?

Her phone began to dance across the kitchen counter.

"That's going to be your office. You'll have to fix some emergency," Josh said with a frightening lack of emotion. "I'm going back to my game."

As she watched him go, Gwen admitted feeling relieved. Her son created a veritable tornado of tension inside her sometimes. Better to answer her phone and fix an emergency.

"Gwen Haverty," she said after she brought the BlackBerry to her ear.

"Hi, Gwen. It's Aaron."

She had no idea why he had called her now, but her first thought was that Aaron would save her. He would help her figure out what to do about the karate class so she could let Josh take it. Aaron was her knight in shining armor and he'd make everything okay again. But as these thoughts dashed through her mind, another part of her brain quite sensibly told her to leave Aaron out of her problems, avoid making him into her savior, push him away. Because if she let herself lean on Aaron, she'd probably never stop.

"I have a question for you," he said when she didn't respond to his greeting. "And don't say no until you've heard me out."

CHAPTER SEVEN

GUMPTION. AARON HAD NEEDED a lot of it to make the call. Ben was the instigator, of course. When Aaron told him about scoring two more tickets, one thing led to another. Now Aaron found himself inviting his courtroom archenemy on what sounded far too much like a date. He did his best to make the invitation seem like something simply for the kids.

"Ben is pretty much insisting that we go to the show together and dinner beforehand. I know what you said before about not getting too friendly, but he won't let up. Says he hasn't been around kids his own age since we moved to the new house. So I'm issuing a formal invitation. Will you and Josh please join me and Ben for dinner Friday night?"

He knew she would decline and he wasn't sure how he would explain things to Ben. The silence resonated so loudly he wanted to hold the phone away from his ear. But he forced himself to wait through the endless seconds.

Finally, she said, "Yes, thank you. That would be lovely."

He let the air out of his lungs. Then her words registered. Her turn to listen to some silence. At last, he said, "Oh. That's great. Good. Okay, then."

She laughed. "Okay, then."

"Um, show is at seven, so how about we pick you up at four-thirty. You and Josh choose the place to eat."

"Deal."

"Um, Gwen?"

"Yes?"

"Why did you accept? Earlier you seemed dead set against this kind of thing."

"Let's just say you called at the right moment. You seem to have a knack for that. Plus, I'm pretty sure Clayton is already in New York so he won't catch me out with you. But this isn't a date. It's for Josh. And Ben. Okay?"

"Of course." But he smiled. He was counting it as a date. His first since Beth's death. Despite his angst earlier in the evening, this felt like a good beginning.

FRIDAY EVENING, GWEN gave thanks that Clayton was out of town. The last thing she needed was to have him see her going out with Aaron. Clay would be sure to make as much of it as he could, perhaps using it to accuse her of bad judgment. While she wasn't exactly breaking any rules by being friendly with her courtroom opposition, going out socially with him could be twisted into seeming like a conflict of interest and therefore a violation of government ethics. Appearances were everything for government employees.

As she put on the earrings that were the last touch to her usual theater attire of black silk suit and red heels, she told herself she was doing this for Josh's sake. It had nothing to do with Aaron at all. Funny, though, that she was determined to look her best.

The man was right on time. As she headed for the front door, the house phone rang. She grabbed the receiver and answered while Joshua's footsteps pounded down the stairs toward the entrance.

"Hi, Gweny dear. How are things?"

"Hi, Mom. Everything is fine. But I was just on my way out the door. Can I call you back?"

"You're going out on a Friday night? On a date? Hallelujah! Finally!"

"Mom, it's not—"

"Pleeease don't tell me it's not a date. Let your mother cling to one shred of hope that you will have some fun with a nice man, let him court you, maybe fall madly in love."

"Uh, yeah, okay. I gotta go. Love to you and Dad."

"No, wait!" Judy Masoner would not be put off if she had something to say. "Your father and I are long overdue for a visit. I've emailed you with a few possible weeks, but I haven't heard back. We need to spend some quality time with you and our grandson."

"I've been busy. But I'll look at the email and get back to you. It'd be nice to see you both," she added, even though a weight settled in her chest at the prospect.

"Great! Have a wonderful time on your date!" And she clicked off the phone.

No time to think about how much she would rather her parents did not come visit while she was coping with a custody battle. Their boundless energy and exuberance and adoration of each other would only serve to remind her of all that she didn't have in her own life.

Chatter came to her from the foyer. Josh had let Aaron and Ben into the house and introductions had clearly been made.

"Hello," she said as she came to a stop in the entryway. "Sorry I didn't come to the door. My mother just called."

"Mom, look," Josh said with a dramatic whine. He indicated the casual attire of Aaron and his son. Ben was wearing a button-up shirt, but no tie.

"Fine," she said. "You can leave the tie at home, I guess."

As Josh yanked off the offending garment and tossed it on the entry table, Gwen eyed Aaron. He wore a shirt with no tie, blazer, khakis. Nothing fancy. He'd obviously felt no desire to dress up for her. Let that be a lesson, she admonished herself silently.

"You look lovely," Aaron said without taking his eyes from her face.

Gwen thought it was nice of him not to check out her body, and yet that was somehow a little disappointing, too.

"Then again, you always look perfect," he added.

She resisted the urge to defend herself. Taking care with one's clothing didn't need to be explained. Instead she said, "We can go as soon as Josh takes his tie upstairs."

"C'mon, Ben, I'll show you my room." Josh grabbed his tie and headed for the stairs.

It was hard for Gwen not to say, *Never mind,* the instant she realized the kids would be leaving her with Aaron. Being alone with him now, in her home, seemed far too intimate. But the boys scampered up the stairs, sounding like a herd of bison. She stood in her own foyer, feeling very awkward.

"They seem to have hit it off," Aaron said. "That's good. Ben could use a friend his own age since he's starting in a new school."

"They're in the same school?" she asked, incredulous.

"No. You're in a different zone. But we could get them together on weekends now and then."

She thought of the karate class being held at Joshua's school. Had she read that the class was open to the whole district? Did she dare ask Aaron if Ben would be interested so they could share the driving? But her thought was cut off before she could decide. To her horror, she saw through the sidelights that Clayton Haverty III was walking up to her door. She groaned.

"Clayton is here. He's supposed to be in New York. I can't imagine what he wants, but this isn't going to be good."

"Too bad we're not already on our way," Aaron said. "But I'm here, so he won't behave too badly."

"You don't know the man very well." She opened the door for Joshua's father.

Without a greeting or even acknowledging that Aaron was there, Clay said, "I came to see Joshua before I go to New York. I want to explain why I'm not taking him with me." He glanced at his watch as he shifted from one foot to the other on the porch.

She stared at him and words simply would not come to her lips. But Aaron stood by calmly, quietly.

"Clayton," she said, finally. "Josh knows about your petition for custody. He's pretty upset about that. I don't think this is a good time for you to see him. And we're about to leave for dinner out."

"I want to talk to my son. Is he up in his room?" He walked past her and would have headed up the stairs, but Aaron casually moved into his path and put out his hand.

"Nice to see you again, Clay," Aaron said with a smile that seemed genuine. Clay shook Aaron's hand automatically, but there was no sign of recognition in his expression.

"I'm here to see Josh," Clay said.

"We have to leave or we'll be late for our show," Gwen said firmly as she moved around the two men to stand beside Aaron and block the way to the stairs. "You are not allowed to barge into my home and demand to see Josh whenever you want. You have to call first and schedule a time."

Clay glared at her. "This is the problem,

Gwendolyn. You make everything so difficult. I'm heading out of town for a week and I have a half hour to spend with my boy before I have to go. Are you seriously saying I can't see my son when my schedule allows for it? That's insane. As usual, you're complicating things. I don't get to spend enough time with him as it is. You've said so yourself." He glanced over at Aaron, as if registering his presence for the first time. "You think Josh is going to want to spend time with this yahoo instead of his own father?"

She refused to defend the company she was keeping and instead focused on the real issues. "Our custody agreement clearly requires you to abide by the court-ordered schedule and to make arrangements in advance and with my agreement. I don't agree to you ruining our evening by making us late tonight."

"You know, I'd have been done saying goodbye to him by now if you just let me go up without all this protesting. So now, you're the one making you late. I'm going up to see Joshua now." He stepped forward as if to blow right past the two adults guarding the stairway.

Gwen and Aaron moved closer together to more effectively block Clay's path. "This isn't your house anymore, Clay," she said. "And I'm simply not going to let you behave as if you own the place—or me. You need to go now—without talking to Josh."

"Who the hell are *you,* anyway?" Clay said directly to Aaron. "What are you doing in my wife's house? And you have about ten seconds to get out of my way."

Aaron's expression remained calm. "Gwen asked you very clearly to leave her house. She explained that you are required by court order to make arrangements to see Josh ahead of time. So you need to go now." He spoke so quietly but so firmly that even Gwen was a little taken aback. This was not the cheerful, almost carefree person she knew.

Clay glared at Aaron, then returned his attention to Gwen. "Get this guy out of my face and bring Josh down now. I'll talk to him outside, if that'll make you happy."

"I'm not going to do that, Clay." Her defiance seemed to surprise Clay. She wondered if he'd become used to her trying to keep things peaceful for Joshua's sake. She'd conceded to him more often than not during their rocky marriage. And lately, she'd fallen back into that bad habit in an effort to avoid a custody battle. But giving in to Clay hadn't gotten her anywhere, she realized. He'd filed the petition anyway. With Aaron beside her, it felt right to let Clay know that enough was enough.

Clayton's face began to turn red. He put his hand on Gwen's shoulder to push her out of the way, but Aaron grasped the man's wrist and stepped forward. The action seemed to take place in slow motion, yet in seconds, Clay was pinned to the wall by Aaron's body. There was no arm across Clay's throat or knee to groin. Aaron simply had hold of Clay's wrist in an awkward twist while he pressed his shoulder into Clay's chest. Gwen wasn't sure what would have happened if Clay had struggled, but he didn't. Perhaps he was as shocked as she was by Aaron's maneuver.

AARON COULDN'T BELIEVE he was in this position. He had rarely had any reason to use his defensive skills, but here he was with the excessively annoying Clayton Haverty up against the wall. The instant the man had laid hands on Gwen, his reflexes had kicked in. He wondered if there had been different choices, but none came to mind as he stood there holding Clay in place and looking into the man's cold, angry eyes.

"Back off, asshole," Clay said.

"Are we all going to remain calm and avoid shoving?" Aaron asked, trying not to sound as though he were speaking to a child.

Clay nodded. Aaron stepped back, rejoining Gwen to protect the stairs.

"That was assault," Clay said. "You're in a lot of trouble, buddy."

Aaron squinted at him. "You don't remember who I am, do you? Cuz I can tell you with complete certainty that what just happened will not get me in any trouble."

From the top of the stairs behind them, a small voice said, "Dad? What's going on? We're supposed to be going to see the Blue Man Group."

"Maybe we should take Joshua's wishes into account," Aaron suggested, eyes still locked with Clay's. "He doesn't want to be late."

"Shut up," Clay said, nearly spitting the words as he pointed a finger under Aaron's nose.

Aaron didn't take his attention off Clay, but he asked Gwen, "Do you want to get the boys back to Josh's bedroom while I see Clay out the door? We can leave as soon as he's on his way to New York."

"Good idea." She turned and ran up the stairs. Over her shoulder, she called back, "Don't make me call the authorities, Clay."

His voice strident, Clay called after her, "You're leaving me no choice, Gwendolyn. I'll take him out of Maryland if I have to. New

York courts will agree I can provide for him better than you've been. Between his sliding grades and the long hours he has to spend with babysitters, you barely even see him. You're not the primary caretaker we all thought you'd be when custody was figured out two years ago. If he lived with me in New York, he'd spend quality time with me."

Aaron heard Gwen's feet hesitate but then she moved on, ushering the boys ahead of her. Clay didn't try to go up for Josh again, but Aaron could feel the urge to do so pouring off the man.

"Taking Josh out of Maryland would be kidnapping," Aaron said. "That's a felony. Can you continue to practice law in New York if you're convicted of that? I know you'd be disbarred in Maryland. You're working in both states right now. And I'm sure you don't want to jeopardize your career."

"I only work in Maryland so I can see my son. And I could pick him up from school one day and take him to my condo in New York to live. By the time Gwen got the authorities to do anything about it, I'd have him established in the best school."

Aaron wondered about the level of truth to that threat. Maryland would likely be slow to move in any meaningful way to retrieve Josh from his own father if the boy went willingly, given Clay had visitation rights, despite her current full custody. But he knew little of New York custody law.

"What good could come of that? Don't you want what's best for Joshua?"

"Don't you tell me what's best for my son. I lived my whole life under the thumb of a tyrannical mother and I won't let Joshua suffer through that. He'll grow up to be a strong man with me instead of the weak, whiny little gamer-zombie she's turning him into."

"Josh seems like a good kid to me."

"Of course he's a good kid, no thanks to his mother," Clay said.

"And you seem like you want to be a good father. But you have to leave now."

Clay squared his shoulders. "I paid for this house. My son lives here. I have more right here than you do."

Aaron couldn't keep himself from taking a step closer to Clay. He wasn't as tall as Gwen's ex, but Aaron knew he could have a certain presence when he wanted to. Clay took the expected step back. "This isn't your house anymore and Gwen asked you to leave."

Clay finally moved across the foyer. He grasped the doorknob. "This isn't over. Tell Gwen I'm watching her. I've noted the time she's spent with you, Zimmerman, and I'll make sure everyone else knows about it, too. Sleeping with the enemy. That'll look great to her colleagues. She won't keep her job with that kind of conflict of interest out in the open. Tell her. I'm taking my son."

He slammed the door hard enough to rattle the decorative glass panes in the center. Aaron walked over and threw the dead bolt, not trusting Clay. He turned immediately and raced up the stairs, hurrying to get to Gwen so he could ease her mind. He didn't realize she'd already begun to come down.

"Is he gone?" she asked, sounding more vulnerable than he would have expected.

"Yes." He slowed his pace and took the last step to her. He wanted—needed—to comfort her, and he hoped she wouldn't retreat from him.

Going on instinct, he gradually encircled her with his arms. She didn't resist and instead put her head on his shoulder and held on. It felt good to give another human being the benefit of his strength, to offer the comfort of a physical embrace. He hadn't realized how much he'd missed this kind of contact.

"Thank you." Her breath whispered over his ear, awakening long-dormant sensations along his nerve endings, making his skin tighten.

His desire to comfort her shifted to just desire.
It felt so unutterably good to have a woman in
his arms—and not just any woman, but Gwen,
who had invaded his dreams lately.

"I'm glad I could help," he whispered back
as he resisted the urge to breathe deeply of the
clean scent of her hair.

While he struggled to shut down his own
needs, he noted the smoothness of her jacket
and the soft yet firm quality of her body beneath the silk. In his arms, she was much
smaller than she'd seemed before. She fit him
well, her cheek at the level of his throat and
her breasts pressed to his chest. He could kiss
her easily or, with the slightest uplift onto her
toes, she could kiss him. How long had it been
since he'd been kissed by a woman? Too damn
long.

He wanted, wanted, wanted to feel her
mouth against his, to taste and feel the flavor
and heat of kissing her. Right now.

Without conscious thought, his hand drifted
to the nape of her neck. His face turned very
gently toward hers, and his body shifted ever
so slightly as he made ready to give in to his
desire. Did she feel the heat building between
them? Did she want what he wanted? Had she
purposefully turned so that her breath slipped
across the skin above his collar? Was she lift-

ing her head to move away from him or to give him access? Would he be able to wait to be sure?

No waiting. She lifted her gaze to his in unmistakable invitation. And he accepted, bringing his mouth to hers, first gently, but then with growing urgency spurred by long abstinence and by the peppermint taste of her. He felt her hands clutching his shoulders and the warmth of her body pressed along the length of him, one breath chasing the next as fast as his own.

Until he sensed her withdrawal and he eased his embrace.

"No," she whispered. "This is all wrong."

He would have asked her why it was wrong, how it could possibly be wrong. But the sound of giggling trickled into his consciousness. He wanted to shut it out, but more giggles came from above them. Something that sounded suspiciously like a boyish "ee-ew" told Aaron they'd been caught.

Gwen groaned quietly as the same realization must have come to her.

"Are we going or not?" Ben asked, laughter in his voice. Josh cracked up.

Aaron couldn't make himself look at the top of the stairs just yet. "Caught," he said as he took a step down and away from her.

She turned to the boys. "Yes, we're going. But not until I check to make sure you cleaned up after yourselves in your room." With her heels tapping on the wooden flooring, she chased the boys into Josh's room.

Aaron headed down to the foyer, grateful she'd given him a moment to collect himself before he'd have to face his son and hers. Wow, he'd reacted quite decisively to that brief encounter. He hoped he could get himself under control and stay that way for the rest of the evening.

The clomp of many feet warned him that Gwen and the kids were approaching. As they walked out to the car, the chatter between the boys filled the silence, so there was no need to actually talk to the woman he'd just kissed so passionately.

GWEN FELT THE SILENCE to her very bones. More like nontalking instead of silence because the kids were having a deep conversation in the backseat.

"Dude, your mom kissed my dad," Ben whispered.

"Other way around," Josh countered. "I just hope *my* dad doesn't catch 'em, cuz he wouldn't be nice about it."

"Aw, don't worry about it. My dad can take

care of himself and everyone else. You worried about your dad?"

"No," Josh said a little too quickly. Then in a smaller voice, "Maybe."

"What'll he do?"

Gwen didn't want Joshua to think too hard about what Clay might do, so she jumped into the conversation. "You know your dad just gets upset sometimes, right, Josh? He'll calm down like he always does." She turned in her seat to look directly at her son. "I won't let anything happen, okay?"

"Okay."

She faced forward again, once more immersed in the adult silence while Ben and Josh drifted off into a discussion about video games. Aaron was driving them in his older Jeep Wrangler so she had nothing to think about other than that kiss and the many, many issues the evening had already created. Clay's threats weighed on her. She'd have to alert the school and Misha would have to be better prepared. This might even cause the babysitter to finally quit. Should Gwen tell her soon-to-be-visiting parents? Would anyone believe Clay could be so rotten? Too many questions. She leaned on the armrest and rubbed her temple.

She also couldn't stop thinking about how she'd willingly kissed Aaron.

Yes, she had to admit, at least to herself, that she had encouraged him. Not that he'd needed much. He'd probably intended merely to comfort her with his initial hug, but it had only taken seconds for comfort to become passion.

Did she regret the kiss? Yes. No. She should. But she didn't. Not yet, anyway. She was certain Clayton would make her very, very sorry for even having Aaron in her home. And if Clay started spreading stories about her and Aaron, there would need to be serious damage control. No matter how innocent they kept their friendship—and that might be difficult now that they'd breached certain boundaries by kissing—people would make assumptions and then question her willingness to fight him in court as tenaciously as she should. But she set that worry aside for now. At this very moment, she was grateful for the memory of that lovely kiss, for his company in the aftermath of Clayton's tirade, and for his calm and silent presence beside her.

The restaurant wasn't far. As soon as he parked, Aaron cheerfully urged them all to get inside and eat fast so they didn't miss the opening of the show. The kids ran ahead. Aaron walked beside Gwen. He gently took her hand in his. And even though the gesture

both scared her and excited her, she let him. No one else was around to see her moment of weakness.

As they walked, he said, "You've probably already thought of this—you should talk to Josh about what to do if his father tries to pick him up at school. He needs to be prepared. And to understand you care."

She nodded. "Not looking forward to that. He's not quite sure which of us he likes better, though most recently he said it would suck worse to live with his father."

Aaron chuckled. "In kid language, that says he very much wants to stay with you."

They got to the door and he opened it for her. The boys were already inside. Aaron gave his first name to the hostess, then turned back to Gwen.

"I could talk to him, if you want. Might work better. Might be worse."

She thought about it. "I think if you get a chance to say something to him, go ahead. He might see you as more neutral than me. He might take advice from a man better than he takes it from his mom."

He smiled. "Or he'll assume I'm saying what you told me to say in the hopes of buttering you up for another kiss."

CHAPTER EIGHT

BEFORE SHE COULD GET Aaron to agree that kissing was something that couldn't be repeated, they were called to the table.

"Dad," Ben said as soon as they were settled into seats and had ordered their food. "Josh is going to take karate as soon as school starts. It's an after-school program at Joshua's middle school. Can I go, too?"

"Sure," Aaron told his son, even as Gwen stifled a groan.

"Josh, I told you I'd see if I could work it out." She looked at Aaron. "He knows I can't always get home in time to pick him up."

Aaron grinned. "And you wonder why I don't want a government job? Your work hours are too long. I'll pick him up when I get Ben. Or Phyllis can do it."

"That's my grandmother. She lives with us," Ben volunteered. "Ever since my mom died."

Josh sat up straight. "Your mom died?" he whispered.

"I was really little, so I don't remember it much."

Gwen shook her head. "We couldn't impose. I'd never be able to return the favor." Or deal with the added closeness that would develop between Josh and Aaron's son.

"It'll be no trouble," Aaron said as if it was a done deal. "I have a hunch Josh will be coming over to visit Ben before school starts, so he'll get to know Phyllis. It's all good."

"I don't know," she began. While she wanted Josh to be able to go to the after-school classes, she now knew she couldn't trust herself with Aaron. And surely she would be running into him all the time if he was dropping off her son every week. Then there was the issue of what people would think, what her boss would say, whether Clay would be able to make her look bad because of Aaron during their custody battle. She sighed deeply.

Aaron reached across the table and placed his hand on hers. "Really, Gwen. It's no big deal. I might even join in the class, if they work with adults. I used to do a lot of jujitsu. Have Josh send us the information so I can sign Ben up for the class, too."

"I can scan it in and send it to your email," Josh said.

Gwen hadn't realized Josh even knew how

to do such things. She stared at his smiling face and wondered where this capable, animated young man had been hiding. Before she could come up with other reasons this was a bad plan, she nodded.

Josh whooped, then settled down to punch Ben's email address into his iPod. "No Wi-Fi here. This place sucks." That was the Josh she knew. "I'll email you from home."

The kids launched into a discussion of Wi-Fi and the county schools banning iPods but not cell phones and then detoured into talking about some of the classes they'd likely both have to take. They paid no attention to the adults at all.

"Is that what you did to Clay?" she asked Aaron. "Jujitsu?"

"More or less," he agreed with a smile. "Pretty macho for a guy like me, right?"

"Unexpected, at least," she said with a small laugh. The last thing she would have thought this hippie public defender would be was trained in a martial art. "Where'd you learn that?"

"Hey, I have two older brothers. My parents were sure I'd need to know how to defend myself. While they were at basketball practice, I went to a dojo."

"Did it work or did your brothers still mess with you?"

He grinned. "Depended on the day."

"Where are your parents and brothers now?" she asked, wishing this was just small talk while they waited instead of a subject she truly wanted to discuss. She wanted to tell herself she needed background information on Aaron to better understand how to defeat him in court, but she knew it was more than that. She actually wanted to hear about his childhood. Which meant she was in big trouble.

Their food came, and the boys chatted happily. Eventually her anxiety over Clay's appearance and the kiss that had followed abated. There was no time for dessert. They had just long enough to walk to the Hippodrome without missing anything. When they were finally inside and an usher indicated their seats, Ben and Aaron were only five rows ahead of Josh and Gwen.

"Well, we'll see you when the show's over," she said.

"Can Josh sit with me, Dad?" Ben asked. "You and Gwen would be able to see us from those seats back there."

To her relief, Aaron didn't even ask. "Josh and his mom have planned to come to this together for a long time. They want to enjoy the show with each other." He turned to Gwen. "But let me know if Josh can't see the stage and we'll switch."

Almost as if he'd willed it to be so, the people sitting directly in front of Gwen and Josh were tall and had lots of hair. If the woman had been a cast member from *Hairspray,* she wouldn't have had a bigger do. Gwen leaned toward her son. "What do you want to do? If Ben comes back here with Aaron, he won't get to see any better than you."

"Would you mind if I sat up there with Ben?" he asked.

She smiled. "It's so nice of you to ask, Josh. You can sit with Ben on one condition." He scowled, so she rushed to finish her thought. "At intermission and after it's over, you have to tell me all your favorite parts."

His scowl evaporated. "Deal." He stood. "I'll send Aaron back here to keep you company." He turned to go, but then leaned down to whisper with devilish humor, "But no kissing when the lights go down."

"Joshua Clayton!" she said. But he was already out of the row and making his way down to the lower seats. Horror and humor got all mixed up together inside her. Horror that Josh had reason to tell her to behave. Humor that he could tease her about it, something he hadn't

done in a long, long time. She missed the easy banter they used to share.

"We meet again," Aaron said as he took Josh's seat. "Did you miss me?"

Gwen felt a blush creeping up to her cheeks. "Did Josh say anything to you?"

"He said he couldn't see from back here and asked if I would switch seats. He said it was okay with you. You said that, right?"

"Yes. He wouldn't have been able to see much." She indicated the couple in front of her.

He leaned toward her. "We can just look between them."

Gwen shifted the other way, away from Aaron. "Yes, that works," she agreed.

"Oh, and Josh also said no kissing when the lights go out."

Her face felt very hot now. "I'm gonna make him pay when he has a girlfriend some day."

"I told him already that he needs to be careful about mentioning what he saw. He agreed that it's private."

"Thank you. If Clay finds out—not to mention the people I work with—and...and..." She trailed off, not sure where she was going with that sentence. "Look," she said. "We have to make sure that kind of thing doesn't happen again, okay?"

A fleeting disappointment seemed to cross his features, which gave her a moment of satisfaction.

"That kind of thing?" he asked. "You mean us kissing? Yeah, that was crazy." He looked out toward the stage.

"Seriously, Aaron. It's more than just my concerns about Clay. There's our work, too. Let's just be two single parents helping each other now and then, like you said before. That way, we can both be our usual relentless selves in court."

"That makes sense." But he ruined his consent by placing his hand gently over hers.

She looked down at their hands and realized she'd inadvertently placed hers on his arm as she'd spoken. As she drew away and turned to face forward, Gwen wondered why she couldn't just behave logically with this man. He was all wrong for her, with his bleeding-heart liberalism that led him to free convicts and his haphazard manner of dress that bespoke a lack of discipline. And yet she did things like unconsciously rest her hand on his forearm as she spoke. It made no sense. While she could see he was decent and could be a good influence on Josh, she didn't even like Aaron much. So why did she have all the symptoms of being attracted to him?

"WHEN CAN WE DO THE deposition for my hospice witness?" Aaron asked her as he pulled into her driveway after the show. He hated to talk about work, but he needed to get her scheduled before his witness died.

The boys had both dozed off in the backseat and, after the initial excitement about how cool the show was, the ride home had been sweetly quiet. He hadn't wanted to break that calm. But now that Gwen was about to go inside, he was out of time and had to ask about the appointment.

"Um," she said. "I have to check my schedule."

"My witness doesn't have much time, Gwen." The glow from the streetlight created a halo of her hair and cast interesting shadows across her face, making her look like a painting instead of the very real flesh-and-blood woman she was. He wanted to reach out and touch her cheek, but he knew she wouldn't welcome that. She'd been very clear on that point.

She nodded. "I know. And I want to comply with the court order. I could do it tomorrow, except I don't have a sitter for Josh."

"No problem. You can bring him over to hang out with Ben. My mother-in-law will be glad to have someone for Ben to play with."

"That just doesn't seem right, somehow. My boss expects me to do what I can to keep the convicted prisoner behind bars. How conflicted would I appear if I got babysitting services through you when you're working to get that same prisoner freed?"

He leaned his head against the backrest of the driver's seat. Frustrated in so many ways, he felt edgier than he had in a long time. "It's no one's business if Josh and Ben are friends. And if it gets us closer to justice, no one will care. Seriously, Gwen. The witness is going to die."

A long silence passed.

"Fine," she said, relenting at last. "I'll bring him over to your house and we can drive together out to the hospice. You're responsible for getting the court reporter to meet us there. Are you happy now?"

He turned toward her again and grinned. "Very," he said, and this time he lifted his hand and gently swept hair away from her cheek.

She didn't move, just stared at him. Was that longing he saw? He leaned ever so slightly toward her. Gwen shifted a fraction toward him. Yearning and doubt filled her eyes and she hesitated just long enough for Josh to awaken and ask groggily if they were home yet.

"Yes, we're home. Let's get inside and into bed."

Aaron recognized a fleeting wish that he could go there with her, but then he recalled that the last woman he'd slept with was Beth and all hell broke loose in his guts.

To Josh, he said, "Hey, you can come over to our house and hang out with Ben tomorrow. Sound good?"

"Yeah, sure," Josh said. "See you tomorrow then." At least he sounded happier about it than his mother.

THE NEXT MORNING, GWEN had second thoughts. But there was no turning back when Josh was that excited about spending the day with his new friend. Weird the two boys had hit it off so well. They seemed perfect opposites to Gwen. What did they see in each other? How would they make a friendship work? Or were these questions she wished she could answer about herself and Ben's father?

"I'll drive," she said when Aaron opened the door. The boys immediately took off to Aaron's basement rec room.

"Sure, but that means you'll have to obey my directions to get there," he said with a grin.

Before she could retort that she had GPS, an older woman walked out of the kitchen.

"Introduce me to your colleague, Aaron," she said. But she didn't wait for him to speak and instead held out her hand. "I'm Phyllis. It'll be so nice for Ben to have a friend over. He doesn't know anyone in the new neighborhood yet."

"Gwen Haverty," she said as she shook hands with Phyllis. "Please call if Josh is any trouble. I left my card on the table." She indicated where she'd put her business card.

"It'll be fine. Just do the work you need to get done."

"Bye, Mom," Aaron said. "Thanks." And he gave her a peck on the cheek.

In the car, Gwen thought about him calling his mother-in-law "Mom" and how intertwined Phyllis was in the little family. It would be awkward for Aaron to introduce a new woman into his life. She wondered if that was why he was still alone, more than three years after his wife's death.

"You're quiet again this morning," he observed.

"So do you date much?" Her musings spilled out of her mouth by accident. She glanced sideways and saw his eyebrows shoot upward in surprise.

"Uh, no. Why do you ask?" By the time he got to "why" he was nearly laughing.

She felt her cheeks grow hot, but figured that since she couldn't gracefully wiggle out of the embarrassment now, she might as well have her curiosity satisfied. "Because you're very close to your mother-in-law. She's part of your family. Wouldn't it be hard for you—and for her—if you introduced a new woman into your lives?"

"Yup, it would." He didn't say anything else for a moment, then added, "But I'd find a way to make it work for the right woman."

"Huh," was all she could think to reply. She would not let herself wonder if she could be the right woman. The idea of a relationship with Aaron still seemed absurd, despite the lingering memory of his kiss.

"Well, now that we have that awkwardness out of the way," he said, "how about if I review the file out loud so we'll have the context clear in our minds once we get there. We don't want to waste time and tire out Mrs. Warren, sick as she is."

"Okay," Gwen agreed, happy to have work to focus on while trapped in the car with Aaron.

THE COURT REPORTER WAS late, so Gwen waited with Aaron, sitting quietly in the reception area of the hospice center. The place was surprisingly lively. Somber, but with a steady stream of people, including children, coming and going. Mrs. Warren's daughter came out to talk to them when they first arrived.

"She needs to get this off her chest before… before…"

"We understand," Aaron said, resting his hand gently on the young woman's shoulder. Rona Warren looked into his eyes, saw the compassion that Gwen had found there, and began to spill a great deal of her sadness about her mother's impending death onto Aaron's shoulders. He seemed willing to take it on. He listened intently, commented appropriately, even held the woman's hand as she wept.

Gwen felt her own eyes tearing up for reasons she couldn't completely explain to herself. She'd seen worse situations, known of deeper tragedies, heard stories far more poignant. She suspected her emotion had something to do with Aaron and his sensitivity to this near stranger. Watching him, she thought about what a good spirit he had inside him and wondered how he managed to make compassion seem strong and manly. More than that, he was so accepting of Rona's tears. There was no hint that he believed the young woman to be weak or childish or annoying.

Gwen had never met a man like Aaron.

Other than her own father, perhaps. She'd always dismissed her dad as too tenderhearted and not very strong. Was that why she'd been drawn to jerks like Clayton? Had she somehow developed the wrong impression about sensitive men?

"Sorry I'm late," gushed the court reporter as she swept into the room. "I had no idea how far this place is from Baltimore."

"Rona, would it be okay if we talk to your mother now?" Aaron asked gently.

"Yes. This is the only reason she's hung on so long." She led the way toward Mrs. Warren's room.

Gwen didn't know what she expected, but the skeletal woman in the bed with translucent skin and random wisps of hair wasn't it. Mrs. Warren was barely alive. Even though Aaron had told her as much, seeing the woman in person made Gwen realize the defense attorney had not been exaggerating. If anything, he'd underplayed the situation. Remorse swept through her for not doing the interview sooner.

"I'm glad you've come," Mrs. Warren said in a paper-thin voice that rasped and wheezed. "I need to be sure you understand." She paused to cough and cough.

Aaron took the older woman's frail hand in

his own. "We need to wait for the reporter to set up her equipment. It'll only be a moment."

She nodded and then noticed Gwen.

"I'm Gwen Haverty," Gwen told her. "From the Attorney General's Office."

Mrs. Warren nodded. "I used to work for the government. Federal. Labor Department. Long time ago." She wheezed and hacked for a time after saying so much.

"Save your breath, Mama," Rona urged her.

"Got a daughter," said Mrs. Warren as she squeezed Rona's hand. "Got a grandson. Sang in a choir. Laughed a lot." She coughed again. "Just need to set the record straight 'bout what I really saw that day without that—that man twisting my words and confusing me."

Gwen wanted to know what man had twisted her words, but Aaron indicated that the reporter was ready. They swore in the witness and made sure she understood the purpose of the deposition. The two attorneys agreed to the usual stipulations. Aaron began to take Mrs. Warren through the night when she'd witnessed a black male attack and rob another man at gunpoint.

After a series of questions leading up to the most important one, Aaron asked, "Can you describe the man with the gun, Mrs. Warren?"

"He was dark African-American, tall and skinny, just a kid, I think."

"In the courtroom, you agreed with the prosecutor that the man with the gun was sitting at the defendant's table in the courtroom. Do you remember that?"

"Well, see, that's the thing I've wrestled with all this time." She had to cough, then went on. "I didn't really think the boy at the table was the right one. That man twisted my words around. I agreed the defendant looked a lot like the robber I'd seen, but there were differences, too. No one asked me about that. And when I tried to explain, that man cut me off and told me I could go." This time, her coughing sounded weak and unproductive. She didn't appear to have the strength to cough anything from her lungs now.

Aaron looked at Gwen as he asked the woman to explain why the defendant at the table probably wasn't the robber. Mrs. Warren haltingly told them that the defendant was much bigger, wider in the shoulders, that his skin seemed lighter, his hair shorter. She provided quite a comprehensive list of differences.

Gwen had to ask. "Why didn't you tell the prosecutor any of this?"

"I told the other lawyer. The worthless one

with the defendant. And I tried to tell the prosecutor. That man didn't want to hear any of it. He wanted to convict the boy he had in the courtroom."

Once the woman's coughing subsided, Gwen asked, "Who was the prosecutor?"

"Free or Fray. Something like that."

"Fry? John Fry?" She was sorry she'd asked. Now it was in a public record, dutifully typed by the court reporter, that her boss had put his conviction record above actual justice.

"Yes, that's who it was," said Mrs. Warren triumphantly. "But the boy in the courtroom wasn't the right one."

CHAPTER NINE

THE DEPOSITION WENT ON for another half hour. By then, Mrs. Warren was coughing and wheezing more than speaking. But Gwen was determined to get everything she could from the woman, tying up every possible thread so that there would be no way for her boss to criticize her if she ended up agreeing that releasing Omar Kingston was the right thing to do.

Aaron didn't speak as they drove back toward Baltimore. At least not until Gwen said, "Why would John push for Kingston's conviction if he wasn't the right criminal?"

"First, let's assume for the moment that Omar isn't a criminal at all, as opposed to just not being the *right* criminal. Second, let's think for a moment about John's ego, how devoted to a high conviction rate your boss is, and why you were hired."

"Why I was hired?"

"To create the appearance that your office cares about justice."

"How could you know that?"

"Quite honestly, I read your bio and looked into how things were going at the time you were brought in. I put two and two together. But you just confirmed my suspicion."

She shot daggers from her eyes, then focused on the road again. After a moment, she said, "You make sure you come across as such a beta male, all caring and cuddly and kind. But you're as calculating and cold as the rest of us lawyers. When you want to be."

"Awesome alliteration!"

She had to laugh. "That's all you got out of my observation?"

"No. I got that you think I'm cuddly. I am, you know."

She did not want to think about Aaron's cuddly side. Or what it would be like to go beyond cuddles. She turned her thoughts back to why John would have pursued conviction without pausing to consider justice in Kingston's case. Answers eluded her. Her boss wasn't a racist, at least not that she'd ever observed. Could it be that he was just so hell-bent on winning he couldn't bother digging for the truth? To find out, she'd have to confront him, and she did not feel able to risk her continued employment with Clay gathering evidence against her parenting. Yet, how could she just look the other way?

"So are you going to help me get Omar out of prison now?" Aaron asked.

"I don't know. I need to read the file again and then the transcripts of the deposition."

"Gwen—"

"Don't start. I know that every day an innocent person stays in prison is a very bad day. Got it. Seriously. But if I don't make his release order ironclad slam-dunk solid, John isn't going to go along. How far do you think I'll get if I piss him off?"

Aaron sighed. "We can work on that this afternoon."

"No, I can't. I have to meet my attorney. I'm getting a restraining order against Clay. He threatened to kidnap Josh. I'm not just going to wait until he actually tries it. And I have a strategy to work out on the countersuit for custody."

He nodded. "Okay. That's important. But so is Omar."

"I won't forget that. Trust me."

"I want to," he said.

But she heard the worry in his voice. No matter how much time they spent together, no matter how attracted they might be, they were still on opposite sides of the legal system, not to mention their opposing ideology.

It would never work. Her fantasies about Aaron needed to be quashed completely, ruthlessly. To do that, she had to find someone else to think about. She'd have to start dating. Carefully and publicly, so as not to give Clayton anything to crow about in court regarding her suitability as a mother. And dating now and then would help mitigate any accusations Clay could make about her and Aaron. On top of that, she realized from her strange gravitation toward Aaron that she must be yearning for companionship without realizing it. Yes, she needed a date. But with whom?

HE HADN'T SEEN HER IN two weeks. But he'd been thinking of her even though he didn't want to. He wondered if she'd be here tonight, in the gym where the karate class was held. She'd refused his offer to bring Josh home after his first class. So either she'd be here herself or Josh wouldn't be here. Ben would be disappointed if his friend didn't show.

But there she was. Standing to one side of the gym, she looked completely out of place in her gray pin-striped suit and heels. A briefcase stood on the floor beside her. Her Black-

Berry was pressed to her ear, though she didn't appear to be talking.

He lifted his hand to wave, but she turned to one side without seeing him. She put her palm over her free ear, blocking out the cacophony of excited boys and girls. Ben ran to greet Josh and he saw Gwen smile at his son as he went by. It warmed his heart that she could be kind to his offspring even though she wouldn't take his calls.

He'd have stormed her office, insisting on seeing her, except she'd signed Omar's documents and the judge had promptly ordered him released. He and Opal had picked up Omar together. It was good to see the young man in the bright sunlight instead of under the glare of unshaded fluorescents in a windowless concrete room. The big man had limped toward him and hadn't stopped until he had Aaron in a bear hug.

"I knew you'd get me outta there," he'd said. Aaron didn't tell him how close he'd come to failure. But he gave him a lecture about not gravitating back to the company of thugs, the very same crowd that had made him a target for prosecution by John Fry.

Now, Aaron walked directly to Gwen, knowing she couldn't avoid him here without looking extremely ungracious. She produced a smile, then returned to her phone call. He wondered if there was actually anyone on the other end. Was she using the phone as a prop to avoid talking to him—or anyone else, for that matter? Looking around at the other parents, mostly women in jeans or sweats, he realized how out of place Gwen might feel. This wasn't an environment where she would be comfortable.

At last, he heard her speak into her cell. "I'll be there first thing in the morning to go over the documents." Then she turned off the BlackBerry.

"Hello," he said, before she could find another excuse to avoid him. "How are you?"

"I've been better."

"Anything I can do?"

She eyed him warily. She shifted from foot to foot, her gaze drifting away. She tossed her phone from one hand to the other. Agitated. Maybe even frightened.

"Has Clayton done something? Maybe renewed his threats?"

She took in a deep breath and held it a second before letting it out. "You guessed it."

"You know we could have Josh stay at my house for a while until things settle down. I'm still willing to do that." When she hesitated, another thought crossed his mind that made him want to go out and make Clayton sorry he was alive. "Did he threaten to hurt you in some other way?"

"Plotting to steal my son hurts me enough to satisfy even Clayton. He's been out of town and my parents are visiting, so I haven't been worried. But they have some things they need to take care of over the next few days and won't be at the house after school. I don't want Josh going home alone. So I think I need to take you up on your offer to keep him. Just for a couple of days. Clay has been rattling his saber a lot lately through his attorney and... I'm afraid I..."

Her voice had dropped to nearly a whisper. She didn't want to have to admit she was afraid or that she needed help. Aaron didn't want to make it harder for her.

"I understand. We'll take Josh home with us tonight, if you want."

Gwen looked into his eyes. There was gratitude in her gaze, maybe more than that. Or was he fooling himself? Wishful thinking? Sometimes, when he was able to persuade himself that Beth would want him to fall in love again, he found himself hoping she'd realize the spark between them was mutual and undeniable. So far, he'd seen little to indicate she felt that way at all. Until this moment.

To his delight, she placed her hand gently against his upper arm. "Thank you," she said. "I don't really deserve your kindness. I've done nothing but push you away. Yet here you still are, offering me help just because I need it. You're a good friend."

Those last words froze him solid. A good friend? That was not what he'd wanted to hear. This confirmed that he'd been imagining the desire he thought he'd seen in her eyes. What a fool he'd been. Pretending there could be someone with whom he could connect the way he had with Beth. Waiting, hoping, longing.

If he could be honest, he'd say *I want to be more than friends.* But he was too conflicted to get those words out of his mouth. He still couldn't shake the sense that a full-on pursuit of Gwen was some kind of betrayal of Beth. But he couldn't deny that he thought about Gwen all the time. He had begun to tell himself that Beth would want him to find another woman. Beth had never been the least bit selfish and he'd considered the idea that his late wife would expect him to find love with someone else.

"I know you've kept your distance for good reasons, Gwen," he said, realizing the words solidified his position as her "good friend."

"You need to look out for your job and for your son. I understand that."

"They're starting," she said, nodding toward the instructor and the group of boys and girls who'd gathered to begin their lesson. "I had to be very devious at work to be here for this. But Josh wanted me to see the first class, so I made it happen."

"You're a good mom." He liked that his comment brought a tiny smile to her face. But as he stood beside her watching their sons, frustration built inside him. He couldn't stop thinking about being in the friend zone with Gwen.

Fortunately, he was acquainted with the instructor of the karate class, and when the kids divided into groups, Mike asked if he would help with demonstrations for the various levels. Aaron quickly shucked off his shoes and headed out toward the center of the gym, grateful to be able to do something physical.

GWEN HAD TO STAND THROUGH the entire karate class. Other moms sat on the floor along the walls and took care of younger children, or chatted together, or read books. But she couldn't very well sit down on the floor in her suit. Even if she did manage to get down there in her snug skirt, getting up would have been impossible. So she stayed standing, all the while trying not to stare too much as Aaron helped the instructor with demonstrations.

Besides beginners like Josh and Ben, there were kids who had been taking karate for a long time. The newbies wore gym clothes and had been given information sheets about where to buy white gis and white belts. The more seasoned had come in their uniforms and wore belts of various colors. At the moment, Aaron and the instructor were with a group of older kids wearing dark blue and brown belts. And the demonstration the men gave was far more involved than the ones she'd just seen. It was quite a sight to behold the ever gentle Aaron Zimmerman duking it out with the black belt instructor. Though Aaron hadn't come in a gi of his own and wore no belt to show his level, he was clearly as skilled as his opponent. The two of them punched, kicked and blocked each other with impressive speed and seemingly choreographed precision. Aaron's style was smoother, more flowing, more bob-and-weave like a dance. The class instructor was more about linear form—or perhaps that's what he wanted to demonstrate to his students.

She wondered how a peacenik like Aaron learned karate, or jujitsu, she remembered he'd called it. But mostly, she watched the bulge and flex of his muscles, the washboard abs visible under his sweat-dampened T-shirt, the unwavering focus of his attention on his opponent. That was his most attractive feature, she decided. His ability to pay attention to the person in front of him with such complete absorption. When she talked to him, she never, ever felt that she had to compete with other things that might be on his mind. He gave his whole mind over to her when they spoke.

Still, she'd managed to do what she'd planned—she had made it clear to him that they were only friends. She'd seen his understanding register on his face. He hadn't been overly surprised or even disappointed. Which had disappointed *her*. Deep down, she'd hoped he'd say he wanted more than just friendship between them. But he'd made appropriate comments, watched the kids in the class for a while, then gone over to help when the instructor had beckoned. Watching him now, feeling his sex appeal to her very core, she wished she could take back her words, wished she could…

Never mind. It was done. There could be no taking anything back without paying a high price. And all for the best. Even though she knew she needed to date, a romance was the last thing she needed to mix into the chaos of her life—the custody issue, her parents staying at her house, her boss's anger about Kingston's prison release, and the usual worries as the mother of a preteen boy. She would not think about Aaron Zimmerman.

But thinking about him became unavoidable. Just before class ended for the boys, he bowed to the class instructor and walked back over to her. His shirt was damp now, clinging in all the right places. Somehow he appeared even more attractive than before. And the eyes of all the moms followed him as he made his way across the room. She heard some distinctly appreciative sighs, which resulted in an almost overpowering protectiveness in Gwen. Or was that jealousy? Hard to tell the difference sometimes.

"I should have brought a towel and a fresh shirt," he said apologetically when he drew close enough.

Gwen made a dismissive gesture. Ben and Josh came running to them, both in bare feet. They immediately sat on the floor to put on their socks and shoes.

"Did you see me, Mom?" Josh asked. "I got pretty good at those blocks, right?"

"Yup, I saw you. And you were very good at the blocks. Pretty good kicks, too." She waited until the boys were upright and then broached the subject of Josh staying at Ben's for a few days. The kids whooped with pleasure at the idea.

"You want me to follow you home," Aaron asked, "so Josh can get his school gear and some extra clothes?"

"That's a good idea," she agreed.

"I want to ride with them," Josh said.

This stung a little, but Gwen knew he didn't mean to be thoughtless. "Okay," she said.

She drove home alone with the car full of males behind her. Whenever they came to a stoplight, she could see them laughing and talking together in her rearview mirror. Gwen resisted the urge to sulk about being left out of the fun. She told herself it was normal for a boy Josh's age to want to be with a friend instead of his mother. But by the time she pulled into her driveway, she was feeling sorry for herself.

The minute she was inside the house with Aaron and the boys, she realized things were not going to get any better. Her mother and father had returned home from dinner with friends. Before Gwen had finished telling Josh to go pack some clothes, her mother was hovering inches away, waiting not very patiently to be introduced to Aaron and Ben.

Ben escaped by running upstairs with Josh. Aaron wasn't so lucky.

"This must be the nice man you went out on the date with the other night," Judy declared as she approached Aaron with a big welcoming smile. She clasped his hand with both of hers as if he might be the answer to all her prayers.

"Aaron Zimmerman, this is my mother Judy Masoner. And my father Edward," she added as her dad ambled over to see what the fuss was about.

"Nice to meet you both," Aaron said, exuding all his usual charm. He wore a T-shirt, sweatpants and beat-up sneakers, but somehow all anyone would notice was his smile.

Gwen wished he'd stayed in the car. Now she'd never hear the end of her mother's encouragement to "go out with that nice man." Her mom would have a face to put with her other notions about Gwen finding a soul mate. "You have to get out onto the water to catch the right fish," she'd say. Or "you've got to put the wares on exhibit if you want to bring in the right buyer." Gwen couldn't seem to make her mother realize that she had no time for dating, unless she gave up sleeping altogether.

"And what do you and your wife do for a living, Aaron?" her mother asked, clearly fishing for his marital status.

"My wife was a nurse before she died," he said. "I'm a lawyer, like Gwen."

"Not at all like me," Gwen muttered, even as her mother said, "I'm sorry for your loss."

"It was a long time ago," Aaron said.

"Are you a prosecutor with Gwen?" Judy asked casually as she picked up Joshua's discarded jacket and hung it in the coat closet.

"No, not a prosecutor. But I know Gwen is an excellent attorney and much admired in the legal community. You can be proud of your daughter, Mr. and Mrs. Masoner."

Gwen noted how he'd skillfully given her mother as little information as possible. She'd have to remember to thank him later.

With a great rumble of feet, Josh and Ben came back down the stairs. Josh carried a gym bag, presumably packed with clothes. Ben carried Josh's school backpack.

"Where are you going, Josh?" Judy asked her grandson.

"Staying with Ben for a while."

"On a school night?" Judy looked at Gwen for an explanation.

"I don't like Josh coming home to an empty house, and you and Dad have things to do. Misha is off on her college trip. I thought this would be a good solution."

"We could have rearranged—"

Gwen held up her hand. "This will work out fine, Mom. We can talk more about it later.

Let me get Aaron and the kids on their way, okay?" She followed man and boys out to the car, then hugged and kissed her son before he got into the backseat with his friend.

She turned to Aaron. "Sorry I forgot to warn you about my parents. I was hoping they'd still be out and you'd be spared the inquisition."

"They seem like lovely people," he said with a smile. "I hope I get to see them again sometime." He seemed to wince slightly after he said that.

Somehow, she felt she had to explain to Aaron, even as she told herself he didn't need to know the details behind her decisions. "The thing is, my parents have always liked Clayton. And I've never wanted to try to change their opinion. He's Joshua's father, after all.

"And not really such a bad person, except when it comes to his relationship with you," Aaron put in.

Gwen looked at him, stunned silent for a moment. "Not such a bad person? He's a—" She kept the epithet from spilling out of her mouth, remembering that Josh was in the car and might overhear. "Friends aren't supposed to defend the other side," she said.

"Maybe you two don't have to be on opposite sides. You have Josh together. Why can't you try to get along?"

"That's my business and not yours, Aaron," she said, feeling the heat of anger in her cheeks. Then she remembered she'd been telling him her business before he'd made his comment about Clay. She waved her hand, as if to erase the words. "I was just trying to explain that I don't want to put my parents at odds with Clay if I can help it. So that's why I accepted your offer to take Josh to your house."

"I understand," he said. But Gwen didn't believe him and had to resist the urge to explain further.

"I'll call with updates on Josh," he added. Then he got into his car. "G'night, Gwen."

She watched as they backed out and drove away. Standing in the driveway under the dark sky renewed that lonely, left-out-of-the-fun feeling she'd had earlier. Dispirited, she went back into the house to deal with her parents and then read some case files before bed.

AARON GOT THE BOYS SETTLED in the kitchen to work on homework before bed. They'd eaten a fast-food dinner on the way home, so he offered them some cookies Phyllis had made. As Josh reached for one from the plate Aaron held out, he said, "My mom is worried my dad is going to kidnap me."

Aaron and Ben both looked at Josh with

wide eyes. "Dude, then we couldn't hang out," said Ben.

"Are *you* worried your father might do something like that?" Aaron asked gently.

"Yeah. I guess. Last time I saw him, he told me he would come get me soon. He said living with my mom was turning me into a mama's boy. I told him I was going to karate, but he didn't think much of that. He said being a real man was all up here." Josh tapped his finger on his forehead.

"Your dad is right that most of who we are is in our brains and not about whether we can deck someone with karate skills," Aaron said after searching for a way to explain.

"So what should I do if he wants to take me away?" Josh asked. "I mean, it would be cool to hang out with him for a while. I love my dad. But if he didn't let me see my mom— well, that would make her sad."

"And you're man enough to not want to make her sad," Aaron said approvingly.

Josh nodded, worry and eager attention in his eyes. He bit into the cookie without taking his focus away from Aaron's face. Both he and Ben waited for an answer.

Aaron didn't want to blow it. This boy needed guidance, but Josh didn't need another adult mixed into the chaos that his parents had created around him. "Well, what would *you* want to do?" he tried.

"I want to make him see that I should live mostly with my mom. But I know I can't make him do anything. Even my mom can't make him understand."

"You could do karate on him," Ben offered.

Josh laughed. "My dad's a good guy. He just wants what's best for me. Same with Mom. They just can't seem to agree on what's best."

"And besides, Ben," Aaron said pointedly, "we need to use our words, not karate, when we have disputes. Josh, talk to your dad and tell him how you feel. Maybe it would help if he knew you like your school and your friends here. Promise you'll do better with your grades. Tell him it wouldn't be good for you to change schools in the middle of the year."

Josh looked skeptical. "Maybe."

"Okay, well, let's think about this some more later. Right now, finish up your homework and get upstairs to brush teeth and go to bed." Aaron doubted the boys would fall asleep any time soon. They were too excited to be together. But he had to at least try in the hope they'd get enough rest before school in the morning.

Much later, Aaron lay in his own bed and

thought about what Josh had asked him. He couldn't begin to imagine how hard it must be for the boy to worry that his own father would disrupt his life—and his mother's—so profoundly and without his consent. He thought about Gwen and how hard she worked at avoiding any activity that would give Clay ammunition or provocation. He doubted Clay would actually be as underhanded as Gwen feared. Aaron's gentle inquiries within their legal circles had revealed Clay to be a decent attorney who tried to give back to the community. The man loved his son, even if he hadn't been able to remain faithful to his wife. But Aaron couldn't know for sure about Clay. Regardless, it was unfair Gwen had to live under the tyranny of a man she'd divorced. As he drifted to sleep, he knew that he'd dream about her again, even though she'd made it clear they were just friends. His dreams didn't seem to care.

In the middle of the night, a few hours before dawn, his phone began to ring. He ignored it at first and it stopped. But then it started up again, happily singing "Puff the Magic Dragon" over and over, and finally he turned on the bedside light and picked up the BlackBerry.

CHAPTER TEN

GWEN DIDN'T GET THE UPDATE from Aaron, despite his promise to call. But she rang his house and was able to speak directly to her son. Phyllis had picked up both boys from their schools. Josh sounded happy and was doing his homework, so Gwen had nothing to worry about. Except her own mother, who didn't understand why her only grandson would stay somewhere else while they were visiting. That's because Gwen had never revealed to her mother—her own mother—the details of her marriage to Clayton or any of the many small torments he'd put her through over the years. And it was too late to start explaining.

Why had she kept so much to herself for so long? She didn't fully know the answer to that. Perhaps she was embarrassed she'd let him treat her so badly. Maybe she worried others would realize how weak she'd been—and believe she still was. Gwen waved that thought away. She didn't care what others be-

lieved. And the things she'd endured in her
marriage were no one else's business. Not even
her mother's. But that meant Judy didn't fully
appreciate why Gwen would be concerned for
Joshua's safety.

Her custody attorney had not been successful with the request for the restraining order.
She'd warned Gwen that this would be the outcome, explaining there was no real evidence
that Clay had been anything but a good father
to Josh. Gwen hadn't wanted to bring Aaron in
as a witness, knowing there would have been
too many questions about why the defense attorney had been at her house at night. And
she didn't have complete confidence in what
Aaron would say about Clay's threats. He'd
defended Clay before. Maybe he'd say Clay's
words were in the heat of anger.

Melody had wondered aloud if that might
have been the case. But Gwen had never been
able to think clearly when it came to her ex
and insisted he was out to steal her son from
her. And she couldn't understand why no one
else saw his evil side the way she did. But
at least Melody had alerted the school about
Clay's threats, both by phone and in writing,
with a copy of Gwen's custody documents.
The administration wouldn't allow Clay to
take Josh from the school grounds. Melody

assured Gwen that they were building a strong case for custody to remain as it was and that Clay's allegations about her mothering were meaningless.

"How can you be so confident?" she said as she sat across from the family lawyer's desk. "Clay is manipulative and will stoop to anything to get his way."

"I've been doing this for a long time, Gwen," Melody said. "Do you think this is the first time we've faced someone like your ex? Trust me."

"I do. But it's funny how much harder it is to face a courtroom hearing when I'm the defendant instead of the prosecutor."

Melody chuckled. "You're not a defendant. You're a mom who wants to keep her son in a stable environment. That's the best thing for Joshua. The court will see that."

"What of Clay's allegations about Josh's grades? And how he says I'm never home to spend time with him?"

Melody calmly looked at her for a moment. "Josh is doing well enough in school. If you want to worry about something, worry about the long hours you work. And take that as a suggestion to spend more time with your son, not as a lack of confidence in your case."

Gwen sank down in her seat, feeling like a

scolded child. "I have him staying at a friend's house until Clay goes back to New York."

"You think Clay would break into your house to kidnap Josh? That doesn't sound like something he'd risk. Clay isn't stupid."

"My parents are visiting and Clay knows it. He also knows I wouldn't want to tell my parents much about what's going on. So he'd figure he could cajole them into letting him take Josh for a little while. That 'little while' would turn into forever because he knows enough New York judges to make it happen. I just don't want to give him a chance to try."

"So where is Josh staying?" Melody asked as she picked up her pen to make a note.

Gwen sank a little deeper into her chair. "Aaron Zimmerman's," she said in a small voice.

Melody looked up from her notepad. "You're kidding, right?"

Gwen shook her head. "He's got a son the same age. It's not a crime for the boys to be friends."

"Uh-oh."

"What's that supposed to mean?" Gwen asked defensively.

"You've got it bad for the Release Initiative lawyer. Jeez, Gwen, how are you going to make *that* work? And let's hope Clayton doesn't find out. He might not be able to make much out of it in court, but I wouldn't want him chatting it up with your boss. Your job is where you're most vulnerable—because of the inordinate amount of time it takes from your home life and because if you lost it, Clay could claim you can't provide adequately for Josh."

"First, I have a good amount in savings and retirement that I could tap into if I needed to find another job." She said this bravely, but the very thought of losing her job and having to live off savings made her feel sick. "Second, I don't have to worry, because there's nothing going on between me and Aaron. Third, our kids are friends and there's nothing wrong with that. Fourth—"

Melody held up her hand. "Spare me. You're not fooling me for a single minute. And you couldn't possibly look guiltier. Just don't tell me you're in love with him."

"Don't be absurd," Gwen said.

"Ha—you *are,*" Melody crowed. "He must be great in bed, because you two are complete opposites."

Gwen stood up and tugged her suit jacket into place. "I haven't slept with him, for God's sake. And I am most certainly not in love with him."

Melody laughed. "Well you're in something

with him," she insisted. "But be careful. This would not be a good time to lose your job, despite your savings."

Gwen rolled her eyes, hoping the dramatic expression would help get her attorney off this subject. "I'm going now. And leaving our case in your hands. We have to get this right, Melody."

Still sitting at her desk, Melody went serious. "We'll do fine. Just promise me no more surprises like Aaron Zimmerman. Seriously, Gwen. Stay away from him until we get the hearing behind us."

Gwen left without explaining how hard staying away from Aaron was proving to be.

AARON WENT THROUGH THE day without thinking or feeling much of anything. The phone call in the middle of the night had been his undoing. With Phyllis taking care of Ben and Josh, there was no urgent need to pull himself together. So he didn't. And when Omar and Opal Kingston came to his office to see how he was holding up, he fell apart completely.

"Look, man, it wasn't your fault," Omar said after explaining they'd heard the news through his network of acquaintances, many of whom drifted in and out of the legal system so often they knew what was going on. "No one is to blame."

Aaron leaned forward, his forehead cradled in his hands. He rocked back and forth, wishing the motion would ease the pain a little. "I am to blame, Omar. There's no other way to see it."

Opal patted his shoulder. "But you do so much good for people. This doesn't wipe out all of that goodness. It's just something that happened."

Aaron continued rocking and holding his head. If he didn't hang on, his skull might explode. If he didn't keep moving, his limbs might freeze up and stop working. That's how out of control his world seemed at the moment.

"William Nepher was my client. And he raped and killed a little girl, Opal. It's not 'just something that happened.' It's a hideous, evil crime, perpetrated on an innocent kid. By a man I got out of prison. My fault. All my fault."

"It's done and over, man. You gotta get ahold of yourself. That motherfu—" Omar stopped the curse in time. "The bastard was caught. He's gonna pay for his crime. You're not helping by beating yourself this way."

Aaron looked up into the young man's eyes. "I put him back on the street, Omar. I worked hard to do it. I was so sure he was innocent. But Bill Nepher is a very bad man. What he did to that kid..." He couldn't speak of it. Couldn't think of it. Yet he had no way of getting the images out of his head. The police had been keen on making sure he'd viewed all the photos of the crime scene—punishment for being the one who'd gotten Nepher back into society. The pictures were now burned onto his retina.

"I know, I know," Opal murmured, still patting his shoulder.

"You need to go home, be with your kid," Omar said. He looked toward his sister. "He have a girlfriend? That'd help."

She shrugged. "We could get his boss to make him go home, at least."

The two of them put that plan into action. In another moment, Opal returned to his small office with Janice Cook in tow.

"Aaron, you need to go home, take a few days off if you have to. You're not doing any good here."

Aaron nodded, but he couldn't make himself move.

Janice sat beside him. "We go back a long way. We've been building the reputation of Release Initiative for a long time. But this isn't the first time one of our clients turned to crime after we got them out. It's part of the job—at least that's what you've said to our other attorneys when something like this happened to them."

Aaron couldn't look at her. "Those clients didn't do what Nepher did to that kid."

Janice had little she could say to that. After a moment, she tried again. "We'll get past this in time, Aaron. Just go home for now and surround yourself with your family and friends. Talk it out. I'll come over and check on you later. Okay?"

In another half hour, after thanking Omar and Opal for their concern and walking out of the building with them, Aaron was heading home alone in his car. He barely focused on his driving, thinking about how he needed to be strong for Ben and Phyllis, but unable to get a grip. He wondered if there was enough alcohol at home to drown the horror, at least until time wore the jagged edge off the nightmare. Time, he knew, would blunt the vividness of the snapshots he'd been shown. The blood, the contorted limbs, the broken body.

He remembered his mother-in-law's seldom-used stash of medicinal marijuana prescribed when she'd lived in California. He craved the numbing effects it might offer. But his son was at the house, and Gwen's son, too. Maybe he could buy the time he needed—a period of not thinking or feeling—with the three bottles of wine Phyllis had won at her card games last week. By the time he got home, his plan was to gather the wine, maybe some weed, and retreat to his bedroom, where he would do his best to blot out the images of a little girl whose life had been so brutally snuffed. If he could get some distance, make the truth less fresh and crisp, perhaps he would be able to focus on his obligations. But he doubted he'd ever be able to do his job again, trust in the rightness of freeing someone wrongfully incarcerated, believe in the validity of his beloved career, which had seen him through after Beth had died. If he wasn't ever able to go back to work, what would he do? Who would he be? And what did any of that matter after what Nepher had done?

"MOM, YOU NEED TO COME over here. There's something wrong with Aaron." It was Josh on her cell phone, calling her after school on his third evening with the Zimmermans. He sounded genuinely worried. But Melody's warnings about staying away from Aaron swam through her mind.

"What do you mean, 'there's something wrong'? Where's Phyllis?"

"She's here. And she told us it's not our business and to just be quiet and do our homework. But Ben is worried. So am I."

"Exactly what has you worried, Josh?"

"Aaron is locked in his room. Since he came home from work early yesterday. He looked bad when he went in there—like he's sick or something—and now he won't come out. When Ben knocked, he yelled at him to go away."

"Hmm," she said. She'd heard about Aaron's client killing a child, but she hadn't wanted to think about how he might be coping with the guilt. She told herself he would rely on his friends and coworkers to put it into perspective. He must have had to deal with similar experiences in the past. She hadn't expected him to fall apart.

"Okay. I can pick you up and bring you home." She had hoped Josh could stay one more day until she was sure Clay had gone back to New York, but whatever was happening at the Zimmerman house didn't need an extra kid to complicate things.

"No," Josh said. "You're his friend. You need to come help him."

"Oh." This startled her. She hadn't expected it. There was a lot of truth in what her son said. She and Aaron had become friends. She didn't have many of those anymore. But she remembered that friends helped each other in times of trouble, no matter what. Just as Aaron was helping her by watching Josh. But the responsibility of friendship warred with her worry about what could happen if people at her work found out. Still, Josh rarely made a request on someone else's behalf. How could she say no?

"Okay. I...I guess I could try."

"Thanks, Mom." He sounded sincerely relieved. "Come as soon as you can."

After she clicked off the phone, she thought for a moment about the transformation Josh seemed to be undergoing. He'd just shown more caring for another human being than she'd ever seen before. Was that natural maturity, or was exposure to Aaron and his family having a positive effect on her son? Whatever the reason, Gwen liked the new Josh a great deal. She called her mother and explained why she would be late coming home.

"Stay as long as you need to, my dear," Judy said. "Aaron seems like such a nice man. Maybe you two will be more than friends someday."

"I'm just going over to find out if there's anything I can do. Please don't read too much into this." Her ever hopeful mother never missed a chance to push her toward a new relationship. "Not everyone can have your storybook life where the hero and heroine live happily ever after."

"Yes, they can. Especially you, Gwen. Your father and I showed you how. Now you just need to believe you deserve it."

This was more sounds-like-the-truth than Gwen could stand at the moment. "I've got to go," she said. "Listen, Mom. Don't tell anyone where I've gone, okay?"

"I understand, dear. And I won't worry if you end up staying the night. You can update me in the morning."

With a groan, Gwen thumbed the phone off a little horrified that her mother was so desperate for her to find love that she'd suggest her daughter sleep over at Aaron's.

Her parents had, indeed, modeled a loving and happy relationship all her life. So it was an eternal mystery to everyone as to why Gwen had always fallen for the bad boys and then ended up marrying one—while presenting a very different image to her parents. Clay had been a player with women, a charismatic, adventure-seeking chance-taker. And she'd fallen hard for him, despite his self-indulgent personality. It made no sense.

A psychologist friend had suggested maybe

Gwen felt neglected in her childhood because her parents were absorbed with each other. But that didn't seem right. Her parents had been wonderful, her childhood happy. But she'd still been inexplicably drawn to the wrong kind of men. At least until she'd met Aaron.

And he was wrong in a completely different way. Why, oh, why, was she attracted to him? He didn't come close to her usual type. And while that might seem like progress, given that he was kind and decent, Aaron Zimmerman couldn't be more wrong for her at this juncture of her life. Almost everything about him irritated her, from his sloppy clothes to his liberal politics. He stood firmly in opposition to her career goals and deep-seated views about justice. He was disorganized, didn't care about setting boundaries for Ben, had a Pollyanna view of the world and couldn't muster enthusiasm for a passionate discussion about anything beyond his clients or saving the environment. The man drove her crazy when she was with him. Plus, he could cost her the job she needed to show the court she could take care of her son. And yet, she couldn't shake the effects of that one kiss they'd shared.

She grabbed her briefcase and headed out into the cool September night. She drove to Aaron's house, hoping she wouldn't have to spend too much time figuring out what was up with the Release Initiative counselor. In and out, she hoped. Maybe she'd take Josh back home so she wouldn't have to deal with the Zimmerman family again—at least until after the custody hearing.

But when she arrived, she saw quickly that things were not good. Phyllis and the boys were in the family room, tense and worried. Ben bounced a baseball against a wall repeatedly without looking up, anxiety in every annoying throw. He'd made several shallow dents in the wall. Calmly, Gwen intercepted the ball and kept it.

"Hey," Ben cried, but Gwen shot him one of her most chilling expressions and he quieted immediately.

Phyllis stood in the room, looking helpless. "I haven't seen Aaron like this since my Beth died," she said. "It started yesterday morning after Josh came, right before I brought the kids to school." She glanced over at the boys and amended, "Not that this could have anything to do with Josh. He's been wonderful. A delight to have in the house."

At that moment, something thudded on the floor above and all of them looked up.

"He won't eat, won't talk to me, won't come out of his room," Phyllis said. "He just storms around up there pacing and sometimes throwing things. I don't know what to do."

"I think I know what happened. A former client—" She stopped herself from spilling the story, worried the truth would be too much. "A former client ended up back in jail and Aaron's blaming himself, I think."

"I only know what I was told by that young man you two got out of prison. Omar, I think he called himself. He came by after Aaron went to work yesterday—without saying a word to any of us, which isn't like him. The young man was looking for Aaron. Asked if he was okay. He mentioned Aaron got a call from his boss late the previous evening. Something about a client getting into more trouble. I explained Aaron had gone to his office, though he'd looked like a zombie." Phyllis paused, then added in a hushed, reverent tone, "After Beth died, Aaron threw himself into work. That's how he got past the initial pain and found the strength to take care of Ben. I wouldn't ever have guessed he'd behave this way in a crisis."

"I'm not sure I'm going to be any help, Phyllis, but I'll try to talk to him, if you want me to." She felt very deeply that she'd be the last person who could help Aaron. She was on the side that had wanted to keep Nepher in prison, even though she hadn't been the attorney to prosecute the case.

"He doesn't have anyone since Beth passed. Friends, of course, but no one special. So if you'd try, I'd be grateful."

"I want you to talk to him, too," Ben said.

Josh nodded his agreement.

Gwen tossed the baseball back to Ben. "Take it outside if you need to throw it. You're not going to help your dad by driving him crazy."

This time, Ben nodded.

"Maybe Ben and I should go to our house," Josh suggested. "Grandma and Grandpa are there. He could stay the night and we could play with *my* stuff for a change. It'd take Ben's mind off things. And Phyllis was supposed to go to her card game with her friends tonight. They play poker." He said the last part with deep admiration in his voice.

Ben looked at his sneakers. "I don't want to go. I need to stay and make sure my dad's okay."

Josh moved a little closer to his friend. Gently, he said, "He'll be okay with my mom. She can fix things like this. We just need to get out of her way."

Ben looked into Joshua's eyes a moment, then nodded.

Gwen was surprised by her son's confidence. She so frequently felt that she could do nothing right in his eyes. But here he was, saying she'd fix things for Ben's father. She couldn't let Josh down now, regardless of Melody's warnings to stay away from Aaron.

Gwen looked questioningly at Phyllis, who said, "I don't mind either way. I'll stay with the boys here or I could drop them off."

Gwen mulled over options for a moment. "Let's wait and see how things go with Aaron first. He might not let me in, and even if he does, I might not be able to get him to talk to me." She turned to Josh. "If I'm not down in an hour, then call your grandparents and see if they'd mind. If they're cool with it, then Phyllis can drop you off there for the night."

She took a deep breath and turned toward the stairs as more banging and sounds of stumbling emanated from above. Three pairs of hope-filled eyes were trained on her and she felt the pressure of responsibility in a situation far outside her comfort zone. As she placed one foot onto the first step, she acknowledged how very much she did not want to involve herself in this man's personal hell. Then she marched up the flight toward the closed door of his bedroom without a single clue of how to comfort him.

AARON TOLD HER TO GO away, but she came in anyway. Hadn't he locked the door? Through the fog of his despair, he saw her hold up the little key that had rested above the doorjamb. He knew a lot of people stored their keys there. He'd forgotten about them. But Gwen must've fished around until she found one.

"You need to go," he said again. "I'm not fit to be around people."

"I'm not people, Aaron," she said. "I'm your friend."

He watched her swish her hand in front of her face as if that would dissipate the faint odor of smoke. The scent of the weed he'd toked earlier still lingered. He'd indulged after an internal battle about being an officer of the court versus the relief from memories it might give him. But it had given him nothing but a craving for Cheetos.

"Yeah, my friend," he said. "So be a pal and get out."

"Your son is worried about you. So is Josh. And Phyllis. And me." Then she coughed and waved her hand in front of her face again. "What have you been doing, Aaron?"

"Anything that I thought might release me into oblivion."

"How's it worked out, so far?" She went to the window and struggled to open it.

"Not at all." He couldn't muster enough concern to help her lift the sash. He just sat there next to the nearly depleted stash of wine and the recently attempted blunt until she got the window slightly ajar.

"Oh, Aaron," she said in that what-am-I-going-to-do-with-you tone that mothers the world over had perfected. "What if Ben saw you? You'd scare him. And he's smart enough to figure out you've been smoking an illegal substance. Why is it even in your house?"

"Phyllis brought it with her when she moved here from California. She didn't know it wasn't legal here and I didn't have the heart to tell her. It's for her glaucoma. Her other meditation has been effective so she hardly uses it."

"So it's not yours, thank heaven," she said as she picked up the ashtray and matching silver box and set it on top of the dresser, out of his reach.

"It didn't help." He dropped to sit on the edge of his bed and realized he was in the same clothes he'd been wearing since he'd arrived home the day before. He plucked at his shirt, wondering if it smelled.

"Good idea," she said. "First order of business is a shower for you."

At that suggestion, his mental fog lifted slightly. He remembered enough of his former self to say, "I'll need help with that."

She laughed. "Get up and into the bathroom," she ordered. He heard her turn on the water while he stripped off his shirt and socks. Then he just stood there. Inertia set in once again, along with the blessed tranquility of not thinking.

She reappeared before him like magic and ushered him into the bathroom. The male inside him had a fleeting image of her stripping him naked and helping him with the shower, and his body reacted halfheartedly to that. Depression and her brusque manner killed any further progress in that direction.

"Put these on when you're done." She set a pile of fresh clothing on the countertop, nudged him toward the steaming shower and left.

The sound of the door closing motivated him enough to finish undressing and get himself under the water. He moved like a robot, without thought or care, until the next thing he knew, he'd turned the water off and stood outside the shower, clean and dripping. But he couldn't think what to do now. He wasn't drunk. Not anymore. But his brain didn't want to function.

Intellectually, he knew he had to get past the tormented state he'd spiraled into. But every time he tried to shake it off, the memories returned. Those crime-scene images would emerge out of the mental recesses where he kept trying to shove them and he could only focus on finding a way to make them retreat again. Even now, the numbing effects of the wine were beginning to wear off again. He couldn't let that happen.

He put on the clothes Gwen had left for him, then went in search of something to help him forget again, though he knew he shouldn't. But when he opened the door, a distraction of a different sort confronted him.

"I wish I knew how to help you feel better, but I'm no good at this. All I know is you don't have the luxury of immersing yourself in self-pity, Aaron. You have a son to take care of. And right now, you're freaking him out." She stood there with her hands on her hips, dressed in a sleek black suit and crisp white blouse, her expression stern.

"You have no idea what I've done," he said.

"I know exactly what you've done. The story is all over the legal community. I heard the horrible details." She looked at the floor. "I'm so sorry."

He rubbed the heels of his hands into his eyes, wishing that action would blur the images. "You didn't see the pictures. What he did to that little kid. I...I can't...I—"

He felt her hands on his shoulders but he didn't open his eyes. He heard her voice, gentle and kind. "Aaron, stop. You cannot blame yourself. That crime—that horrible crime—is the price we pay for our legal system. It's the best in the world, but nonetheless flawed and terrible things happen. Sometimes because a lawyer like me fails to get someone convicted who should have been. Or the cops screw up evidence. Or a judge isn't doing a good job. Or a jury is blinded by some irrelevant aspect of a case. Bad people walk out into society all the time. And they commit heinous crimes. That's just a fact of living in our world."

He wanted to internalize her words. If he could do that, he might find a way to move past the nightmare. For his son's sake, if nothing else, he knew he had to snap out of it. Letting his hands fall from his face, he opened his eyes, tried to make sense of what she was saying. But he couldn't get past it. "Annie Bell Shaker. That was her name. She was twelve years old. She had a little brother and parents who loved her." The last words came out cracked and brittle. His eyes began to burn again and his throat went tight.

"Oh, Aaron," she whispered. Then she pulled him into her embrace.

CHAPTER ELEVEN

"IT'S GONNA BE OKAY," she heard herself murmur to him as he dropped his head to her shoulder. She did her best to comfort him by stroking her palm over his back and whispering soothing words. But holding him aroused more in her than a nurturing instinct. Even in his weakest moment, he was strong and male and she wanted him wrapped around her entire body.

She knew she needed to fight off the sexual desire for his sake as well as her own. But there was a mild buzzing inside her head and her body felt somehow disconnected from her thoughts, as if her body and her brain weren't part of the same person. Worse, she felt growing awareness of the man she held so intimately. The warmth of him, the clean scent, the hard muscles were nearly irresistible. It had been a long time since she'd been touched intimately by a man, and she sensed if he did anything even slightly erotic, she'd be lost.

"I need you," he whispered into her ear.

Those simple words, spoken almost as a question, melted her insides and sent tendrils of desire to the most sensitive parts of her body. The buzzing in her head blotted out any thoughts about why she shouldn't be in his arms. She kissed his unshaven cheek near his ear, then slowly moved to place another at his jaw, closer to his mouth.

His response was slow, but sure. He lifted his head enough to show her he was paying attention. Brazenly, she kissed him again, at the corner of his mouth this time. Heat suffused her, and a sensual awareness blossomed. She heard him suck in a breath and he shifted his form more firmly against her. She could feel him completely now, pressed flush to her from breast to thigh. The slightest movement of her hips confirmed for her that he also felt the same desire that had overtaken her. Her sluggish thoughts lazily questioned the wisdom of what her body was doing, but she shifted again anyway and he groaned. His hands moved to her shoulder blades, down her spine, cupped her bottom, drew her closer still.

In the instant before his mouth slid into position over hers, she took in a deep breath of the sweet, oddly scented air permeating the room. Then she gave herself over to kissing Aaron, who tasted like wine and who kissed her with the wholehearted attention of a man who could think of nothing other than finding and giving pleasure. He made her believe she was the center of his universe, the only thought, the only desire.

Even as his kiss deepened, she felt him step backward. And then she was falling with him, landing on his bed while his lips and tongue explored her mouth and made every one of her nerve endings come alive.

"Gwen," he murmured. "Tell me you want this."

"I want this—I want you," she said before she could think too much about her answer. A small part of her mind held on to worry that she shouldn't feel this way for this man, wasn't even supposed to be with him at all. She couldn't allow herself to want him, to crave his body and his touch upon her skin. But she couldn't make herself care about conflicts of interest and risks to her job. Not now. Not while she was lying on his bed, allowing him to unbutton her jacket and blouse, to slide his hands over the skin he uncovered, to kiss her throat and the swell of her breast. Wrong, she knew. Taboo. But it didn't matter. If anything, that aroused her more.

Her desire flared as the word *forbidden* slipped into her consciousness. She'd always

wanted what she shouldn't want or have. The
bad boys, the hoodlums, were the only ones
who could make her crave sex like an addict.
But this was Aaron—safe and sweet and kind
and honest. Still, she wasn't supposed to have
him. So she wanted him now, desperately, ach-
ingly, passionately.

"So beautiful," she heard him whisper as
one of his hands stroked her leg from knee to
thigh, pushing her skirt upward so that only
the thin strip of her panties and the fleece of
his sweatpants lay between them. "What do
you want, Gwen? What do you need right
now? Do you want me to keep touching you?
Do you want to make love with me?"

She didn't want him to ask her permission,
so she didn't know what to say. She wished he
would just take his fill of her, giving her no
choice other than to accept the glorious sensations. She didn't understand her own desire
to be overtaken sexually, but she'd accepted
it. And had always found men who thought
nothing of taking from her without ever asking
what she wanted.

Aaron didn't seem willing to go further
until she'd consented. She rebelled against
this demand for her permission. "Don't ask
me," she said, hoping those words would be
enough to spur him.

"I've already asked," he whispered into her ear. "I need to hear your answer. What do you want, right now, right here?" As if to persuade her to give him the answer he preferred, he kissed along her jaw and down her throat, sending sensations skittering over her skin and making her arch her back in a silent plea for more.

Words. He wanted words. Permissive words that would make her an equal partner in this activity. As she searched beneath the overwhelming sensations of his kisses for words that would encourage him without owning too much responsibility herself, she knew she should stop this now.

"I can't," she tried.

"Tell me," he insisted.

How could she leave him? Even her half-formed thoughts about leaving sent a hot flame of possessiveness storming through her and she reflexively held on to him more tightly, wrapping one leg around him, holding him to her.

With a defeated groan—as though the speech was being torn from her—she gave him back his own words. "I want you to make love with me, Aaron. Right now, right here."

And there was no turning back after that.

HER SKIN WAS THE SOFTEST, her scent the most provocative, her breathless moans the sexiest he'd heard. Aaron had gone well beyond wanting into the realm of needing, but he'd refused himself until she'd given her spoken consent. Somehow he would have found the strength to pull away from her if she hadn't given it. But she'd spoken the words asking him to love her. It had taken seconds to get rid of the remaining clothes. Now he gave himself over completely to insuring she wouldn't regret her decision.

She demanded fast and furious from him, wanting the sex intense and carnal. He delivered all the intensity he'd been storing during his three long years without a woman in his bed. He heard her call out his name when her whole body tightened and convulsed, then she'd writhed beneath him while he found his own bliss.

Still, he wanted far more with her than a reckless, breakneck tumble. And he found himself almost immediately ready for a calmer, more tender lovemaking. He started by kissing her slowly, gently, from lips to shoulder to breast, to stomach. He kept his hands busy, too. And she purred as he coaxed her patiently once again to that state of mind and body where pleasure grew steadily. He slid lower, and found his way to where she would be most sensitive, and he stayed there, giving her what she needed. His reward was her complete surrender. She gave herself over to the sensations and soon cried out in ecstasy.

Only then did he shift and fit his body into her. Still, he forced himself to go slowly, to make love to her with gentleness. She welcomed him, arching and undulating as she made soft sounds of wonder and delight. And when he was so close to his own climax he could barely stand it, she held on to him tightly and rocked her hips for him, bringing him still higher, before he crested and soared on waves of pleasure.

Exhaustion overtook him and he dropped to the bed beside her. His body thrummed in the wake of what they'd just experienced together.

That's when he realized she lay beside him, weeping.

"WHY ARE YOU CRYING?" Aaron asked carefully, and Gwen wasn't sure how to explain.

"I'm happy?" she tried. This sounded ridiculous and funny, but instead of the chuckle she'd meant to give, her throat tightened again and more tears welled.

"And you cry when you're happy?" he asked after a moment.

"Not usually. But this wasn't a usual experience for me."

"Say no more. I'm just *that* good." When she didn't laugh, he added, "Seriously, tell me what's brought on tears. That's not a reaction I expected. You're not sorry, are you?" He seemed afraid to know the answer.

"I'm not sorry. Maybe I will be later. But I'm not sorry now. I needed that. I needed you."

"We needed each other," he added.

"Yes. Each other. That was the first thing that was different. It was so…so…mutual." She sighed at her inability to find the right word. "I'm not sure that makes much sense."

"Keep talking. I'll catch on eventually."

She rolled to her side so she could snuggle against him with her cheek on his shoulder, enjoying the solid warmth of him even as an ill-defined sense of wrongness continued to nag at her. "First, I'm not used to anyone looking out so completely for *my* needs. Second, I'm not used to anyone asking me what I want."

"Yet you tried to avoid answering me when I asked."

"I know. There's the paradox that is me." And she cracked up, finally, at how odd the word *paradox* sounded just then. "I…I didn't really want the responsibility, the ownership in what we were doing. I wanted it to be all you. I've always been that way. But after I answered, after I knew I was as responsible as you, it was good. Really good." The urge to laugh came over her again, for no good reason.

"Why do you think that is?"

"I have no idea. All I know is the tears came because I realized I'd never been asked for my permission or what I wanted. I was touched that you'd insisted on my answer. That just seemed so...so...kind."

"Ugh. Don't you know men never want to be 'kind' or 'nice' or 'a good friend' even if they are?"

"Well, you're the first kind, nice, good friend I've ever gotten into bed with. I had no idea I'd like it so much."

"I'm glad," he said, and then he yawned. "Sorry. Your good friend is about to go unconscious for a while. I haven't been able to sleep since... Will you stay with me?" She hesitated, so he added very softly, "You'll keep away the nightmares."

"I'll stay," she whispered as she pulled the sheets and blankets over them both. Her brain just didn't seem to want to work well enough to figure out a good reason to leave, even though she knew she shouldn't spend the night. She curled herself against him, ready to slay any dragons from his dreams.

But a few hours later, she was the one who woke up from a nightmare. She sat bolt upright, disoriented about her surroundings and terrified that there was a man beside her in the bed. When Aaron reached out to her, she scrambled away, clutching the sheet to her chin.

"Gwen," he said. "It's me, Aaron. I'm not going to hurt you. I'd never hurt you."

"Aaron?" Her heart rate began to stabilize, the fear turned to confusion. "What...?"

"A nightmare? You kept mine away, but I didn't do the same for you." He sounded very disappointed by this.

"I...I don't ever have nightmares." At least not for a long time. "Except..."

"Except what?"

And then a flood of memory came storming back from behind the thick doors she'd constructed in her mind for her own protection. "Oh, God," she said, and she bolted out of the bed and stumbled to the bathroom. She made it as far as the sink before she was violently sick.

Aaron was right behind her. He gave her a moment to be sure she wouldn't be sick again and then wrapped a blanket around her and handed her a warm damp washcloth. He closed the toilet seat and eased her to sit on top. She sat there, hunched over, her head hanging so her hair hid her face.

"Oh, God," she whispered again.

Aaron waited without speaking. He handed her a paper cup of water so she could rinse her mouth.

After another few moments she was able to translate her bone-chilling fears into objective words. "I got this overload of memories. Stuff I hid away, I guess. Crazy things from my awful marriage. Clayton was pretty much a tyrant. A cheating tyrant. And he's good with words, wields them like weapons. He'd work his black magic on me with a combination of accusations and half-truths, insisting I was always imagining things, making me question my own mind. Even when we were still married, he was threatening to take Joshua from me." She rested her forehead in her palms with her elbows propped on her knees. She could hardly understand why she was reacting like this. Why here? Why now?

Aaron sat on the edge of the tub, protectively near. "If memories are bad enough for us to suppress, they're bad. If they come back to bite us when we least expect it, that might be a form of post-traumatic stress disorder."

She looked up at him in horror. "No, that's crazy. Clayton never hit me, never hit Joshua. Though he had to stop himself once or twice. He used words—mean conniving words, but still just words."

Aaron leaned forward so he could look her in the eyes. For the first time, she noticed he'd been thoughtful enough to wrap a towel around his waist. "You're a well-educated and very intelligent woman, Gwen. You *know* that trauma can come from words. Mental and emotional abuse can have similar effects to physical abuse. I know you know that."

She stared into his calm, patient eyes, so full of certainty. And she nodded. "But he didn't really *do* anything to me," she protested weakly.

"If I'm understanding what you've told me, Clayton worked on you relentlessly over a span of years until you didn't trust your own convictions. He eroded your confidence, like a constant drip of water can wear away stone. For a woman as naturally strong and clear-headed as you are, that had to have been torture."

"I didn't have to stay. Why did I stay so long?"

"Why did you?" he gently asked her back.

"Josh," she said. "I kept thinking it would

be better for Joshua to be with both parents."
She looked away, thinking of her son. "But
one day I decided it wasn't better for him. I
was turning bitter and resentful. I was angry
all the time, even at Josh. So I finally got Clay
out of our house, finally got a divorce."

Aaron nodded. After a moment he asked,
"Did you ever talk to anyone about what
went on in your marriage? Did you confide
in anyone?"

She met his gaze again and held on to
the quiet strength she saw there. "Not until
now. How do you know so much about post-
traumatic stress disorder?"

"I was a psych major in college. Then,
before you'd joined the D.A.'s office, I had
two different clients who suffered from it. A
Gulf War vet who beat the crap out of a guy in
a bar. His was a more standard case. But later,
I had a woman who poisoned her husband. She
went to a mental hospital instead of prison. I
hear she's out now and doing okay. Even got
custody of her kids back from the State."

She nodded, taking in what he said. But her
situation was different to his clients'. She was
a strong woman with a high-profile career.
She coped with enormous stress every day.
Surely she didn't suffer from PTSD. On the

other hand, she hated the idea of Clayton renting space in her head this way.

"Maybe I'll talk to someone about my crazy marriage," she said. "Couldn't hurt."

He gave her a half smile as he stood, urging her upright with him. "Will you come back to bed with me? I'd like to just curl up there together for a while. We have the house to ourselves, it seems. I went downstairs while you were sleeping and found a note saying the boys are at your house for the night and Phyllis is at her friend's."

"Yes," she said, and allowed herself to be led back to where they'd been before she'd startled awake from a dream in which she was married once again to Clayton and he was asking a court to commit her to a mental hospital because she had no clear grasp on reality. He'd never done anything close to that, but there had been so many times he'd made her doubt her own intuition, her own sanity, that it felt as if he had. She could now recall how frequently she'd questioned the small indications of his infidelity, how often she'd wondered if she could trust her mind, how well he'd manipulated her psyche. With those memories unlocked, she wasn't sure she would ever be able to sleep again for fear more would be released from the vault of her subconscious.

But when she came violently awake again hours later, she could not deny she was going to have to do something about her emotional equilibrium now that her mind had unlocked these recollections about her marriage. Maybe Aaron was right about PTSD. She hated comparing her own difficulty to people with far worse traumas, but she knew it was more important to get help than to go on sleeplessly or to allow these revealed memories to take over her life. Otherwise, she wouldn't be much of a mom, or much of a lawyer, either.

Aaron slept quietly beside her and she wondered if terrible dreams still tormented him. His features were calm, and she thought perhaps he was sleeping dreamlessly. She lay there staring at his profile and wondered how she'd failed to notice before that he had a perfect balance to his features. His nose was straight and lifted perfectly into a strong brow. His lips were sensuous without being girly. He had a firm jaw, but his charm and humor kept him from ever appearing overbearing. An attractive man, Aaron. Why had it taken her so long to notice?

Because he'd always struck her as a beta male. He was the kind of man she usually dismissed, as a rule. His hair was too long because he only got it cut when he felt like it. His clothing was anything but the quintessential power suit, his demeanor casual and relaxed. The opposite of everything she'd ever admired in a man. Yet circumstances had brought them together anyway. Was she glad? When she recalled their lovemaking, she was very glad. She wanted more of that. But how could they make anything work between them? Especially now?

Melody's warnings came flooding into her mind, along with the many reasons she shouldn't be in this man's bed. She pulled a pillow over her face as if she could hide from her own shame. Could she blame the effects of secondhand weed? The room had smelled of marijuana when she'd arrived. Oh, hell.

When a phone began to ring, she lifted the pillow that was doing nothing to help her think more clearly. She realized light streamed through a window, filtering through the drawn shade.

"That must be your phone," Aaron said in a sleep-raspy voice.

His tone made her think of how he'd sounded when he'd whispered in her ear the night before and liquid heat began to pool inside her. Damn. Could she still blame the secondhand marijuana? Nope.

When she didn't get up right away—she

was very aware she was naked beneath the sheets—he pushed back the covers and walked over to her briefcase. He fished the phone out, but it stopped ringing. He brought it back to her anyway, unconcerned about his own nudity. He sprawled stomach down onto the bed beside her and handed her the now-silent PDA.

"Good morning," he said with a lopsided grin. "And thank you for pulling me back from the edge of darkness." With that, he sobered and his gaze drifted away for a moment. She knew he had slipped into terrible memories again.

"Come back," she said simply. And he did. His eyes refocused on her and some of the pain there faded.

"What time is it?" he asked her.

She held up her phone to check, but instead of answering his question, she sat up fast and sucked in air. "Damn," she blurted. "I was supposed to be in court twenty minutes ago."

CHAPTER TWELVE

GWEN PULLED ON CLOTHING as fast as she could. It took Aaron ten seconds to don his sweatpants from the night before, while she struggled with one button after another on her blouse. All the while, she couldn't make eye contact with the man she'd made love to the night before.

"Slow down, Gwen. You're already late, so a few more minutes won't matter."

There was truth in that, so she paused. But she still couldn't look at him. "This was a mistake, Aaron."

"What? No. Don't say that. We're great together. In a hundred different ways."

"My family lawyer specifically told me to stay away from you. She said you were a threat to my job, which I need to retain custody of Josh. But I dismissed her concern. Until now."

Finally, she forced herself to meet his gaze. She wished with all her heart she could take back the words that had brought the hurt into his eyes. But her son's future was at stake.

She'd allowed herself to forget about that last night. She'd allowed passion to overtake her better sense. And now her job was in real jeopardy. Missing a hearing without just cause—in the hospital, under arrest, or being held hostage—was enough to get her fired.

"I'm sorry, Aaron. I didn't mean for this to happen." She gestured vaguely toward the bed. "I thought I could help you and—"

"You *have* helped me. More than I deserve."

"But this went too far. It was a mistake." As she picked up her suit jacket, her gaze fell upon the photo of a woman on the far nightstand. She presumed it was Beth and she couldn't believe she hadn't noticed the deceased woman's eyes upon her while she'd made love with Aaron. The idea made her shudder. Cold words came to her then—words that she knew would make Aaron back off. "Besides, you're still in love with your wife." She gestured toward the photo as she took hold of her briefcase and headed toward the door.

When she looked back, she saw that he had frozen in place and was staring at his wife's picture.

"I'm sorry," she said. "But we can't see each other again."

As she put her hand on the knob to let herself out, he moved with swift determination to her side and placed his hand over hers. "Thank you for helping me get through the night."

He looked into her eyes a moment, and she saw a thousand emotions warring beneath the surface. Gwen bolted out of the room, afraid that if she stayed one more second, she'd fall apart. She had to get out of his bedroom, out of his house, out of his life, and go salvage her job so she could keep her son.

She should have carried her shoes, she realized. Her heels clattered noisily down the stairs in rapid staccato and a sleepy-eyed Phyllis came to investigate. It was too late for Gwen to avoid her.

"You stayed the night," Phyllis said as she stared at Gwen with bewilderment in her eyes. "Is Aaron going to be okay?"

Was he? Gwen would have liked to find out the answer to that, too. But she had no right to such information. She was walking out of his life. And even though he might be fooling himself that there could come a time when they could explore the possibilities of their mutual attraction, she knew better. Clayton might lose this next custody battle, as Melody had promised, but he would never give up. She would never be truly free of him. To keep Joshua, she'd have to sacrifice any possible future with Aaron.

Standing before Phyllis as these dark thoughts went through her mind, Gwen couldn't find the right words to answer. "I'm sorry" was what came out of her mouth. She all but ran to the door and out into the blinding morning light.

AARON SAT FOR A MOMENT on the edge of the bed where he and Gwen had made love the night before. He looked at the photo of Beth and couldn't understand how he could feel so much guilt and still want so badly to pursue Gwen until she relented in her determination to stay away from him. Yet, as he looked at his beloved wife's image, he could hear the echoes of her voice telling him to go after what he wanted in life. He wanted to believe she would approve of Gwen. What confused him was how he could love Beth, long for her, need her, grieve over her—and still be falling in love with Gwen. The quandary made him stay sitting there for long moments.

But after a while, he decided that the time to sit idle, wallowing in his own pain, was past. He would cling to the words Gwen had given him the night before, about the justice system being flawed yet still the best. He would try to get beyond his self-recrimination and sorrow for Annie Bell's death and her parents' grief.

He would do what he could to make certain her killer paid a price for what he'd done. And he'd try to resolve his inner turmoil over the woman who'd been taken from him years ago and the woman who didn't want to be with him now.

But first, he had to go for a run. Until he did that, his mind would keep trying to return to that dark place he'd been in before Gwen had rescued him. He couldn't let that happen after she'd risked so much to help him. He knew from his experience after Beth had died that his best defenses against depression were physical exercise and work. He wasn't quite ready for work again, but he could run.

As he downed a yogurt standing next the refrigerator, he assured Phyllis that he would be okay now, that he'd pulled himself together. He apologized for worrying her. But he pretended he didn't know that she'd seen Gwen leave this morning. He simply couldn't deal with a discussion about his disastrous love life with the mother of his deceased wife. Hell, he didn't even want to think about it. His head was still spinning over the Nepher horror and the hurt from Gwen's parting words. He desperately wanted to believe she would come back to him after she won final custody. Still, as he stood in his kitchen with his mother-in-law, guilt flooded through him.

While he knew he needed to move on with his life, he also knew he should have found a way to ease Phyllis toward such a big and painful change. Allowing her to discover that her beloved daughter had been replaced by a new love as Gwen made her morning escape from his bedroom—that was beyond cruel. He felt the weight of what he'd allowed to happen and wanted to find a way to make it better. But how? It seemed like an impossible situation.

He needed to go running so he could clear his mind of everything painful and confusing and sad. He left Phyllis standing in the kitchen with a stricken expression on her face. Just as the door shut and locked behind him, he heard his cell phone chirping its merry tune from the foyer table where he'd left it. His office, no doubt, wondering what had become of him. He decided not to go back in to answer it. He needed to run.

SHE MANAGED TO SAVE HER job, going straight to the office without stopping home to shower and change clothes. A brush through her hair and a touch-up with some lip gloss in the car mirror was all she had time for. No one noticed anything was amiss, outside of the fact that she'd been a no-show in Judge Baker's courtroom.

"I'm not going to fire you," John told her. "But you owe me. And what I want is your undivided attention on the Nepher case. That scumbag goes to prison for the rest of his life, or you're looking for another job. And the same goes for all the other cases Release Initiative is pushing."

Her phone began to ring from inside her briefcase, but she ignored it. She should have kept her mouth shut, but she couldn't do it. "Release Initiative isn't defending Nepher. He's a sociopath and no one could have known he would do what he did."

"*I* did. *I* knew."

She ignored that arrogant comment. "He did not commit the crime for which he was originally convicted. His release was appropriate."

"Appropriate? Do you know what he did to that kid as soon as he got out?"

"Again, there was no way to predict that. His psych evaluation, done far too late, paints a picture of a sociopath. This time, he'll be convicted of a crime he's actually guilty of. But you can't blame the nonprofit for what happened."

"The hell I can't." He looked at her closely, suspicion in his eyes. "Where were you this morning, anyway? You've never missed a court appearance in your life. I heard you were in court a few hours before you gave birth to your son. So what the hell kept you from the hearing today?"

Yes, she should have kept her mouth shut and accepted John's ranting for what it was. What had compelled her to defend Aaron's employer to her boss, who would never, ever understand? And what was she supposed to say now. An outright lie could ruin her if he already suspected. She could not underestimate the power of the rumor mill, especially when Logan was among the rumormongers. But she couldn't tell John the truth, either.

"I can't tell you without revealing confidences. Please don't ask me to. You said yourself I've had a perfect record until now. I assure you there will be no other incidents."

Like a volcano about to erupt, John's whole body seemed to expand with rage the instant she begged him not to ask her. But he didn't get out a single word. Logan rushed into the office without knocking. The young man's expression was grim.

"Gwen, you need to go home right now," Logan said. "Your mother has been trying to reach you. Your son and his friend are missing."

Her whole focus riveted on Logan's announcement even as she reached for her cell and saw she'd accidentally turned off the sound. Missing? What did that mean? For how long? Were the boys hiding from her parents? Why would they do that? She thumbed through the twenty missed calls and saw they were all from her own home phone. She wanted to throw the phone across the room in her fury and angst as she wondered if Clayton had finally made good on his threats to take Josh? If so, what did he think he could gain by taking Benjamin, too?

She didn't think about her words or who was in the room to hear. She just wanted to marshal all possible resources as soon as possible. "Logan, call Aaron Zimmerman right away and tell him everything my mother told you. Ask him to meet me at my house."

"Why?" Logan asked. John stood by, stunned to silence.

"Because his son is the friend who's missing along with Josh. If Clay kidnapped them together, he'll want to help find them to bring them home."

"Your ex wouldn't be that stupid," John said, leaving unacknowledged the bombshell she'd just revealed by admitting her son was close friends with Aaron's child.

"I've kept you informed of Clay's threats. My mother and father aren't the type to claim the kids are missing if they haven't already called the schools and looked everywhere. What else could have happened?"

John had no answer and Logan said nothing. He just held her briefcase, retrieved from her own office for her, as she rushed toward the exit. Before she got onto the elevator, she turned back to the two men.

"Can you call the police and anyone else who could help find Clay? I have to contact Melody and try to reach Clay by phone while I drive home."

She saw their two heads nod in unison before the elevator door closed. As she descended to the lobby, it seemed her stomach remained on the fifteenth floor, but she refused to give in to the gut twisting sensation and just focused on problem solving, remaining in control, and dialing her phone as she marched with determination to her car.

Clay didn't answer his line and she left him a voice message filled with icy threats about what would happen when she found him and their son. Melody answered her phone, but she urged Gwen to focus on driving. They would meet to discuss strategies and options at Gwen's house, where they could get more details from her parents.

Gwen did her best to shut everything other than driving out of mind. But Logan's voice kept ringing in her ears. "Your son and his friend are missing."

AARON DIDN'T TAKE THE time to shower and change after his run. The instant Phyllis told him what had happened, he grabbed his car keys and his cell and took off. Phyllis had wanted to go with him, but he persuaded her to stay at the house in case one of the boys called or showed up there. He promised he'd keep her informed. After he got his car under way, he glanced at his phone and realized it was full of messages, starting with Gwen's landline number. Presumably her mother had been trying to get in touch with him. Tossing the PDA onto the passenger seat in disgust, he wondered how he and Gwen could have missed finding out about the kids sooner when they both were glued to their cell phones.

It crossed his mind that she would blame their passionate night together for keeping her from protecting Josh. She might even blame him. As he pulled into her driveway, behind Gwen's car and next to a police vehicle, he prepared himself for the possibility she would direct her anger toward him. He would quietly take whatever she needed to dish out because he'd do anything to help her through this.

He knocked gently at the front door, but when no one answered, he let himself in. He found Gwen standing rigidly by her fireplace in the same clothes she'd had on the day before. Her parents were seated on one sofa with two police officers on the other. The cops had notebooks out and were clearly getting down the details from Gwen's mother and father. They all looked up at him for the barest second and Gwen announced to the room, "This is Benjamin's father." Then the questions and answers resumed while Gwen walked over to where he stood. She stopped a few feet away and stood there awkwardly, looking at the floor and the officers and the nearest chair, but not at him.

"No one can reach Clayton and everyone is assuming the boys are with him," she said. "But I'm not so sure anymore."

"Why is that?"

"Small things don't add up. Both kids seem to have taken their backpacks, but they took their homework out of them first. I'm not sure what they put back in, but if Clay had to sneak them out of the house without my parents noticing, I'd think he wouldn't take the time to prep backpacks for each of them."

"Yes, that's odd. We should try to figure out what they took in those backpacks. Is any money missing?"

"I can check. Josh knows where I keep cash for emergencies."

She turned to go look but stopped when the male cop said, "Excuse me."

"Mr. Zimmerman, we need to talk to you next," his female partner said. "Do you mind coming in here with us?"

"Go ahead and look around," he whispered to Gwen. But the cops heard anyway.

"Go ahead and look for what?" the female asked.

He let Gwen field that question. "I wanted to see if any of the emergency money is missing."

"Why would money be missing if Joshua's father took him?" the male cop asked.

Aaron interjected, "Our kids are missing. She just wants to make sure we're on the right track. So unless you want to question us together..."

The officers exchanged glances and said they'd prefer to speak to him alone first. Gwen hesitated, then left on her mission to see about the money and to try to figure out what Josh had taken in his backpack. Aaron moved to the living room and sat in a wing chair that looked as if it had never been used before.

From here he could see the female cop's name tag said Clark. Officer Clark looked over to Gwen's distraught parents, who sat like stones on the formal couch. They were in shock. Aaron wondered if he would end up that way, too. So far, he'd been in problem-solving mode, running on the assumption that the boys were safe and would be back soon. Either the kids were with Clayton Haverty and no real harm would come to them or they were on some adventure of Benjamin's making and would be back before nightfall. After all, he'd suffered through many of Benjamin's antics in the past and knew it was probably too early to give in to real fear. Or perhaps that's what he was telling himself so he could continue to function.

"Mr. and Mrs. Masoner, we're done for now. Call us if you think of anything else that might be important to locating your grandson and his friend, okay?"

Judy Masoner nodded and Edward didn't do or say anything. Neither one made as if to leave the room. Aaron leaned toward them, put his hand gently on Ed Masoner's shoulder. "Sir, I think the officers want to speak to me alone for a moment. Perhaps you could make everyone some coffee?"

Judy responded immediately. "Yes, we'll make coffee. Perhaps some sandwiches for later." She got to her feet and headed toward the kitchen. Edward followed like a lost puppy.

Aaron returned his attention to Officer Clark and her colleague. He didn't recognize either one of them, but they probably knew who he was and what he did for a living. They most certainly knew Gwen, perhaps even worked with her on cases.

Clark flipped backward through her notebook and seemed to study an entry she'd made earlier. Then she looked up and said, "I understand you and Ms. Haverty spent the night alone together at your home, Mr. Zimmerman. Can you provide details on the activities of your time together."

A single word ran through Aaron's mind. *Damn.*

CHAPTER THIRTEEN

AARON HAD NO WAY OF KNOWING whether
Gwen had told the police the whole truth about
what they'd been doing the night before, but he
remembered that she did not want anyone to
know about their tryst for fear it would harm
her chances for permanent custody of Josh.
That meant he'd have to hedge, something he
didn't like to do with cops. Especially cops
like officer Clark, who seemed able to pen-
etrate to your very soul with one deep look
into your eyes.

"Gwen's son was worried about me and
asked her to come over to see what she could
do," he said. He couldn't seem to keep still
and watched the jittery jackhammer motion of
his knee. It seemed that part of him must be
under the control of an alien. He couldn't stop
this physical exhibition of his frantic worry.
Where were the boys? Who were they with?
How would he get them back safely?

"Why was her son worried about you?"

The question jolted Aaron out of his

thoughts. "Surely you heard about Nepher and what he did." His knee kept up its anxious vibration.

"You mean what he did after *you* got him out of prison."

Aaron sighed, fighting once again the sickening feeling that kept threatening to overtake him when he thought about his part in the crime. "Yes, that's what I mean. It's not going to be an easy thing to live with. I was a mess for a day." Deep inside, he knew he was still a mess. But he would keep that to himself until the current crisis was resolved. His son needed him. Gwen and Josh needed him. He'd do his best to keep himself together.

"And Ms. Haverty helped you through the worst of it."

"Yes, exactly." Maybe this woman was more sympathetic than he had any right to hope for.

"And her helping you through it took all night while your children were...where?"

Nix the sympathy. "They came here to stay with Gwen's parents for the night. I wasn't really fit for them to be around."

The officer made a note of that and Aaron's knee continued its jackhammering. He wanted to be looking for his son.

"But you somehow figured you were fit to

spend the night with Ms. Haverty?" The male cop spoke for the first time.

From his tone, Aaron could tell the cop felt protective of Gwen and her reputation in the legal community. Could that protectiveness be used to persuade these two to keep the previous night's details to themselves?

"Look, we need to stay focused on finding the boys," Aaron said. "And I don't want to have Gwen's reputation tarnished because she tried to help me. You've worked with her, I'm sure. So you know she does important work. None of us want to jeopardize her ability to continue doing that, right?"

They exchanged glances again, then both nodded. Clark got back to business right away. "Did you ever hear Clayton Haverty threaten to take the boys?"

"I heard him threaten to take Josh from Gwen. But I have no idea why he'd take my son, too. Why not just leave him here?"

"That's what we'd like to know, too. We have an APB out on Mr. Haverty and we're trying to get a reading on his cell phone location, if it's on."

"He hasn't been answering his—"

He was interrupted by Judy Masoner calling up the stairwell to her daughter. "Gwen, please come to the kitchen. Your father thinks he found something."

GWEN LOOKED AT HER FATHER, who stood staring at the refrigerator door. The police officers stood behind her. "Was that there before? What does it mean?"

"What is it, Dad?" she said as she approached. All she could see were the twenty or so drawings, homework assignments, schedules and notes from Joshua that were pinned to the fridge with magnets.

Edward Masoner turned slowly, showing every moment of his age. Gwen noticed for the first time that there was a slight tremor making his head nod, almost imperceptibly.

He looked at her. "Oh, well, this note here. I don't remember it being there yesterday."

She focused where his unsteady hand indicated. There was a note in Joshua's scrawl. And it didn't look familiar to her, either. She plucked it off the door, sending the magnet clattering. Aaron, her parents and the two cops huddled around her to read what it said.

"Mom, don't worry. Gramma Char will fix things with Dad. Love, Josh"

No one spoke as they stared at the page with

the youthful handwriting on it and tried to make sense of the message.

"Did they try go to this grandmother on their own?" Clark asked.

Gwen whispered, "She lives in Pittsburgh. How could they believe they'd get there?"

"Maybe that ex of yours took them there," Edward said. "I'd like to punch him in the nose for causing so much worry."

Gwen shared her father's sentiments, but she was feeling more and more certain that Clay wasn't the cause of this particular worry. Aaron stood across the room and she looked over at him, wondering what he made of the situation. "Do you think they could have run away on their own?" she asked him.

A stricken expression crossed Aaron's face. No one else noticed, but Gwen had a connection with this man now, whether that was a good idea or not. She took several steps in his direction. "What?" she asked him, afraid to hear his thoughts.

"I talked to Josh about dealing with his father's threats, remember? I told him he needed to take on some of the responsibility for making sure his dad didn't take him away from you. We were talking about not going with Clay unless he knew for sure, directly from you, that it was okay. I meant he should go to school officials or another trusted adult if his father showed up unexpectedly." Aaron pushed all of his fingers through his shaggy hair and turned in a slow circle, his body language filled with anguish. "What if he misunderstood me? What if he thought I meant that he had to figure out a way to fix things once and for all?"

"Sounds like that's exactly what he thought you meant," said Officer Clark. "You're just not having a good week, Counselor."

"Shut up," Gwen snapped. Everyone went into stunned silence, including Gwen. Her stomach was pitching as she stared at Aaron. As much as she knew she ought to tell him this wasn't his fault, she couldn't get past the realization that even the man she thought she could rely on had let her down. Aaron had screwed things up and now her son was lost out in the dangerous world.

Mustering some control over her voice, she said, "I need to think." But her mind didn't seem to want to work.

"Call Charlotte and see if she knows anything about this," suggested Judy.

Glad to have a clear, sensible direction, Gwen immediately turned to the phone sitting on the counter and dialed her former mother-in-law's number. She let it ring a long time, but there was no answer, not even a voice mail pickup. In frustration, she slammed the receiver back into its cradle. It was maddening to have phones so ubiquitous in society, and still be unable to get in touch with Clayton or his mother.

"If you can get me this grandmother's address, we can amend the Amber Alert," Officer Clark offered.

"I have no idea how they would think they could get all that way," Gwen said. She definitely preferred the idea of Clayton absconding with the boys. But in her heart, she knew the kids had gone off together, just as Aaron feared. They were out there somewhere, trying to get to Clay's mother, hoping she would make her son behave better.

"I know where the address book is," Judy said, and she went to get it out of the drawer in the study.

"It's still possible they're with Clay," Edward offered. "The man threatened to steal Josh away, after all."

Gwen knew her father hated his own lack of awareness about Clayton's threats. It had taken the interview with the police to make him accept the full extent of his former son-in-law's ill treatment of Gwen. And now he struggled with anger at himself for not listening well enough to his daughter, as well as rage at her ex-husband. "If I get my hands on him…"

"We're still trying to track him down," assured the male cop. "We'll find these kids. We'll be in touch."

Edward showed the cops to the door. They heard Judy giving them Charlotte Haverty's address, then the door clicked shut, and the police were gone. Gwen felt bereft. Their presence had given her the sense that someone was doing something to find the boys. Now she couldn't shake the feeling that their case would be just another number on the police blotter.

Alone in the kitchen together, Aaron and Gwen turned to each other.

"They know about us, I think," Aaron said. "About last night. The cops put it together, and probably would have come to the same conclusions even if nothing had happened between us."

"I don't care much about that now. All that really matters is getting Josh and Ben back safely." She looked up into his eyes, hoping he'd recovered some of his famous calm, wishing she could still count on him to bolster her own strength. But he'd made this happen with his stupid, thoughtless counsel to Josh. She didn't think she could ever forgive him. Still, until the boys were found, she had to be civil.

"I can't just wait here, doing nothing, while the boys are out there somewhere. They're just little boys." Her voice broke on the last word and she had to blink away the sudden stinging tears in her eyes.

Aaron stepped close, but when she shifted away from him, he kept himself from touching her. Gwen didn't want him near her. She couldn't get out of her mind the possibility he'd caused this by persuading her son to take matters into his own hands. Whether he'd intended to or not, he'd encouraged Josh in this direction. And Aaron's involvement underscored for her some of what made him so frustrating. He clung to his belief that talking and hugging and being kind and open with everyone could solve the world's problems. Her son had listened to him, and now he was out there in the world all alone, possibly trying to make his way to his grandmother to persuade her to help them with Clay.

"I don't know if this will comfort you, but Ben has some experience traveling on his own. He's flown out to visit my father in California. And this isn't the first time he's taken off on a crazy adventure."

"That isn't a comfort at all," she snapped.

Unfair to lay blame. But if someone else was responsible, then she didn't have to be.

He spun away and held on to the sides of his head as if he feared it would crack open. "God, I'm so sorry, Gwen. If not for the Zimmerman clan, Joshua would most likely be at school right now. But—" he squared his shoulders and became the man she'd admired so many times in the courtroom "—I'm going to do everything in my power to make this right by finding our kids. We're going to call everyone we know and get them searching for the boys. Some of my clients have extensive networks. It's time to activate them all."

"Yes," she said, relieved to have something to do. "Yes, we need to start calling people."

BY THE TIME SHE REMEMBERED to contact her boss, she was a frazzled mess. She'd been on the phone alerting everyone she knew between her home and Pittsburgh about the missing boys. Each person had been appropriately concerned and sympathetic, but Gwen felt none of them grasped the full seriousness of the situation. As a result, she became even more frantic. It didn't help that hours were passing without any news. John made himself sound concerned for her son, but he also asked her whether he needed to find replacements for her on pending cases. By the end of their conversation, she was ready to scream.

It didn't help that Aaron had gone to his own home once he'd exhausted the numbers in his cell phone. She now had mixed feelings toward him and Benjamin and their roles in persuading Joshua to go off like this. Sometime during the day, it had popped into her head that maybe no one was at fault. Not even Clay. As badly as he'd treated her during their marriage, he had always been an attentive father. His threats about Josh and custody had come from concern for his son. How many times had Clay tried to talk to her about Joshua's grades? How many times had he begged her to cut back her hours?

The idea that Clay might not be as evil as she liked to paint him made her feel powerless and angry. If Clay had a decent side to him, he'd have a real chance at winning custody. The idea made her stomach roil, so she put it out of her mind and turned her anger toward Aaron and his too-adventurous son.

Even now, though, she'd found some comfort in having Aaron in the house. His son was also missing and they had to work through this ordeal together.

"Coffee?" her mother asked. Her parents had been rock solid as the hours passed, fighting off their own despair and feelings of guilt. After the initial shock, they had reluctantly agreed with Gwen that they couldn't have seen this coming, so they couldn't have prevented it. They had been providing food and coffee to anyone who came to help. Gwen realized that a number of people, mostly from her office, had come. They were networking with their own friends and family, calling in every possible favor to try to find the boys.

She declined the coffee with a shake of her head. But as her mother turned to ask others about refills, Gwen called her back. "Mom, I—"

Judy looked at her daughter. "I wish I could fix this for you."

"You're helping so much. I wanted to say thank you. I feel I'm not alone in this. Before…I always felt so isolated."

"You've always been surrounded by people who care, Gwen. The change is in your ability to see how much we love you."

Gwen nodded, feeling her throat tighten again for the hundredth time. As her mother walked away, Gwen silently acknowledged the truth in her words— and that Aaron and Ben had opened her heart to the possibility that she might possibly be worthy of the love that had always been available to her.

"Logan," she said into her phone, contacting him for what had to be the hundredth time in the past three hours. "I was hoping I'd have that phone list I asked you for by now."

"The one from your office computer?" he asked. "I printed that an hour ago and sent it over. I figured I'd be more use to you here. It should be there by now."

"You could have emailed it. Who's bringing it?" But even as she asked the question, the answer walked through the front door.

As Gwen made eye contact with her boss, Logan said, "Mr. Fry insisted on taking it to you himself. He wanted to see how you were holding up."

CHAPTER FOURTEEN

WHEN HE ARRIVED HOME, Aaron found his mother-in-law coping with a steady stream of people who wanted to help. She had put them to work right away, sending them off to bus and train stations, the airport and other public places. Some had ideas of their own about where to look and she'd started a list so she could help people avoid duplication. He was grateful.

"Folks want to feel they're doing something to help you, Aaron," she told him. "You have a lot of people who want to return your kindness any way they can."

"Well, you've been amazingly resourceful and organized. Thank you."

"I'm the one responsible for losing them, so it's the least I can do."

Aaron sighed. Fatigue kept nipping at his heels, but he had to ignore it and keep going. He couldn't let Ben's grandmother go on thinking this way.

"Phyllis, you didn't lose them. We're pretty

sure they ran away. I told you on the phone, you aren't responsible." In his mind he added, *Because I am.*

"If I'd kept them here with me, this wouldn't have happened. Mr. And Mrs. Masoner didn't know about Benjamin's tendency to get into trouble. But I wanted to go to my card game and left them with those poor people. They must feel just terrible!"

"They do," Aaron said. "We all do. Let's stay focused on finding the boys instead of blaming ourselves."

"That's what we're here for," came another voice from behind him.

Aaron turned to see Omar Kingston and his sister walking through the front door.

"We want to help look for your son," added Opal. "We're just sorry we couldn't get here sooner."

"I couldn't get off from work," Omar said apologetically.

Aaron still couldn't fully understand how Omar always knew what was going on. It was as if he had informants everywhere. Regardless, he was a good man to know when knowledge of the streets was needed. Aaron grasped Omar's offered hand, and they drew each other into a man-hug. "Thank you for coming. We've got as many people as possible looking for them. The police are a little pissed about that, but they haven't come up with anything, so there's not much they can say."

"I heard it was your girlfriend's ex who took 'em," Omar said.

Aaron didn't bother to correct the misconception that Gwen was his girlfriend. He had hopes. "We aren't so sure," he said. "Either they ran away on their own or the note they left was to cover up that they're with the ex. But I'm certain Ben wouldn't have gone willingly."

"Could the ex have forced his kid to write the note?"

"One of the police officers believes that's possible. I think they like the theory because it's easier than runaway ten-year-olds. If they find Clayton Haverty—and they're bound to find him sooner or later—they're sure they'll have the kids, too."

"You don't believe the police are doing everything possible?" Phyllis asked. Aaron knew she wanted to trust the authorities were doing their jobs well.

Aaron put his hand on her arm to comfort her. "I'm sure they're turning over every stone. I just think they may be focused on some possibilities more than others."

"So we do the things they aren't so focused on," Omar said.

Aaron nodded. "That's what we've been working on all day."

"We know a lot of people," Opal said. "Omar's got connections."

Aaron had doubts that Omar's particular connections would be of any help in finding two little boys trying to make their way to Pittsburgh.

"HOW ARE THINGS GOING?" John asked. He'd handed Gwen the phone list as soon as he arrived and she immediately started dialing numbers. He'd wandered off somewhere, but now he was back.

She looked at him and wondered why he'd stayed. More than that, why had he come? Suspicions began to crawl up her spine, and with them rage blossomed. He was scoping out whether she would be able to get back to work sometime soon.

"I'm clinging to self-control by my fingertips, John. My son has been missing all day. We have no idea where he is." She managed to say this calmly but was sure he'd have seen the anger in her eyes if he'd been more aware.

"The police say he's with Clayton, so that's something to be thankful for."

She stared at him. Had he been talking to the people stationed in the house, trying to find out whether the situation was as serious as she claimed? Was he questioning her instincts, the way Clay always did?

"Thank you for bringing the phone list," she said. "Maybe you should go back to the office, review the files on my desk so you can take over or reassign my cases."

"You think that's necessary?" he asked.

He sounded so innocent. So reasonable. But Gwen had been trained by J. Clayton Haverty, who was a master at making his point without saying anything he could be held accountable for. Somehow, she kept the screams of rage confined to the inside of her head.

"I can't know when this nightmare is going to end, John," she said. This time, there was an edge of hysteria to her voice. She took in a deep breath, trying to regain control.

"They'll find Clay soon. And he's not going to hurt his own son. I'm sure everything will be fine."

She couldn't stand it another moment. Nothing else mattered as much as forcing this pompous ass to see she would not be treated like an overreacting fool. Not again. Never again.

"Are you suggesting I'm making too much

of all this, that I shouldn't be so upset because my son is missing? That he must be with his father and everything will be fine? Am I seeing danger that's not really there? Is that what you're saying, Cla—John?" As she spoke, she stalked closer to him, each step punctuating another of her words. By the time she said his name, almost slipping in her ex-husband's instead, she was directly in front of him.

He held up his hands, palms out, as if to show he wasn't armed. Or perhaps to defend himself in case she became violent. "Well, the police are saying he's with Clay. Clay has always taken good care of the kid, right?" He looked confused, as if he didn't understand what was wrong with his logic.

Gwen knew he was right, had even had similar thoughts of her own. But she wasn't ready to let go of the image of Clay she'd been building over the years since their divorce. "Clay is a monster in an Armani suit," she cried. "He's sneaky, devious, cruel and an egomaniac of enormous proportions. He will do anything to get his way, no matter who it hurts. And you think my son would be safe with him?" She knew she was shrieking, knew she'd lost control, knew she should turn and run away before she did irreparable harm. But somehow, she had to make John and everyone else understand that Clay was the bad guy in all this. That way, none of it was her responsibility.

"Calm down, Gwen. You're overreacting."

Something snapped—the last thread of her control, perhaps—and she lunged at him. With balled fists, she went at him, beating his chest, trying for his jaw or nose or eye. He dodged the worst of her attempts, shock making his eyes wide and mouth slack. A feral sound came out of her own mouth, interspersed with half sentences about this being the last time anyone would tell her to calm down or question her sanity or assert she was overreacting.

He backed up, but she kept going for him, striking out at him with all her might, kicking his shin once and hearing a satisfying yelp. But then her vision blurred and she felt wetness on her face. She paused in her assault to swipe beneath her nose, which gave John the chance to grasp the other wrist so she couldn't keep hitting him.

"It's okay, Gwen," she heard him say. "It's gonna be okay."

She found herself weeping against the lapel of his suit in gut-wrenching sobs, falling completely apart as her beleaguered boss awkwardly patted her shoulder and repeated his assurances that everything would be okay.

Even as embarrassment seeped into her consciousness, she couldn't stop the tears.

A door opened nearby; a familiar scent came to her. Through the fog, she knew Aaron had come, bringing the hope that she would be able to pull together the shattered pieces of herself. She allowed herself to be eased into Aaron's arms. He enveloped her in the safety of his embrace and simply stood there with her for a while. She couldn't tell how long. Things like time had no meaning for her.

"Judy, can you show me the way to her bedroom?" Aaron said, speaking to her mother, who must now be close by even though his voice seemed faraway. The most prominent sound was the beating of her own heart, too fast still, even though her physical outburst had ended.

He held her close to his side as he led her up the stairway and down the hall. She couldn't feel her limbs, thinking she must have floated to her room. Then she really was floating, because he'd lifted her into the cradle of his arms and set her on the lofted comforter covering her bed. She saw through the fog that his eyes were full of concern. Her mother, too, hovered nearby, worry deepening every line in her face. Her father hunkered in the doorway, helpless and perhaps a little afraid.

"I'm okay," she tried to say. But it sounded like mumbling. What the hell was wrong with her? What had happened down there with John? Why couldn't she hear anything except her own pulse or see clearly?

"Sleep awhile, Gwen. Close your eyes. I'll wake you before too long." Aaron's voice, so soothing. So full of promise. So honest and faithful. She trusted him. And he asked so little of her. She would do as he asked. It felt good to close her eyes, to block out the fog and fade to black.

"SHE'S SLEEPING NOW." Aaron had never liked John Fry much, but he'd been kind to Gwen even as she tried to beat the crap out of him. He owed the man an explanation of some kind. "But she'd never forgive me if I let her rest too long. She'll remember soon enough that Josh is still missing."

"What the hell was that all about?" John asked, looking more like his pompous self than he had when Aaron had walked in on his very awkward attempt to comfort a sobbing woman.

"She's been under a great deal of stress. I think it all became too much for her. She'll be back to herself in no time." He did not want to say that what had happened to Gwen looked very much like a PTSD-induced breakdown. People still didn't understand the causes of post-traumatic stress disorder and often blamed the person suffering from it or believed it could easily be treated. He wanted Gwen to have the chance to get help without being stigmatized as bat-shit crazy.

"From what I've pieced together from all of you about the incident, I'd say she misunderstood what you were saying and freaked out. Any mother would. Whether Josh and Ben ran away and are out there on their own or Clay abducted them in the night, this is a serous situation and she needs everyone to treat it that way."

"C'mon, Zimmerman. You're not that worried about your own boy, are you? You know he's with Clay, so he'll be okay."

Aaron wanted to punch his lights out. But he hadn't endured years of insidious mental and emotional abuse from an ex-spouse, as Gwen had, so he didn't cave in to the desire. "No one knows whether the boys are with Clay. We still can't find him. They could be anywhere, possibly alone and unprotected. Do you have kids, John?"

The attorney nodded and looked away. "I guess ten years old is pretty young if they've run away on their own."

"Then you see why Gwen might have lost control for a moment?" She'd probably succumbed to a flashback of Clayton's subtle manipulations that made her question her own sanity. But Aaron wouldn't be saying those thoughts aloud. He could only hope she would seek help and work out these things with a trained therapist.

"Well, besides all that, I need to get a better understanding of how you know so much about her. You talk like you're best friends when you're supposed to be on opposite sides. What the hell is going on with that?" John spoke in a low voice so he wouldn't be overheard.

"Our kids are friends from a karate class they take together," he said, sticking to Gwen's main reason for being around him socially. He didn't mention that she'd comforted him during one of his worst times, or that they'd spent a night together.

"And that's all? Sure looks like more than that."

"Whatever you're trying to insinuate, this isn't the time."

John stepped back as if slapped. His cheeks flushed. "There will come a time and I'll want an explanation. You got that? We have our reputation to maintain and having one of my attorneys consorting with a Release Initiative attorney will not be tolerated. I'll be getting to the bottom of this after the boys are safe."

Aaron stared at him. It was no wonder Gwen's subconscious mind had flashed back to her ex and led to her meltdown. Fry was nearly as self-centered as Clay. "Well, thank you for your confidence that we'll find them," he said, putting the best spin he could on the attorney's words. "Keep those positive thoughts going out into the universe."

John squinted at him, dismissing the metaphysical mumbo jumbo, as he would call it. "I'll be at home if anything develops. Keep in mind I need Gwen back in the office as soon as possible." And he left.

It took Aaron a moment to realize the man hadn't said he'd be at the office. He'd said he was going home. Sure enough, the sun had begun to set. The day had slipped away with no word about the boys. A wave of panic made his heart beat faster. He stood there doing yoga breathing until it passed and he had some measure of control again.

Then he did something insane. He went through the same motions he'd already tried a hundred times during the day, hoping for a different result. That was Einstein's definition of insanity, right? Doing something over and over, hoping for a different result? But he couldn't help himself. He hit the keys to automatically dial Benjamin's cell phone. He listened to it ring. He listened to his son's cheerful voice telling the caller that he was trekking to Antarctica and would return the call when he got back from his adventure.

At the beep, Aaron repeated what he'd already said to his son many times that day. "I love you, Ben. Please call and tell me you're safe." His voice broke and the last words came out little more than a whisper.

He put the phone away, resisting the urge to redial. Futile, he knew, but it comforted him to hear his son's voice, even on the recording made months ago. That voice made him certain Benjamin was alive and would be home soon.

As darkness began to close in, Judy went from room to room, turning on lamps for the people who had come to help search for the children. For the first time, Aaron felt there was nothing more he could do. So he trudged up the stairs to check on Gwen. Perhaps he should wake her and see if she needed more serious medical care. He'd already found one physician, a neighbor who happened to be in the house shortly after Gwen's meltdown, to check her vitals as she slept. The woman declared Gwen wasn't in any danger and should simply rest. Aaron had let Gwen do just that, but his worry remained.

When he walked into her bedroom, she opened her eyes. A small smile flickered across her lips as she caught his gaze. Aaron's throat tightened. He recalled all the times he'd come home and inadvertently wakened Beth, who was trying to sleep because of her shift work as a nurse. She'd smile at him in that same wistful, welcoming way. But Gwen's expression was quickly replaced by abject terror. She bolted upright. "Josh!"

He went to her and sat beside her. "We'll find them soon," he promised, even though he knew it was a hollow vow.

"It wasn't just a nightmare?" she asked, searching his face, begging him with her eyes to tell her it was all a dream.

"No." He took her hand into both of his and held it, hoping to give her strength. "But everyone we know is doing everything humanly possible to find them."

"What time is it?" she asked. He could hear the panic just under the surface of her voice, but she kept it in check.

"Just after seven."

"Oh, God. So many hours have passed.

Statistically, kids not found in the first four hours are gone for good."

"Our boys will not be confirming that statistic, Gwen. We'll find them. If nothing else, they'll show up on Mrs. Haverty's doorstep and she'll call. But it takes a long time to get to Pittsburgh from here."

"I hate the waiting," she admitted.

"I know. We all do. It was easier when we had something to do. But I've exhausted my calling list. Now we simply have to wait."

She eyed him speculatively. "You're very brave."

"It's the least I can do when my son and I are the cause of the whole thing."

"Are you?" She stared at him a moment, then memories seemed to flood back into her mind. She withdrew her hand and looked away. "Maybe I could have been a better mom, stayed home more, made him feel more secure. Hell, we could blame it on Nepher. If he hadn't committed his horrendous crime, the kids wouldn't have been together last night with my parents so they could run away or be taken by Clay. I'm not even sure now which one is more likely."

"No one is. The fact that both Clay's and Ben's cell phones are off makes everyone believe they're together."

"It doesn't matter anymore. I just want them

home. Make them come home, Aaron." She hugged her arms tightly around herself.

He wished he could comfort her. "They'll be home soon," he said. And longed to make it true.

Without looking at him, she whispered, "Can you also erase that debacle with John, superman? If you can't make him forget it ever happened, I'm pretty sure I'm out of a job. Which I deserve. I have no idea what happened to me. It was as if he was Clayton and I needed to fight back for once."

"We talked about this before, Gwen," Aaron said gently. "I know a great psychiatrist who specializes in PTSD, particularly from domestic abuse."

She didn't respond at first. After a long moment, she said simply, "Okay."

Relief washed through him. If she could accept talking to a professional, she'd probably be okay in the long run. He hated the possibility that Clay would overshadow her life forever. If she talked to Dr. Rousseau, there was hope she could rid herself of Clayton Haverty's shadow.

"WE'VE GOT HIM ON THE phone!" a police officer shouted.

Gwen heard her father call her name. She and Aaron just about flew down the stairs.

"He says he doesn't have them," the man said to the gathered crowd as he listened to Clay on the other end of the line. He called out Clay's location to another officer, who wrote it into his notebook.

"He's in D.C.?" Aaron said. "I thought he was in New York."

"So did I." Disappointment washed through Gwen as she realized her intuition had been right when she'd concluded the boys were on their own. Until now, she'd been able to tell herself they might be with Clay, which was safer than being alone. And as this thought crossed her mind, she realized that somewhere deep down, she knew Clay wouldn't hurt Josh, wouldn't actually kidnap him, wouldn't have taken Ben, wouldn't be the terrible person her psyche sometimes made him out to be. She knew she'd have to think more deeply about her ex when this was over. Maybe that psychiatrist would help her.

"May I speak to him?" she asked the cop. She experienced a split second of hesitation before putting the phone to her ear, then took a breath, steeling herself for this difficult conversation. "Clayton," she said, trying to sound strong and in control.

"Gwen, is it true?" Clay said, and for a split second, Gwen thought he would share her parental worry and be supportive as they continued the search. "Did you lose Joshua? Are you really such an utter failure as a mother that you lost my son?"

CHAPTER FIFTEEN

GWEN GLANCED TOWARD AARON, knowing he'd overheard Clayton's accusation. His expression remained neutral, but he placed a comforting hand on her upper arm. With this simple gesture, she was somehow reminded that she was not a bad mother. For once, she didn't let her ex-husband get under her skin.

"Do you know why your mother isn't answering her phone, Clay?" she asked, staying focused on getting her son and Benjamin to safety.

"She's in Italy. I told you she was going. You don't pay attention to anything I say. That's why we could never get along. You won't listen. I need someone who will give a damn about what I think, what I want. But you just do whatever you think is best, no matter what."

She couldn't remember him ever telling her anything about Charlotte in recent months, and for the first time while talking to this man, she didn't question her own certainty. She just moved on to the next question.

"Do you know why Josh would want to go see her? He left a note saying Gramma Haverty would fix things."

Clay's voice became less accusing. "My mother is good at fixing things, but Josh wouldn't go see her by himself when he knows she's in Europe."

"He's with his friend and I'm not sure he would remember that she went overseas. They aren't with you, so they must have gone off on their own. We're not going to overlook any possibilities. Are you sure you told him about your mother being in Italy?"

Clay didn't answer right away. It was the first time she'd questioned his memory. And because of the gravity of the situation, he was complying. He might have been an awful husband, but she could no longer doubt his love for his son.

"Maybe he didn't hear me," he admitted. Gwen knew this was as much as she was going to get from him.

"The police in Pittsburgh have been to her house and no one is there. So if that's where the kids are going, they're still in transit."

He gave a derisive laugh. "Or they've run away because Josh can't stand living with you and they're hiding out somewhere until I get back."

She saw Aaron spin away and turn in a tight circle of frustration as he heard this latest accusation from Clay. Somehow, his reaction helped her stay calm. "None of us know for sure why they took off. The focus needs to stay on finding them."

Clay hesitated, then said, "I'll be there in an hour to help any way I can."

Gwen couldn't hide her surprise that he'd give up tormenting her so easily. Apparently, Clay lost interest when she didn't react to his gibes. She could have used that knowledge years ago. "Keep your phone on," she said. "I'll call you if anything changes."

She clicked off and Aaron took the borrowed phone and handed it back to the police officer.

"So he's not with his father?" It was Officer Clark.

"No, his dad doesn't know where he is," confirmed Aaron.

Clark called over her shoulder to her partner, "Cancel the Amber Alert."

Gwen gaped at her. "What?"

"This is a runaway situation now," Officer Clark explained. "Amber Alerts are for abductions."

While Gwen understood the police had no choice, the cancellation of the alert was a terrible blow and she could feel herself start to fall apart again. The darkness outside didn't help, either. With a heavy heart, she started back up the stairs and toward Joshua's room.

"Gwen," Aaron started to say.

Without looking at him, she held up her hand for silence. It felt wrong to continue listening to Aaron's promises that the boys would come home safely. She stood in the center of her son's room a moment, just looking at his things. He'd recently replaced a poster of Ironman with one of Stephen Strasburg, a pitching phenomenon playing for the Washington Nationals. It told her he was growing up and shifting to real-life idols instead of pretend ones. But it saddened her that she didn't know when he'd actually made the switch.

She sat on the edge of his unmade bed and let her eyes wander over her son's treasures. After a few moments, she realized she was clutching one of the shirts he'd worn and tossed aside. Lifting the cloth to her face, she breathed in the scent of her child, her boy, her baby. Her eyes filled and her throat tightened. But she didn't allow herself the weakness of letting the tears flow. As she sniffed them back, her gaze fell upon Joshua's laptop, sitting on his desk under the window. For the first time, she realized it was on, even though the screen had gone to sleep. Had anyone checked it?

"Aaron!" she called, ignoring the fact she'd pushed him away only moments before.

Aaron came running. She could hear his feet pounding up the stairs. When he appeared in the doorway, she asked, "Did we check the computer?"

"Do you know his password?"

She thought a moment. Hell, she hadn't even known he revered a Nationals pitcher. She certainly didn't know his password. She shook her head.

"Well, let's see if we can find out something anyway. Maybe it's not locked." He sat down at the desk and woke up the monitor. He tapped away for a few minutes as Gwen looked over his shoulder. After a few moments, he was able to get to the web history.

"Look," she said, leaning over him and pointing to one entry.

"They checked both plane and train schedules for Pittsburgh. I guess that confirms what we figured out from Joshua's note. But it doesn't really tell us anything new."

"No, I guess not," she admitted. "Where would they get enough money to buy tickets?"

"Huh." Aaron's fingers danced over the keyboard. She could see he was calling up his own banking connection, so she looked away, giving him privacy. "Just as I thought," he said. "Ben used my credit card. I keep getting new ones after he figures out the numbers, but somehow, he keeps getting into the accounts."

She stared at the back of Aaron's head as she absorbed her shock at Ben's actions. "What do you do to him when he does that?"

He swiveled the chair so he could look at her. "I do what other parents do. I ground him for a week, take away whatever he bought for a while. But usually it's a book or an educational product, so I don't really have the heart to keep it from him forever. Generally, he's a good kid, and I want him to explore his world. Frankly, I admire his tenacity on the credit card thing."

"So, basically, he gets away with it in the long run," she said. It came out sounding more judgmental than she'd intended. But she was angry again that Ben had provided the means for Josh to run away. If it hadn't been for Ben, Josh would be home right now.

Aaron shrugged. "I guess he does. But it's not like he uses the cards to buy porn or bomb-making equipment."

"No, Aaron. He buys tickets so he and my

son can run away from home." She'd raised her voice, barely able to keep herself from shouting. She remembered how she'd lost complete control of herself with John and took a deep breath, trying to calm herself.

Aaron stood and faced her. "You're right," he said softly. "I can't deny it. Maybe if I'd been a better disciplinarian, none of this would have happened. I've never been good at punishing Ben. After Beth died, he was all that kept me together and I pretty much let him do whatever he wanted, gave him whatever he asked for."

That speech sapped some of her anger. "None of us really have any idea what we're doing as parents," she admitted in a much softer tone. "It's not like there's an owner's manual."

He smiled, despite their mutual worry, and Gwen could see the weariness in the fine lines around his eyes. He'd been hiding his fatigue well until now.

"I could learn a few things from the limits you set with Josh," Aaron told her.

"Ha. Everyone else who knows us tells me I'm too hard on him. You should hear my mother encouraging me to give Josh some freedom." Her eyes began to sting again.

"Look where giving him some freedom got us all."

"It must be human nature to blame ourselves even as we search for someone else to accuse."

She nodded, wiping at her eye. Aaron reached out and placed his hands gently on her shoulders. Against her better judgment, she shifted forward into his embrace. He wrapped his strong arms around her as she rested her cheek against his shoulder. She could hear his heart beating steadily. He smelled like coffee and cinnamon, though she didn't know why. When was the last time she'd eaten anything, she wondered.

As if plucking the thought right out of her head, he said, "Come down to the kitchen and eat something. Your neighbors have brought over enough food for the Chinese army."

Her neighbors? "I don't even know any of my neighbors, other than to wave hello as we rush off to work each day. And I know the kid who mows the lawn for us. Can't remember his name. Oh, and there's the girl who draws in chalk all over the sidewalks. I see her all the time in the summer. I think her name is Kate." She was babbling now but couldn't really stop herself.

She kept on trying to remember names, asking Aaron about the kids in the karate class the boys had been attending, trying to recall more of the weak personal connections she'd never had time to develop. As she rambled, he urged her down the stairs and into the kitchen. He put a plate of oatmeal cookies and a steaming cup of coffee in front of her. He remembered how she liked it and moved a pitcher of cream and the sugar bowl in her direction across the island where she sat. He made her a cheese sandwich, and she ate it without tasting anything at all.

"I need to do something," she announced, as the nonsensical flow of words wound down. "I need to be out there looking for them, even if it's just to make me feel better. I can't just sit here going slowly insane."

"Couldn't agree with you more," he said. "But there's not much to see at this time of night. The local airport and train stations have already been checked and double-checked."

She dropped her head onto her crossed arms, resting on the countertop. "Why doesn't one of them call?"

"Joshua's phone is here, for some reason. Ben's isn't anywhere around, so I think he must have it with him. But he's not answering. It goes right to voice mail, as if it's off. Or the battery is dead. He's always forgetting to charge the thing."

When Aaron's phone rang, both parents jumped. Her heart pounding with hope, Gwen watched him work the BlackBerry out of his pocket and push the talk button.

"Hello?" he said.

Gwen could hear the voice on the other end. It was deep and male. Not a child. Her shoulders slumped once more and she looked away as her vision blurred and a sob threatened.

"Gwen." Aaron said her name very softly. "They've been found."

AARON HELD THE PHONE to his ear and listened intently.

"Me and Opal are on our way to get them," Omar told him. "My friend Rudy saw them sitting in the Philadelphia train station. They missed their connection and weren't sure what to do. So they been sitting there all day, trying to figure out what to do next."

"So, they're okay?"

"Yeah. They're a little shook up. Rudy is an intimidating guy to look at. Teddy bear on the inside, though. He'll stay with them until I get there."

"He should call the police, let them take over—"

"No." There was no room for compromise in Omar's tone. "Rudy's not gonna be comfortable with that and I don't want him finding an excuse to take off."

Fear coursed through Aaron's veins again. Would Rudy the teddy bear take off with or without the kids? "Okay," he said as euphoria drained out of him.

"And I gotta tell you, it'd be better for your boys to not be mixed up with police, if they can help it."

Aaron understood Omar's reluctance.

Gwen had come to stand close to him. "Ask him if he talked to the boys."

"Did you talk to them?"

"Yeah, my buddy put 'em on speakerphone. I told 'em they both had to stay there with Rudy and they said they wouldn't be any trouble. They said they were sorry."

Aaron realized he should switch to speakerphone, too, so Gwen could hear the whole conversation. He pushed the button. "I'll come get them myself. Just tell Rudy to stay put. I'll pay him back if he needs to buy the kids some food or whatever."

"I got it covered, man. And me and Opal were already on Ninety-five North when Rudy called us," Omar added, referring to the highway that joined Baltimore to Philadelphia. "So we're gonna get there before you. I could just drive 'em home."

"Thank you, Omar, but I can't sit here and wait anymore. I'm leaving right now. Will you keep them there until we arrive?"

"Whatever you want."

He kept talking to Omar, asking for more details as he grasped Gwen's hand and led her directly to the front door and out to his car. He realized Judy and Edward had overheard the speakerphone.

"The boys are okay," Gwen called to her parents. "They're about two hours away. We're going to get them now. I'll call from the car with more details, okay?"

As Aaron slid into the driver's seat and buckled up, he saw Officer Clark and her partner sauntering to their squad car. Case closed, as far as they were concerned. Aaron wasn't sorry to see them go. They had done their best to find the boys and he was grateful for that. But the story of Gwen staying the night would surface in the legal community now that the cops knew. And it had been Omar and his connections—not the police—who had finally tracked down the boys.

"Is this really happening?" Gwen asked as he backed the car out of the driveway a little faster than he should have. "Are they really okay? Are we going to have a happy ending to this ordeal?"

Aaron slapped the car in Drive and hit the gas, leaving a little rubber on the pavement but so damn glad to be going toward his son that he didn't care. "We're going to get our kids, Gwen. The hardest part will be to keep from getting a speeding ticket on the way."

"I'll check the GPS and traffic report to make sure we don't run into delays."

Aaron grinned, feeling the smile all the way to his toes. "That's why I love you," he said. "You know exactly what I want, even before I do."

CHAPTER SIXTEEN

SHE WAS SURE HE HADN'T meant to say he loved her. Or he'd said it as a throwaway comment, like "gotta love it." He could not have actually intended to tell her he was in love with her. But just in case her assumption was not on the mark, Gwen avoided speaking to him for a long time, hoping the comment would be forgotten. She made one phone call after another, starting with Phyllis and her own parents. She asked them all to call others so everyone who had been helping could be in on the good news and stop searching.

When she finally got around to calling her ex-husband, he kept it short. Her dad had already phoned to let him know where the boys were. "Apparently your father has had a change of heart about me and doesn't want me darkening the door of the house I paid for."

Gwen smiled. "He said that?"

"Told me to go home, because you had everything under control, as usual. But I'm on my way to the train station in Phillie, of course."

"There's no point in you going there. We're already on our way. I'm taking the kids home immediately. I'm not waiting for you."

"I'll be there before you. I'm in the Porsche with the radar detector. And you drive like an old woman."

She hung up without commenting and filled Aaron in. As she talked, she realized their speed increased. Not so much to cause her to worry, but enough to tell her Aaron definitely wanted to reach their sons before Clayton.

"You don't have to worry. Ben will stay with Omar's friend. He won't go with Clay."

In the light from oncoming traffic, she could see Aaron's jaw tighten and release. "But Josh might be persuaded to go with Clayton. Not going to let that happen." He sounded determined, and Gwen took comfort in that.

"Should I call the police in Phillie? I know Omar didn't want that."

After some thought, Aaron said, "Yes. Call them. It's not an emergency, so it may take them a while to get there. We could arrive before they do, but it would be nice to know they're on the way. Things could get ugly if we all converge on the train station at the same time."

It seemed she'd been on the phone the entire day, but she made more calls. To the police, to her mother for an update, to Phyllis to make sure she knew what was happening.

"Anyone else?" she asked Aaron.

"I don't think so. And we're almost there. Another fifteen, maybe twenty minutes."

"We have to park the car somewhere."

He gave a rueful chuckle. "Sweetheart, I'm leaving the car at the curb in front of the door. If they tow it, we'll rent a car to drive home. I'm not wasting a single second looking for parking."

"Oh." To Gwen, who had always needed order and who had been married to a car fanatic, Aaron's willingness to sacrifice his car to get to the kids faster seemed downright heroic. "Thank you."

"I helped get us into this mess, so I can damned well do my best to get us out."

THEY MADE IT THROUGH streets thick with traffic, even at this late hour. At last, Aaron pulled his car to a stop in front of the gray stone pillars of the 30th Street Train Station. For no good reason that he could see, the station actually stood on Market Street. A cop appeared out of nowhere, telling him he couldn't park there and to move along. Aaron ignored him and got out of the car, making the officer shout.

Gwen got out and flashed some sort of ID. The cop looked confused, but he didn't stop her when she ran to catch up to Aaron as he strode toward the impressive entrance. The place was old and regal, one of those historic buildings from the early twentieth century. Once through the doors, the two stood in a cavernous, vaulted area filled with milling people. It all looked familiar, even though he'd never been here before. He didn't stop to ponder further. Omar had said he and the kids would meet them at the left side of the grand entrance. He was fairly certain they were in the grandest of entrances. But the left side was a distance away, and the people walking in every direction blocked his view. He grasped Gwen's hand and the pair of them started walking.

"I can hear Josh," Gwen said. She picked up her pace until she was running outright, deftly zigzagging around strangers, racing to find her son.

In another moment, Aaron could hear Josh, too. The boy was shouting, protesting. When he made his way through the last of the crowd, Aaron saw the strangest tableau of angry people—with both boys at the center of the storm.

"Don't get too close to him," Ben advised, even as he pulled on Joshua's arm, keeping him out of reach so he wouldn't be captured by Clayton Haverty.

Joshua was shouting at his father, "You're not helping. You never help! I'm not going with you. Not now. Not ever."

Clayton was using his best authoritative voice to order his son to come with him this instant or pay the consequences. When that had no effect, he said, "Your mother let you run off on your own. She's not paying enough attention to you. You need to live with me."

As Gwen approached, she saw two police officers standing more or less between the verbally combative father and son. Their hands were spread as if to keep boxers in their respective corners, and one of the cops was telling everyone to calm down.

To one side stood Omar and Opal, trying to be invisible but refusing to leave the scene after promising Aaron and Gwen they would protect the boys until they arrived. A big man with hundreds of tattoos stood by. He appeared ready to tackle Clayton if Omar gave the word.

Gwen came to an abrupt standstill taking it all in, just as Aaron had frozen in place to assess the situation. Before he could decide how best to approach the contentious gathering, Ben looked up and saw him.

"Dad!" he cried. And then he came barreling at full speed toward Aaron, crashing into him and wrapping his arms tightly around his waist. The hug didn't last long. Ben whirled around and struck a defiant pose with clenched fists and squared shoulders. "Now you're in trouble. My dad's a lawyer and he knows karate!"

"Ben," Aaron protested. And then all hell broke loose.

"MOM!" JOSH CRIED. Aaron saw him begin to run toward her, but Clayton stepped into his path. He got hold of Joshua's upper arm and refused to let go, despite the boy's struggles. "Joshua, stop it this instant. I'm not going to hurt you, I just want to talk about this."

A male officer moved in their direction, but seemed unsure what to do. Gwen didn't hesitate. She went up to Clay and Joshua. Aaron could only imagine what she would have done if the officer hadn't told her to stop. Clay didn't lose his grip on Joshua. Aaron wanted to go to them and protect both woman and child by force, but something stopped him. He somehow knew Gwen needed to work this one out on her own. When Omar shifted his weight, indicating he would try to intervene, Aaron held up his hand, asking him to wait. Instead of going to the fighting parents, he strode over to Aaron and Ben. Omar's friend had disappeared into the shifting sea of people as soon as he'd concluded the kids were with the right people.

Gwen's voice rose above the echoes reverberating under the vaulted ceiling. "Let go of my son," she demanded. If she'd turned that intensity on Aaron, he would have done what she asked immediately. Clay was not as intelligent.

"He's my son, too. For God's sake, Gwendolyn, he ran away from you. He needs to live with a parent who will look after him better. He's coming home with me."

"No!" Josh called out.

"No," Gwen said calmly, firmly. "I have custody, granted by the court of Maryland. He will be going home with me. Now, and always."

Joshua suddenly went slack, a trick he'd learned in karate class but had apparently only just recalled. When Clay looked down at the deadweight he was holding, Josh jerked his arm upward and out of his father's grasp. In another second, he was clinging to Gwen. But

Clayton wasn't willing to accept defeat. He headed straight toward Gwen and Josh.

Aaron didn't register the details of his movements, but in an instant he found himself standing between Gwen and her ex, preventing Clay from reaching them. Ben had let go of him at the exact moment necessary and Aaron shot into action so he could be in the right place at the right time. When Clay's hand lashed out, Aaron's palm was there to stop it and push it back until the two men stood nearly nose to nose.

"Break it up," the cop ordered. "You two step back away from each other."

Aaron did as he was told, but Clay had to be manhandled by the cop and physically pushed away. In another moment, Clay had shrugged his suit coat into place again.

"I wasn't going to hurt them," he insisted. "I wouldn't do that. Tell them, Gwen. I've never hurt you or Josh. I just want her to listen. To see reason. She works all the time. Our son is being raised by a babysitter."

While he ranted, the police officer spoke into the mike at his shoulder. Two more cops were already coming onto the scene.

"You, is that your kid?" one of them asked, pointing first to Aaron and then to Ben.

"Yes," Aaron said.

"Go stand over there with him and don't move."

Aaron did as he was told. Ben had moved closer and they stood watching as the police tried to sort out Joshua and his warring parents. Gwen was already showing the third officer her custody papers.

"WHAT HAPPENED WHEN your friend found the boys?" Aaron asked Omar.

"He was one big scary dude," Ben volunteered.

"You need to be quiet right now and let the adults talk," he said to his son. Ben wasn't used to being told what to do. For that matter, Aaron wasn't used to giving orders. To his surprise, Ben obeyed.

"He told them he was there to keep them safe until their parents showed up. They pretty much just sat on that bench over there until I got here. Ben recognized me."

"He came over to the house when you were upset by what happened with that other client," Ben said.

"Quiet," Aaron said, but he never once took his protective arm from around Ben's shoulders. He needed to feel his son beside him.

"I told both boys they weren't going with anyone until you got here," Omar told Aaron.

"But then that one shows up first." He pointed to Clay. "I didn't expect the short one to go off on his father the way he did. He's been yelling like that since the man showed up. Keeps telling him he needs to go talk to his mother, and from the sound of it, he meant his grandmother, not your girlfriend."

"Gwen is your girlfriend?" Ben asked.

Aaron squeezed his son's shoulder a bit to remind him he was not supposed to be talking. "You performed a miracle by finding them. I owe you."

"No, man. My friends found 'em. I just got 'em looking out for the kids. It's what we do, me and my home boys."

"I'm not ever going to forget how effective your connections can be, Omar," Aaron said. "I may have you work some investigations for me."

Omar grinned and walked away. As he did, Aaron flashed back to Nepher's crime, the horrible photos of a dead child. He couldn't imagine going back to the same job now. As much good as he'd proudly done for people like Omar, he didn't think he'd ever be able to put his heart into the job again. There would always be a doubt lurking in his mind—could this client be another Nepher?

Aaron turned his attention to the wrangling

going on among the other adults. The cop tried to keep the conversation orderly. Gwen was clinging to Josh with one arm and waving her custody documents. At last one of them read what was on those sheets. He conferred with another of the officers.

The third officer said, "We should call social services and let them sort out what should happen with the kid."

"But she has custody papers. We should let her take her son home."

"And she's with the Maryland State Attorney's office. I'm not messing with that. My shift is almost over anyway."

The officers barred Clayton's way while Gwen collected Joshua's things and headed out of the train station with Aaron and Ben. From behind them, they heard Clay shouting that he would see them in court. "I promise you," he called after them, "this isn't over. The judge will give me custody when he finds out you lost your own child!"

Somehow, they found the strength to keep walking away without saying anything. Before another half hour passed, Aaron and Gwen were climbing into his car with their sons. By some miracle, the vehicle had not been towed away, although there was a ticket on the windshield that would undoubtedly cost him. But it was worth it. He had the boys back and that's all that mattered. After he started the car, he adjusted his rearview mirror so he could see the tops of their heads. He wanted to keep an eye on them as he drove home.

Gwen turned to the kids. "If you ever pull a stunt like this again, there will be consequences. That goes for both of you."

Aaron didn't say a word. She sounded so formidable, he didn't dare. And he welcomed the help. Ben needed limitations before he got into trouble he couldn't be rescued from.

"But, Mom," Josh began, as if he would attempt to defend his behavior.

Gwen raised her voice a notch. "I will not stand for any 'buts,' Joshua. What you did was ridiculously dangerous. I don't even want to think about how dangerous. You could have been—" Her voice broke, and Aaron could tell she was succumbing at last to the terrible emotions of the day.

"You could have been kidnapped," he said, speaking for her while she tried to collect herself. "You could have been killed. We might have looked for you for months and years and never been able to find you." He kept his voice calm and steady, trying to impress upon the boys the perilous nature of what they'd done, but hoping not to give them nightmares for the rest of their lives.

"What *were* you thinking?" Gwen asked even as she let herself cry.

"I wanted to get Grandma Char to talk sense into Dad," Josh said. "Dad's her son and she's bossy and tough. We figured she could make him see that he can't take me off to New York when I want to stay where I am. I wanted to…"

"He wanted to protect you," Ben said to Gwen. "Josh knew his dad was giving you trouble. We wanted to make that stop."

Aaron could tell the boys' words were making Gwen cry harder, though she did her best to be quiet about it. Her tears broke his heart.

"Why would you think running away was the answer?" Aaron asked.

"We didn't run away," Joshua said. "Didn't you see my note? I put it in the middle of the fridge. I told you where we were going."

Gwen sniffed. "Gramma Char is in Italy, Josh. That's why she's not answering her phone."

"She'll be back tomorrow. We were planning to be at her house when she got home."

Aaron had to admire the kids for figuring out so much on their own. They'd planned and executed the whole scheme. "Why didn't you just wait and call her on the phone?"

"Because she won't talk about anything important on the phone. She doesn't like phones. That's why she doesn't have a cell phone. She wouldn't have taken me seriously unless I went to explain things face-to-face."

Aaron sighed. From a ten-year-old's perspective, the kids had good reasons for their actions. "Ben, why didn't you keep your cell phone on? At least I would have been able to call and you could have called me. I could have found out you were safe."

"We didn't want it on at first because we figured you'd come after us and ruin our plan. Then I found out the battery was dead. I was planning to call you when we got to Joshua's grandma's house. But then we missed the train and had to wait until morning for the next one."

"I need to get you one of those solar chargers," he said, more to himself than to his son.

"Cool!" Josh and Ben said together.

"Back to the point." Gwen sounded more annoyed than tearful now, to Aaron's relief. "While you may believe you did all this for me, to protect me—and I'm grateful for your concern—it was still a foolish and dangerous plan to travel by yourselves to Pittsburgh, of all places. You need to learn to talk to us as your parents before you go off on adventures of any kind. That's what we're here for, to help you figure out what's okay and what's not. So, you are both grounded. And those video games you love so much. Forget about it. You'll spend some time reflecting on how much you frightened everyone and how much trouble you could have gotten into. You must have overachievers for guardian angels."

"We were doing okay until we missed the second train," Josh insisted. "We were just going to take turns sleeping while the other one watched out for trouble, but then that scary dude Rudy showed up and started telling us not to move until our parents got there."

"He was crazy big and mean-looking," Ben agreed.

"It could have been so much worse," Gwen whispered. "What if that big, mean guy hadn't been a friend of a friend? What if he'd abducted you?"

"We would have done our karate on him?" Ben said it like a question, telling Aaron that his son didn't believe he was skilled enough to have the slightest effect on someone like Rudy.

"There are a lot of good people in the world. Rudy is one of the good guys. But there are some bad people, too." Aaron thought of Nepher and shuddered, realizing that his own son could have met a fate similar to Annie's.

"I guess we shouldn't have gone off on our own," Josh admitted.

"At least not until we're bigger," Ben said.

"Can we get some food?" Josh asked.

"Yeah, we haven't eaten for days."

Aaron reached out his hand and found Gwen's. "They may be grounded for the rest of their lives, but we still have to feed them."

"I suppose you're right," she said as she once again withdrew her hand from his. "I think there was a sign for fast food at the next exit."

It took them an hour to go through the drive-through and return to the highway, the car now filled with the sounds of munching and slurping. Things finally got quiet and Aaron was left with his thoughts.

Glancing over at Gwen, he saw her eyes shining. She was still awake.

"Can't sleep?" he asked.

"I thought I should stay awake to keep you company so *you* wouldn't fall asleep, but I'm not doing a very good job of that."

"I'm just happy to have you and the boys together with me."

"Thank you for this," she said. "For driving,

for setting things in motion to find them, for standing up to Clayton, for being so support-ive."

Guilt made him quiet. He'd been responsible for all this. And yet, as he drove, he began to realize how tired he was of feeling guilty. He'd have to work on letting that go. Even his confusion over his continued feelings for Beth needed to be dealt with. It was time to get on with his life. Beth would want that. Wouldn't she?

His thoughts ran back to what needed to happen next. Foremost in his mind was pro-tecting Josh and Gwen. "I'm worried about how angry Clay is," he said to her. "I know you don't want complications right now, but I think he needs some time to cool down and no opportunities to do anything rash. I'd feel better if you and Josh would stay at my house for the night."

"My mom and dad are at my house. We'll be okay there."

"If Clay shows up at your door, do you really think your father is up to that kind of confrontation?"

After a moment, she said, "No."

"So maybe they should go to a hotel, just for tonight, while tempers cool. And if you're not at your own house, I think Clay will be more likely to get a grip on himself."

"Yes, that makes sense."

"Then you'll stay the night with us?"

"Do you have a guest room Josh and I can share?"

"Of course," he said, trying not to sound surprised or disappointed. "I want you to be safe, that's all."

"Okay. Just for tonight."

CHAPTER SEVENTEEN

ONCE AT AARON'S HOME, the three males united in persuading Gwen to let Josh spend the night in Ben's room. She didn't like the idea of them staying together again after the trouble they'd gotten into, but there was only one bed in the guest room and Josh was getting too big to share with his mom. The only other option would have been to sleep with Aaron again and *that* was out of the question. Aaron didn't even suggest it, so he must have agreed with Gwen. She ignored the twinge of disappointment this gave her.

"I swear, if you don't both stay in this room all night long, quietly and innocently sleeping, there will be hell to pay. Do I make myself clear?"

Both boys stared at her with big eyes and nodded their understanding. Marginally satisfied, she left them there to whisper together until sleep overtook them. Because they'd slept in the car on the way back from Philadelphia, she knew it might be a while before they drifted off. As long as they were quiet and stayed where they belonged, she would let them be.

Aaron stood by her as she watched the two boys from the doorway a moment longer.

"I wish I had your knack for being firm and caring at the same time," he said. "I've never been good at finding that middle place. Phyllis says I'm raising Ben with no healthy boundaries."

"Well, Josh would say I'm way too strict, hemming him in so he has no freedom. Maybe that's why he ran away so easily. His first real break from the many rules that control his life."

As they stood side by side, Aaron slipped his arm across the back of her shoulders companionably. "Going to Joshua's grandmother was Ben's idea."

Giving in to her need for comfort, she leaned her head against his shoulder and tried to absorb some of his calm strength. "But I could tell from how they told the story that Ben was having second thoughts until Josh latched onto the idea with such gusto. It took both of them to get into so much trouble."

"Maybe that's why kids need two parents," he said wistfully.

Gwen drew away from him. It wasn't a good

idea to be overly cozy with Aaron. Whenever she got too close to him, she seemed to find herself hungering for more. She was in enough trouble already with her boss. And she was certain Clayton would do everything in his power to win custody. "Except when one parent is J. Clayton Haverty."

"Clay just wants what's best for Josh," he said. When Gwen shot him a glare, he added, "You're doing a great job, but Clayton can only see what you let him see or what he discovers on his own. In court, he's going to look like a concerned father—which he is."

She didn't respond to that, so he went back to his original point. "It just seems like it would be easier if you had help. I know I'd prefer not to go it alone raising Ben."

"You have Phyllis."

"Not the same as a wife," he said.

Gwen realized he'd turned to face her and was studying her with an odd expression. She took a tiny step back to counteract the magnetic draw. It would be so easy to move into his arms, to kiss him, to love him. But the consequences were too great. She took another small step away. "I should try to sleep."

"Yes, that's a good idea," he agreed, but simply stood there as if he hoped she'd change her mind.

"Is it okay if I use the bathroom first?" she asked, pointing lamely to the door just past him on the right.

"It's all yours. I have my own attached to my bedroom."

She remembered that now. She'd been in that bathroom. She'd made love to him in that bedroom. Spent the night. Shared nightmares with him and learned some new things about herself while in his embrace. She wished…

"No," she whispered to herself as she forced herself past him and into the bathroom. When she emerged shortly after, he was gone. The boys had fallen asleep already, or at least they were silent and unmoving when she checked on them one last time. She went to the guest room. Phyllis had turned down the bedcovers for her, and put a glass of ice, a can of Diet Coke, and some cheese and crackers covered in plastic wrap on the nightstand. How thoughtful.

What would become of Phyllis when Aaron married again, Gwen wondered as she sat on the edge of the bed and nibbled on the snack. But none of this was her business. And anyway, families were configured in all sorts of unusual ways nowadays. Phyllis could easily remain part of the family even when a new wife came along. Assuming she was secure enough to accept the mother of Aaron's first wife. Were there many women who would be willing? Gwen knew she would welcome Phyllis into her life with open arms.

Doesn't matter, she told herself. None of her business. She needed to stick to solving her own problems. And maybe Aaron had no intention of ever marrying again anyway. With a sigh, Gwen took a sip of the water that had accumulated at the bottom of the glass of ice. Exhaustion finally took care of her wayward thoughts about Aaron, and she was asleep almost before she laid her head upon the pillow.

AFTER A SLEEPLESS NIGHT, Aaron rose early. Even so, he had only twenty minutes of peace with his coffee at the kitchen counter before he heard the boys pounding down the staircase. They slid on the tile floor as they rounded the corner, then became abruptly still when they saw him.

"Hey, we're still here," Ben quipped.

Aaron knew he should say something about his son's inappropriate levity. Gwen would know exactly what to say, he was sure. "Not a joking matter, Benjamin."

Ben shrugged and went to the refrigerator. "Why are you up so early?"

"Maybe it has something to do with all the crazy stuff going on around here," he said.

Josh spoke hesitantly. "It's Saturday. Will Mom and I be going home today?"

"That's up to your mom. I'm sure she'll tell you as soon as she decides."

Josh gave one of those preteen shrugs, too. "She never tells me anything." He moved to Ben's side to inspect the breakfast cereal options.

"I'll try to work on that," Gwen said from the threshold. "You're old enough now. I should include you more in planning that involves you."

"I didn't hear you come downstairs. Did the boys wake you?" Aaron asked.

"No. I got a phone call." She was clearly gauging what to say in front of the boys. "A social worker from Child Protective Services needs to interview me and Josh at home today."

"Dad didn't waste any time, did he," Josh observed. He sounded far older than his years. "This is why I wanted Grandma Char to talk some sense in to him. She's the only one who can."

"I don't understand why you think Grandma would help," Gwen said. "She's far more likely to want your dad to have full custody. She and I never got along very well."

Josh shook his head as he poured some milk into his breakfast bowl. "That's because you're too much alike. But when you and dad were divorcing, she told me that if anyone asks me, I should say I want to live with you. She said she doesn't like you much, but you're a better parent than her son."

Gwen stared at Josh. "She said that?"

"More than once."

Aaron looked from mother to son. "So Charlotte might be helpful in your custody hearing?"

"It would be impossible for her to side with me against Clay."

"We may need to do whatever it takes to make sure Josh stays with you," he said gently.

Gwen turned to him, her expression cold and hard. "You have no part in the fight, Aaron."

Her words chilled Aaron to the bone. She looked over at the boys. They sat side by side at the table, spoons raised halfway to their mouths. "Dad's just trying to help," Ben whispered, wide-eyed.

Gwen offered Ben a smile. "I know he is. But Melody and I will do what we need to do to make sure we win our case. Having too many lawyers involved can complicate things."

Aaron thought that sounded like a reasonable explanation for the boys. But he understood the subtext clearly enough. Gwen wanted him out of her life. That hurt. Yet he knew her decision was about protecting her son. He couldn't blame her. He'd do the same if roles were reversed. Still, he wished they could find another answer to the problem.

"Finish your breakfast, Josh. We have to get home in time to wash up and meet this social worker, Mrs. Proux."

"What kind of stuff is she gonna ask?"

"She'll want to know why you ran away," Gwen said.

When it appeared to Aaron that she wasn't going to elaborate, he decided to speak up. "Mrs. Proux is going to be investigating whether your mom is taking good care of you. She's going to question why you would end up running away if everything is okay at home."

"I didn't run away," Josh insisted. "We left a note. We had a plan."

"And it wasn't because of Gwen," Ben added.

"Yeah, my dad strikes again," Josh grumbled.

Gwen moved quickly to stand in front of

her son. "No, Joshua. *You* struck again. If you were worried about your father, you should have talked to me. Taking off on your own for Pittsburgh was the worst judgment I've ever seen you display in a long line of bad judgment."

Aaron could see she was trembling with rage. And her reaction was so out of character and beyond what the situation called for, he knew he had to do something. "Stop," he said softly, even as she opened her mouth to say more. "This isn't helping."

"But—" she began, but Aaron slashed his hand through the air.

"Let's discuss this in the study and let the kids finish eating in peace," he suggested. Before she could disagree, he grasped her hand and led her away. He was glad she didn't resist.

Once in the den with her, he closed the door.

"You have no right to interfere between me and my son," she sputtered.

"Maybe not, but you're in my house and I'm not going to let you take out your own frustration on that boy. He's ten years old and he's not supposed to have good judgment yet. You know that. Blaming him for being a kid isn't going to help the situation."

She stepped back from him as if he'd

slapped her. Then she shook her head. "You're right. Josh isn't to blame. I am. I'm a terrible mother."

Aaron's heart went out to her. He understood how easy it was to feel like a complete failure as a parent. "You're not," he said. "You're a wonderful mother who understands limits and boundaries and discipline better than I ever will. I should take lessons from you."

As he spoke, he slowly drew her into the circle of his arms. She let him enfold her and even rested her head against his shoulder. "But you've been under so much stress. I just don't want you to say things to Josh that I know you don't really mean."

"I'm so angry with him right now. Because of that stupid stunt, I could lose him," she said. "Clay will make the most of this in court. He could win. He'll bring up everything I've ever done wrong as a parent, including letting Josh run away. He'll say I poisoned Josh against him and that's why it's not his fault that Josh took off. The truth is, I could have done a better job to help Josh see his father's reasonable side." Her voice broke.

"It'll be okay, Gwen. Melody won't let him win." He just wished he could be as certain of that as he sounded.

"But this social worker is coming and God

only knows what Josh will say to her and how the situation will be twisted—and the house is a mess."

Aaron laughed. "I'm pretty sure the house being a mess is the least of your troubles, my love. Just do your best with her. And trust Josh to be honest and sensible. He's your son as much as Clayton's. He'll say the right things."

"Sometimes I mix him up with Clay and I lash out at him, even when I don't have a good reason to. He'll say something just so or his facial expression will be exactly like his father's and I'll forget that I'm talking to Josh and not Clay. That's when I say things to him I don't really mean. I'm just so angry all the time. Then Josh does something that reminds me of his father, and…" She paused to sniff back more tears. "That's why I'm a terrible mother."

He held her tight. "I think you're a mother doing her best under extraordinarily difficult circumstances. I want you to know I'll always be here if you need help or just a shoulder to cry on."

She laughed a little at that and swiped her hand over the wet spot she'd created on his shirt. "I think I need more help than even you can give me, Aaron. Thank you. Thank you for everything you've done and keep trying to do."

She pulled away and he let her go reluctantly.

She walked toward the door and paused there, staring down at the floor. "I realize now that I need to talk to a professional therapist about my anger, about my former marriage, about raising Josh. I can't go on with this monster inside me, hoping it won't jump out and hurt my son. The timing is terrible. Clay will use it against me if he can. But I can't control these rages, so I need to do something about them. Maybe you could send me the name of that psychiatrist you mentioned. The one who knows about post-traumatic stress disorder in domestic situations. I mean, I don't have anything that bad going on, but clearly I could use some coaching on how to control my anger and cope with Josh."

"I'll send you her name right away. You'll like her. She'll help you."

At a knock, Gwen opened the door and found Phyllis on the other side.

"Your phone was ringing and ringing. I thought it might be important and it was sitting out on the table." Phyllis handed the Black-Berry to Gwen.

"Thank you." Gwen took the phone and examined the display.

"The boys have both eaten breakfast," Phyllis said. "Josh is ready when you are. He told me he didn't want to cause you any more trouble, so he's sitting on the porch step waiting for you."

Gwen's expression softened. "Okay," she said. "I'll be right there."

Phyllis left them alone, but Gwen kept the door open. She turned to him with sad eyes. "That was Melody calling me. She finally gave up and sent a text. Apparently Clayton persuaded a judge to hold an emergency custody hearing a week from Monday. So the social worker's visit is only the beginning."

"A week isn't much time to prepare," he said.

"We were mostly ready for court before, but now we have to figure out a strategy to deal with the accusations he'll make related to the kids taking off for Pittsburgh."

"I'll help any way I can," he said.

She shook her head. "I can't accept, Aaron. We can't be together at all. It's bad enough everyone knows I spent the night here. You know how Clay will make it look in court. And, honestly, I'm surprised I haven't been fired already."

"I'll quit my job," he offered. "I don't think I can go back to doing the same work anyway."

"No!" she said. "You're too good at what you do. And even if you quit, we still wouldn't work. Too many differences between us, too many complications, particularly my obvious need for psychotherapy."

"I understand," he said.

"You do?" She sounded almost sorry to hear him give up so easily.

Gwen couldn't appreciate what he'd meant by the comment. He understood she needed to focus on her custody battle, but he wasn't giving up on them. If she thought that, then she completely underestimated his determination. Still, he had to let her go for the time being. Just as he had to let go of Beth.

"You need to stay focused on the custody case."

"Okay," she said. "Well, goodbye. And thank you for everything."

Aaron watched her leave the room. He heard her open the front door. Slowly, Aaron made his way to a vantage point in the hallway so he could capture his last glimpse of her.

"Ready to go?" she said to Josh as she stepped onto the porch.

The ten-year-old stood and faced her. "I'll

fix things with the social worker, Mom," Josh promised her.

She rushed forward and hugged him. Joshua's arms circled his mother's waist. "None of this is your fault, Josh. I didn't mean what I said before. Just tell Mrs. Proux the truth and we'll be fine. Just be yourself."

"It'll be okay, Mom," he said.

And Aaron was going to do everything in his power to make sure it really would be.

CHAPTER EIGHTEEN

IF GWEN THOUGHT THE DAY spent with Mrs. Proux had been an ordeal, the day she spent with Melody practicing testimony for court a few days later was absolute torture. Melody pretended to be Clay's attorney and hammered her with accusations while twisting every word she uttered to support the assertion that she was an unfit mother.

"Stop it!" Gwen shouted, having endured the pummeling for as long as she could.

Melody relaxed her expression, turning back into the woman Gwen knew instead of the demon she pretended to be. "I'm getting you ready for what you'll face in court, Gwen. You know it'll be bad. And you need to be prepared. The only way to do that is to practice."

"I know," she admitted. "It's just—"

"Cowboy up, Gwen. You're not going to be able to cry 'stop it!' in the middle of questioning."

She was right, of course. But Gwen had managed to fit in only a few sessions with her psychiatrist, and although the treatments were helping, she sometimes still felt overwhelmed. "I'll be stronger when the meanness is coming from Clay or his lawyer. Coming from you just feels wrong."

Melody nodded. "We've been at this for a long time. Let's review the rest of it without the role-playing."

"We should do whatever you think will get us where we need to be for court," Gwen insisted.

"We're as ready as we can be. And I have a few things brewing that might turn the situation in our favor."

Gwen looked at her attorney. "What things?"

"I can't say yet. I don't know if any of them will come through for us. So best not to count on them."

Gwen nodded. She'd put her trust in this woman and wouldn't question her now. Melody knew Joshua's future was at stake. "Let's get this done. I need to go home to spend some time with my son."

AARON ENDURED THE GOODBYES to the wonderful people he'd worked with at Release Initiative. He suffered through the party they threw for him and then waded through the years of stuff he'd collected in his tiny office—deciding what to box up for home and what to throw away. As he progressed through these rites of passage from one part of his life to another, he worried about how long his savings would last and whether he'd have to dip into his retirement account so he and his family could remain in the new house they'd moved into only months before. He told himself he'd find another position soon and that everything would work out. He could even open his own law practice, if necessary, although he didn't much like the idea of billable hours and grubbing for clients.

He had his résumé in with several nonprofits, and while the pay wouldn't be quite what he'd been making at his old job, he knew he'd enjoy the work. For now, though, he had a lot of time on his hands. He decided to throw his services at Melody Michaels and she immediately put him to work on Gwen's case. She agreed that Gwen didn't need to know about this arrangement. It would only upset and annoy her. But Melody needed the help if she was going to get all her plans in place by the court date.

"I think I might have found some stuff about Clayton on the internet," he told Melody the day before the hearing.

"What kind of stuff?"

"I'm still scouring through all the photos and links. His girlfriend is a party animal and doesn't seem to care about her Facebook privacy settings, but Clay has been more careful. I have to keep digging."

"Can you do that while you're traveling?" Melody asked.

Aaron smiled as he noted the scheming glint in Melody's eye. "When and for how long? And where? Oh, and why?"

Melody grinned back and told him the details of what she hoped he could accomplish.

Aaron was more than game to try.

FOR THE FIRST TIME IN her life, Gwen was nervous as she took her place in the courtroom. Though she wanted to put her trust in the justice system, as she had throughout her career, this time was different. Her son's future was at stake. As she sat beside Melody at the respondent's table, she tapped a pen against her leg in a frantic staccato.

"Give me the pen, please," Melody said calmly. "I'll give it back once things get started. But right now, you're driving me crazy. Take some deep breaths or something."

Gwen tried to stay still. Occasionally, she'd glance at the petitioner's table where Clayton sat with his attorney. Her ex appeared calm, collected, confident. Gwen wanted to strangle him. Her fingers actually tingled with the desire.

Supporters sat in the audience section behind her, which brought her both comfort and added tension. Her parents were directly behind her, ready to testify to her excellent mothering. Logan had come, bearing best wishes from John Fry, who had very kindly allowed her to keep her job, despite her insanity the day the kids had gone missing. He hadn't been happy about all the time she'd taken off from work to prepare for this hearing, but he'd accepted it. Even Phyllis sat nearby, though there was no sign of Aaron. She hadn't wanted him here. She knew Clay would embarrass them both by publicizing that they'd spent the night together, and yet she was disappointed Aaron hadn't come anyway.

"All rise," intoned the bailiff.

She tensed. At last the hearing was beginning. Gwen stood along with everyone else. She'd done this a thousand times before, but today was the first as a client instead of the attorney. As Judge Landau swept in and claimed his place, she took heart that she'd never pissed off this particular judge. And she had no reason to believe he was friendly with

Clayton or his attorney. The man would be neutral, at least.

He smacked his gavel onto its pedestal and looked at the two tables before him. "Are we ready, counselors?"

"Yes, Your Honor," intoned both Melody and the lawyer Clay had hired to represent him—somebody named Parker Fentice.

"I've read your opening statements already, so we'll just get on with witnesses. Petitioner?" This was a hearing before a single judge and he didn't have to let the parties blather on with opening statements. There was no jury to impress and while the audience might be wowed, the spectators had no say in the outcome. Judge Landau clearly wanted to move things along as quickly as possible.

"Your Honor, petitioner calls our first witness, Howard County Police Officer Christina Clark," said Mr. Fentice.

Gwen didn't think the police officer looked very happy to be approaching the witness stand, though she must have done it many times for other cases. As she responded to the preliminary questions to establish her credentials, she didn't sound very happy, either. Gwen appreciated her reluctance and dreaded her testimony. Clay and his attorney were coming out of the starting gate with guns blazing. Gwen knew Officer Clark's information would be damning.

Mr. Fentice brought his witness all the way through the dispatch communication that sent the officers to Gwen's house. Through her, he established that Joshua had gone missing, but failed to bring up the early suspicion that Clayton had kidnapped him. Gwen knew Melody would take care of that on cross-examination.

At last, Fentice got to the questions Gwen dreaded most. "Officer Clark, did you interview the custodial parents of the missing children?"

"Yes, of course," Clark said, glancing toward Gwen with an apology in her eyes.

"Did you ask the mother of Joshua Haverty where she was when her child went missing?"

"Yes." At least Clark was making Fentice work for every scrap of data he got out of her.

"Please tell us—and include any details— exactly what the answers were to this line of questioning."

"Ms. Haverty was with a friend overnight. The boys were with her parents and she would have every reason to assume they were safe and—"

He cut her off. "For what reason did she spend the night with this friend?"

"She said the friend had a difficult experience and she was attempting to be supportive. The friend corroborated this. And everything lined up with what we were told by other family members."

"And who was this friend with whom she spent the night?"

Melody got to her feet. "Objection. Irrelevant."

Judge Landau looked at Melody coolly. "This is a hearing, not a trial. Let's just get all the information out on the table, and quickly. Mr. Fentice, you had best be presenting relevant information only. Answer the question, Officer Clark."

"A fellow attorney," she hedged.

Fentice squinted at Clark, clearly irritated. "But who? What was the name of the fellow attorney?"

"Aaron Zimmerman," she said at last.

The spectators murmured. There were members of the legal community here who might not have heard this new and titillating information. Others may have heard rumors, and now they were confirmed. Only a few had known she'd been with Aaron. Gwen felt her cheeks heat as a blush crept over her face. While she wanted to be defiant about her relationship with Aaron, she knew she'd be judged for sleeping with the enemy. That was the last thing she needed during this hearing.

"Aaron Zimmerman," repeated Fentice. "He's that infamous attorney for Release Initiative, correct? The one Ms. Haverty opposes so frequently in court as part of her duties with the State Attorney's Office?"

To her credit, Officer Clark didn't bother to respond. Fentice wasn't really asking her a question, just making sure he got the most out of the situation. He moved on to questions pertaining to Gwen's outburst with John Fry, forcing the officer to provide details about the meltdown and also about Aaron easing her away and up to a bedroom. The whole thing felt like being pummeled with a baseball bat, yet this was only the first witness.

"Nothing further," Fentice finally told Officer Clark.

"Cross?" asked the judge.

"Yes, Your Honor," said Melody. "Officer Clark, what were your impressions of Ms. Haverty as a mother during the period her son was missing?"

"She was terrified, stressed. But she also worked very hard to find her son, calling everyone she could think of and cooperating with the authorities to the fullest."

Gwen was relieved Clark could be objective

in court, no matter what she thought about Gwen staying with Aaron the night the boys had gone missing.

Melody nodded. "And can you explain to the judge what the police believed had happened to Joshua?"

"We were fairly sure Mr. Haverty had taken him without permission of the custodial parent."

"So you thought he'd been kidnapped by his father?"

"Yes. At first."

"Why were you so certain Mr. Haverty was the one who'd kidnapped Joshua from the home?"

"Because we had several credible witnesses inform us that he'd threatened to do so on previous occasions, including the week prior to the incident. Ms. Haverty had court-ordered full custody of the child, so we put out an Amber Alert for Joshua and Mr. Haverty."

Melody paused, letting that sink in. "Thank you, Officer Clark. Nothing further."

Though Gwen's tension remained high, she smiled a little on the inside. Melody always knew how to make her feel better. She'd established Clayton as the overbearing jerk he was.

Of course, Fentice wasn't done. Not by a

long shot. He called Mrs. Proux, whose testimony was a longer version of "Child Protective Services has concerns about the safety of Joshua Haverty, given his recent success running away from home. We are monitoring the situation closely."

Then he called Misha, Joshua's babysitter, now back from her trip.

"What are your usual hours working for Ms. Haverty?"

"Like, it varies a lot," Misha said. "But she pays me well, so no worries."

"Can you give us an estimate of your usual hours taking care of Joshua?"

"Well, in the summer I'm like there all the time, which is great because I'm putting myself through community college. But when there's school, I show up for when Josh gets off the bus and stay until Gwen gets home, you know?"

"What do you mean when you say you're there all the time? Do you sleep there?"

"Of course not. I go over around seven in the morning."

"And what time do you usually leave?"

"Like, whenever. It varies."

People in the audience understood just how frustrating Misha's answers were becoming for Fentice and soft chuckles could be heard from the back of the room. Even Gwen found it amusing that Misha so innocently refused to give Fentice what he was after.

Fentice moved closer to the witness stand as if he would try to wring the right answers out of the young woman. "Do you sometimes stay at the house through dinner?"

"Sure. But she pays me."

"Do you sometimes have to get Josh into bed?"

"Sometimes. She has that crazy job serving the State. They make her stay. But she always calls and lets me know. And Josh is a good kid. Gwen has done a good job raising him. He's pretty polite with me, kind of a nerd with his video games. He worries about his dad a lot, though and—"

"That's enough. Thank you. No more questions." Fentice said it in a tone that indicated Misha had gotten the better of him and he didn't dare ask her anything else.

But Fentice swung back toward Misha at the last minute. "Oh, wait. I do have one more question. Do you know whether Ms. Haverty is under psychiatric care?"

"What?"

"Does she see a psychiatrist?"

"Objection!" called Melody. But she was too late. Because at the exact same moment,

Misha said, "A shrink? So what? Doesn't everyone talk to one these days? Maybe you should try it. You have some serious control issues."

"That will be all," said Fentice.

Melody moved toward the witness stand for cross-examination without having to be asked. Misha hadn't seemed like a favorable witness during preparations, but she was doing great on the stand. She couldn't be blamed for answering honestly about the psychiatrist.

"You've been with Gwen and Joshua for how long?"

"Since Joshua was in kindergarten. Four years."

"So you were with the Haverty family before the divorce?"

"Yes. And let me tell you, I was glad when she got rid of her husband."

"Why do you say that? Was he violent?"

"Not with his hands. But, man, he could be mean."

Fentice shot to his feet. "Objection!"

Judge Landau's gaze shifted to the petitioner's table. "Uh, this is your witness. You can't really object to what she has to say when you're the one who called her. And you have no grounds."

"She turned hostile."

"I'm not hostile!" Misha said. "I've never had a hostile day in my life! Who are you calling hostile!"

People were laughing out loud now, not even trying to hide their amusement. The judge banged his gavel until everyone settled down.

Misha looked at the judge with big eyes and waited for him to give further instructions.

"Counselor, continue your cross-examination," Landau said to Melody. To Misha he said, "You can answer the questions in your own way."

Gwen thought she detected a glint of amusement in his eyes when he looked at her babysitter, who deserved a raise in her hourly pay after this performance. Her heart filled with appreciation for Misha as Melody walked her through details of Clayton's manipulations of her. The attorney even got Misha to testify that Gwen was a good mother and a caring parent, despite the long work hours. Gwen wanted to hug her babysitter.

"Redirect?" asked the judge, and something in his voice seemed to add, "if you dare."

But Fentice dared. "How was Clayton as a parent?"

"What? Seriously? I just told you how he manipulated his wife."

"But how was he with his son?"

Misha shrugged, glanced at Gwen, then said, "He was okay, I guess." Misha shifted in her chair and appeared unsure of herself for the first time.

"Did they do things together that you saw?"

"Yes. Sometimes he wanted to do things outside with Josh. He'd try taking him out to play catch even. But Josh isn't a sports kind of kid."

"Nothing further," said Fentice smugly. He turned back to his table.

But Misha wasn't done tormenting Fentice. "You know, it's one thing to want to play games with your kid and another thing to do homework with him or make sure he brushes his teeth. Gwen and I do those things with Josh. Who would do them if Josh left us?"

Fentice's shoulders slumped. He didn't even attempt to redeem the situation. Looking at the judge stoically, he said, "May I call my next witness?"

"Sure," Landau said. He told Misha she could go and she resumed her place in the audience, though Gwen hoped she remembered she had to be at the house by the time Joshua got out of school.

Fentice was only just starting to lay the groundwork in his effort to prove she wasn't home much and that Joshua was being raised by the nanny. He called more witnesses who testified well for him, weaving a tapestry that implied Gwen was far more interested in her career than her child. With every witness, he managed to conclude with the implication that her lack of attention to Joshua was the reason he wanted to run away from home. Melody did a good job of mitigating these impressions, but she couldn't thwart them completely.

TRUTH WAS, GWEN HADN'T been spending enough time with Josh and she knew it. She found herself trying to make deals with fate along the lines of, *If I can just get custody, I swear I'll spend more time at home.* But those promises to fate did nothing to change the impressions Fentice built. Especially when he started in on how wonderful J. Clayton Haverty was and what a good father he'd been and how much better and more attentive he'd be if he had custody.

Fentice began to work his way through several witnesses—colleagues, clients, companions of Clay's. But then the hearing broke for a late lunch. Gwen went to a nearby diner with her parents while Melody left to make some phone calls. It was a somber meal during which her parents said very little. They continued to feel responsible for giving Clayton the ammunition he needed to rush the custody hearing. They worried he would win. Gwen couldn't help sharing their fears. Gone were the days when mothers were favored for custody of their children. It was all about the best interest of the child in Maryland. And Clayton, through his attorney, had pointed out Joshua's mediocre grades in school, followed by promises to put him into the best New York City private school available.

When the hearing resumed, Fentice called a psychiatrist Gwen didn't know. This doctor testified about post-traumatic stress disorder and the violent behavior that could result from it. He'd heard about Gwen's attack on John Fry at her home the day the kids were missing, and offered a medical opinion. Gwen didn't know how Clay or Fentice had found out about her therapy sessions, but somehow they knew. And they weren't afraid to use the information. This put Melody in a bind. She hadn't planned on calling Gwen's therapist, but she had to counter the picture Fentice painted about Gwen's mental state. They still had some time to decide what would be best. Fentice wasn't finished with his own witnesses yet.

He called a woman Gwen had seen on the witness list but someone she'd never met—Brenda Voight. Melody had handled the investigation of this witness alone, so Gwen didn't really know anything about her. As a pretty blonde woman in her twenties made her way to the witness stand, Gwen noticed Melody repeatedly glancing toward the doorway in the back of the room as if she anxiously awaited someone's arrival. But then the questioning began and Gwen's attention turned to the witness stand once more.

"Ms. Voight, how do you know Mr. Clayton Haverty?"

"I'm his fiancée," she said.

Gwen tried hard not to let her mouth fall open. Clay had never mentioned a fiancée. Gwen had assumed she was another colleague or perhaps even the elusive girlfriend Josh had once mentioned. But fiancée? That was a surprise.

Parker Fentice led Brenda through a description of her idyllic relationship with Clayton and how much he wanted to raise Joshua and how happy she would be to assist him with Joshua once they'd married. As a website developer, she worked from home and would be able to spend time with a stepson. And she had lots of experience with children because she had three younger brothers. Gwen had to admit the woman seemed charming and smart and probably capable of being a great mother. Which was beyond depressing.

It didn't comfort Gwen to see that Melody was becoming increasingly agitated as Fentice's questioning of Brenda began to wind down. Her glances toward the door had taken on an intensity, as if Melody was willing someone to walk through it. But no one came.

"Cross?" Judge Landau asked.

With one more wishful look at the door and a sigh of resignation, Melody got to her feet and approached the witness stand. "Ms. Voight, do you have a Facebook page?" she asked.

Brenda looked puzzled, then said, "Doesn't everybody?"

"Objection!" cried Fentice.

Judge Landau's gaze pierced the petitioner's attorney. "Again, this is your witness. Just stop it. I'm pretty sure Ms. Michaels is about to provide some interesting details from the beloved and notorious Facebook." He looked to Melody. "Continue."

But Melody turned toward the door instead and paused, glaring at the wooden panels and brass hardware.

"Are you expecting someone, Ms. Michaels?" Landau asked.

She squared her shoulders. "I was hoping

for some visuals that were being prepared for this line of questioning. But I can go on without them." She turned back to Brenda. "Describe for the judge what kind of photos you have on your Facebook page."

"The usual pictures. Family, friends." But the woman squirmed ever so slightly in her seat.

"Are there photos of you at parties and—"

Before Melody could finish her sentence, the door into the courtroom whooshed open on nearly silent hinges. Everyone turned to see who Melody had been waiting for. Gwen turned, too. And saw Aaron Zimmerman striding forward with a sparkling new electronic tablet in his hand. He walked with purpose directly to Melody, who met him at the railing. She was smiling.

"Took you long enough," she whispered to him.

"Plane was delayed," he said.

"How'd it go?"

"Better than expected," he answered with a grin.

"Ahem," said Landau. "Can we get back to business?"

Melody turned to the judge, eTablet in hand. "The visuals have arrived, Your Honor. This line of questioning will go much more quickly now."

"Saints be praised," said the judge.

But Gwen heard this banter without much focus. Her attention was instead glued to Aaron, who smiled at her with serene certainty.

CHAPTER NINETEEN

GWEN WATCHED MELODY AND Fentice approach the bench to discuss the use of the eTablet to question the witness. Fentice objected, of course, but Landau seemed fascinated. The judge scrolled through the apps screens.

"Can I get instant stock trades on this thing?" Gwen heard him ask.

"Um, I think so, but we were hoping to use it to make a legal point," Melody said.

"Sure." He handed it back to her, saying to himself, "I'm gonna have to get a new one of those soon."

Melody brought the eTablet to Brenda. "I've opened the app for you. Would you please tell us what's on the screen, Ms. Voight?"

Brenda squirmed and looked to Fentice for help. Though Clayton nudged his attorney and whispered in his ear, Fentice didn't bother to object. He gave a defeated wave of his hand, indicating Brenda should do as asked.

With great reluctance, Brenda said, "It's a Facebook page."

"To whom does this Facebook page belong?"

"Me," Brenda said in nearly a whisper, sinking deeper into the witness chair as if she wanted to disappear.

"Will you please click on the photos portion of your Facebook page?" Melody asked.

Brenda sighed and did as she was asked.

"Now click on the album marked 'tags,' please."

She did that and sank slightly deeper into her chair.

"Are you in these pictures, Ms. Voight?" Melody asked.

"Yes, some of them," she said quietly. "But they aren't my photos. Someone tagged me in them just because I know the other people. I wouldn't put this kind of thing on my page." She glanced toward Clayton.

Gwen knew Clayton hadn't embraced technology with the enthusiasm of others his age. His expression remained impassive because he had no idea what was coming.

"And what are you doing in this photo?" Melody asked as she pointed to the eTablet.

"Partying?" Brenda tried.

"Does this photo show you holding a mirror with a line of something white and powdery?"

Melody didn't sound smug. In fact, she seemed to feel sorry for the woman.

"I was handing it to someone else," she tried. Then she turned toward the judge. "Can I plead the fifth?" Brenda asked, even as a horrified Clayton shot to his feet.

"I knew nothing about this!"

The judge banged his gavel and Clay sat back down. Melody gently took the eTablet from the witness and handed it to Landau. He flipped through the photos quickly and handed the eTablet back.

"I don't see Mr. Haverty in any of these photos," he said. "So get to your point, Ms. Michaels."

Melody turned to Brenda and held up the eTablet. "The party where this photo was taken—was Mr. Haverty with you at this particular event?"

Brenda's worried eyes shifted to Clay. He gave her the slightest shake of his head, telling her to deny it. But Melody gently reminded Brenda she was under oath and that other witnesses to the party could be called. Gwen felt sure this was a bluff, but it worked.

"He was there, but he wasn't doing any blow, as far as I know. And I was just watching what the others were doing. I didn't do any myself, but I—"

Clayton stood once more. "The engagement is off."

Brenda squinted at Clay. Then in measured words, she said, "You know, come to think of it, I didn't watch him the whole time and there were a lot of drugs at that party, and he stayed to the end, so maybe he did do some. He never complained about any of his friends who used."

As Clay fell back into his chair, Fentice stood. "We all get the point, Ms. Michaels. Can we move on?"

"Sure," Melody said. "I have no further questions of this witness."

Parker Fentice did his best to rehabilitate his client's reputation, spending much of the afternoon bringing in one witness after another to testify that Clayton was an upstanding citizen who would be the better choice for raising Joshua. There were additional witnesses who swore that Gwen was so focused on her career that she couldn't possibly provide for Joshua properly. Others were brought who'd witnessed her tirade against John Fry the day the boys were missing, allowing the lawyer to repeatedly bring up the possibility that Gwen was being treated by a psychiatrist. Melody objected to anything related to PTSD, but Judge Landau overruled her every time. Eventually he told her to sit down and be quiet.

"No additional witnesses, Your Honor," Fentice finally said.

"Really?" asked the judge. "I don't get to hear from Mr. Haverty directly?"

Clayton stood. "I'd be happy to answer any questions you may have, Your Honor. My attorney and I simply felt it best to let others provide unbiased testimony about my devotion to my son and my ability to raise him more appropriately."

"I don't have any questions for you, Mr. Haverty. I'm just surprised you're not taking the witness stand." Landau turned to Melody, then glanced at the clock. "Perhaps we should resume in the morning, Ms. Michaels?"

"I may have only one witness to call, Your Honor," she said. "Depending on how that goes, we could be finished tonight."

"Seriously?"

"Yes, Your Honor. But she wasn't on my witness list. I didn't think we'd persuade her to come or that we could get her here in time."

Landau gestured for the two attorneys to approach the bench. Gwen and her ex-husband stayed at their respective tables, but Clay looked across at her with anger in his eyes. Clay did not like to be thwarted.

This time, the judge reached for a switch and Gwen realized he'd engaged a sound dampening system. Having always been one of the people within the cone of silence at the judge's bench, she now realized how frustrating it was to have them talking without being able to hear them. Fentice appeared agitated and gestured as he spoke. The judge eventually cut him off. When Melody returned to the table, she was smiling.

"Well, let's see if we can get this done, then," he said, ready to push through to completion. "Call your witness, Ms. Michaels."

She wiped the grin from her face before she turned to the judge. Without looking at anyone else, she said, "Respondent calls Mrs. Charlotte Clayton Haverty to the witness stand."

Gwen turned toward the door. She'd swallowed her pride and contacted Charlotte, who had stayed in Italy well beyond her original plans. But Charlotte refused to speak against her son and wouldn't agree to come back to the U.S. for the hearing. Yet here she was, walking down the aisle toward the witness chair. Gwen's gaze met Aaron's once more. He was smiling and Gwen surmised he was responsible for bringing her mother-in-law here. She didn't share his glee, however. Charlotte had never liked Gwen. And she'd almost always sided with her son. Despite Joshua's insistence that his grandmother wanted him to be raised by his mother, Gwen felt certain this was going to be a disaster.

Clayton shot to his feet. "This is outrageous!"

Judge Landau hammered his gavel. But Clay looked down at his still-seated attorney and said, "You call yourself one of the best custody attorneys in the country? You couldn't even make sure my mother stayed in Italy and off the witness stand. You're fired. I'll take it from here."

AARON HAD USED EVERY ounce of his persuasive skills to get Charlotte Haverty to come back from Italy to testify for Gwen. In the end, he'd needed to arrange an international phone conversation between Charlotte and her grandson to finally win her cooperation. Joshua had prepared his plea to his grandmother before he'd run away to find her in Pittsburgh. He hadn't forgotten any of the points he'd wanted to make and Charlotte had been impressed. She would do as her grandson asked of her in court. At least that's what she'd promised.

Seeing the horror in Gwen's expression now made Aaron wonder if he and Melody had done the right thing. For all they knew Charlotte would not hold up her end of the bargain. Given the other evidence Fentice had presented, if Charlotte turned hostile, that could seal Joshua's fate and he'd go to his father. As Aaron's stomach roiled with doubt, he told himself Charlotte was too ornery and blunt to become a turncoat at the last minute. And as much as she didn't care for Gwen, Charlotte loved Joshua and wanted what was best for him. The grandmother had been adamant that being raised by her self-indulgent son would not do Josh any good, and Aaron could only hope she'd stick to that position. He watched the older woman walk with purpose and dignity to the witness stand.

The bailiff swore her to tell the truth, she agreed, and then she took her seat as if claiming her throne. Her brilliant blue eyes, enhanced by her perfectly coifed silver hair, gazed out upon the audience with cool disdain. She did not make eye contact with her son, who was seated alone now at the Petitioner's table.

"Thank you for coming all this way, Mrs. Haverty," Melody said to her.

Charlotte gave a regal nod. "Such are the burdens of a grandmother."

Aaron thought that comment boded well. He glanced at Gwen, sitting at the table. Her back was to him, but he could still see the tension suffusing every muscle. He wished he could reach forward and knead her shoulders to help her relax. Or maybe holding her hand would be enough. But he couldn't do that.

Melody took Charlotte through a series of questions that established her relationship to all the parties. Charlotte responded crisply, without embellishment.

"Mrs. Haverty, I know this may be difficult for you," Melody said. "But would you please tell the judge what you told me on the phone last week about who ought to be raising Joshua?"

"It's not difficult for me. I told you that Gwendolyn is the best person to raise my grandson. She certainly has her deficiencies, but Joshua wants to stay with her and with his friends at school. She's as good a parent as my son would be."

Gwen breathed a sigh of relief.

Naturally, Clayton was on his feet. "I object."

"On what grounds, for heaven's sake?" Landau asked.

"This is my mother. She shouldn't be coerced into serving as a witness for a former daughter-in-law she never liked."

Landau raised his eyebrows at that. Then

he faced Charlotte. "Do you feel in any way coerced, Mrs. Haverty?"

"Of course not. No one makes me do or say anything. Do sit down, Clayton. You're only making things worse."

"This is outrageous," he said to her.

"Nevertheless," she retorted.

The judge sighed. "Enough of the mother-son banter. Ms. Michaels, given that I'm clear on where you're going with this testimony, can you wrap things up soon?"

"Yes, Your Honor. I'd just like to simply ask Mrs. Haverty to explain some of the reasons she told Joshua he should stay with his mother." Melody looked expectantly at her witness.

"You haven't asked me a question yet," Charlotte said. But if this was how she intended to be difficult, Aaron was willing to accept it. Melody was, too, it seemed. She acquiesced to Charlotte's snarky comment.

"Mrs. Haverty, will you please tell the judge why you told Joshua he should remain in Gwendolyn's care?"

And she did. In colorful, detailed terms. She never said anything overtly bad about her son, even mentioned he wanted to be a good father, but pointed out that he tended to be as self-indulgent as she herself had always been. Which made Gwen the better guardian for Joshua.

She wound down after about ten minutes.

"Despite every effort on his father's part, Clayton took after me and has remained devoted mostly to himself. I love him, I suppose, as a mother is required to do. But I believe strongly that his desire for custody is not only about wanting what he believes is best for Joshua, but also because he needs to win a battle against Gwen. He may see her custody of his son as a failure on his part. But the most important thing in all this is that Joshua strongly desires to remain with his mother. He indicated to me that she is controlling and rigid and at home far less than she should be, but he is comfortable with her and his school and his friends."

She looked at her own son, sulking at the Petitioner's table. "If you would simply listen to your son, Clayton. He will tell you what he needs if you pay attention. Your child's future is at stake. Should you not at least hear his views?"

Aaron thought he heard Clayton mumble, "You never listened to *me*," but no one else seemed to catch this childish remark.

Then, bold as could be, Charlotte looked up at the judge. "I assume you will do the right thing by my grandson if it comes to that, sir. But would you be kind enough to allow for a short recess so Clayton can speak to Joshua for a moment? He's waiting outside with his other grandparents, just in case someone cares to consider his opinion in this matter."

Judge Landau was not amused. He scowled at the woman.

Melody shot to her feet. "I request a ten-minute recess, Your Honor."

Landau sighed, declared, "Ten minutes," and smacked his gavel. In another second, he had disappeared through the door behind the bench even before the bailiff could finish intoning "All rise."

"Mother, this is beyond imagination. How could you testify against me when all I want is to be a father to Joshua? I love him. I want what's best for him. I can get him into the best schools, hire the best nanny, introduce him to the best people to know."

Charlotte calmly left the witness stand and approached her son. "You have no idea what you're saying, Clayton. Parenting is a difficult job requiring endless sacrifices. You are not equipped. But more importantly, Joshua will do *best* under Gwen's care."

"You don't even like her. You never liked

her. Why would you side with her now?" Clayton asked.

"I'm not taking Gwendolyn's side, son. Never that. I'm taking Joshua's side. He's doing well enough with Gwen and he would do very badly with you. If you would consider your own lifestyle more objectively, perhaps even listen to what Joshua has to say for himself, you would know how this should all turn out." She stepped closer and lowered her voice. "You're not always a considerate person, Clayton, and I accept some responsibility for how you turned out. But I know I taught you right from wrong. In the end, I'm confident you will do the right thing for your child." She placed her blue-veined hand on Clayton's shoulder. "Talk to him," she urged.

With a reluctant nod, Clayton swept out of the room.

Aaron's gaze shifted to Gwen, who sat there, stunned and speechless, next to her equally silent attorney. But Charlotte walked over to him and he shifted his attention to her.

"Am I free to go?" she asked Aaron.

"Not yet," he told her. "There may be more questions. And Clayton can cross-examine you if he wants to."

"Perhaps you'd like to go back to the witness chair?" Aaron said to Charlotte. Then he escorted her there as if she were royalty. This kind of treatment had gone a long way toward persuading Charlotte to come home from Europe.

Aaron gave Gwen a reassuring look as he passed by to retake his place behind her. His thoughts shifted to the details of the hearing as he watched Gwen sink lower into her seat. Certainly, Charlotte's appearance had been a coup, but it hardly overcame the rest of the evidence. In particular, Gwen's very necessary treatment for PTSD might stand out as reason enough to award Clayton custody. When Melody reached over and plucked the pen from Gwen's hand, Aaron realized she had been nervously clicking it open and closed, open and closed.

"Sorry," she said to Melody.

"Pretend you're sure of the outcome, Gwen," Melody advised. "You know a show of confidence can make a difference."

Gwen nodded and sat up straighter just as the back door to the courtroom opened again and Clayton stormed inside. Scowling, he went to his seat.

In another moment, the bailiff told them to rise and the judge reseated himself at the bench. He brought the gavel down once and said, "Are we going to be finishing this tonight?" He looked from Melody to Clayton and then to Charlotte, as if he couldn't decide who was really running the show.

Melody stood. "We only have one—"

Clayton also got to his feet, cutting off what Melody had been about to say. "Your Honor, I'm withdrawing my petition for custody. I've come to realize belatedly that it would be in Joshua's best interest to remain under the care of his mother."

A stunned silence pervaded the courtroom. Even Judge Landau seemed unable to speak.

After a moment, Charlotte said, "Sometimes you actually come through on the big issues, Clayton. I'll give you that." Then her gaze drifted away as she rose from the witness stand and headed toward the exit.

Judge Landau hammered his gavel. "You haven't been dismissed yet," he said to Charlotte.

She turned and glared at him. "I've done what I came to do," she told him. "What more is there?"

Landau sulked a moment, looked from Petitioner to Respondent and back again. Then sighed. "Fine. Go."

Charlotte walked over to the spectator area and seated herself near Aaron. He had promised to take her to the airport so she could fly to Pittsburgh, now that her sojourn in Europe—and her duty to her grandson—was over. Aaron gave the older woman a reassuring smile. She didn't return it, but nodded slightly, as if accepting her due.

"Are we wrapping this up based on the withdrawal of the petition?" the judge asked.

Apparently, Melody shared Aaron's concern that Clayton would simply renew his claim on custody of Josh at some future date. "Your Honor," she said, "in light of this development, Respondent asks that you dismiss the petition for custody with prejudice and order custody of Joshua Haverty to remain with Gwendolyn Haverty as a matter of the best interest of the child."

"Granted. Petition dismissed with prejudice, barring unforeseen circumstances or significant changes in circumstances. And you'll get your court order in due course. I don't want the boy to have to go through any of this again without some serious cause." He glared at Clayton. To Melody, he said, "Anything else?"

"No, Your Honor." Her tone indicated she could hardly believe things had come to a close so fast. Aaron could hardly believe it himself.

The gavel came down with a resounding clack and the bailiff intoned, "All rise."

Before everyone could get to their feet, the judge was gone again. But this time, the courtroom erupted. Dozens of people moved toward Gwen with congratulatory words and pats on the back for Melody.

Some well-wishers approached Aaron and Charlotte, as well, but he kept his focus on Gwen. He hoped for a look from her, perhaps even a word—something that would help him discern how she felt about things between them now that the custody battle was over. It could go either way with her. She might be annoyed he'd interfered in her case when she'd specifically asked him not to. Or she might be happy he'd ignored her wishes and brought the witness who saved the day.

"Is it time to go to the airport?" Charlotte asked him.

He didn't respond because he saw Gwen begin to turn toward him. She seemed to move in slow motion. After an eternal second, she faced him. Her eyes showed astonishment, followed quickly by joy. A smile transformed her features and she shot out from the center of the crowd nearly enveloping her. Without thinking about it, he rose, too. In another second, she had her arms wrapped tightly around his neck in a stranglehold of happiness. Even though the railing remained between them, this was as close as he'd been able to get to her all week. She was warm and soft and happy and he loved her with all his heart. He'd come to terms with this weeks ago and resolved that loving Gwen didn't take anything away from what he'd had with Beth.

"Ahem!" Charlotte said.

"Get a room," Melody teased. Her comment brought Gwen back to her more restrained self and she retreated a step. Her expression turned uncertain. "Sorry."

She looked down at the floor, then at her mother-in-law and Logan. Her attention shifted to Clayton, who was packing up notes and books. At last, she turned back to Aaron, but only for a moment. In that brief glance, Aaron saw the confusion of emotions she suffered. He knew right then she wasn't ready for him yet. He would have to be patient, give her time. The therapy she'd been having for post-traumatic stress would have been emotionally draining, and she would have to practice a new way of coping with her memories and reactions. She needed time to heal before he asked her to explore their feelings for each other.

"Thank you, Aaron," said Melody. "I couldn't have pulled this off without you."

"Yes, thank you for this," Gwen said softly. "You gave me and Josh the best chance we

could have of never going through this again."
Gwen still wouldn't meet his eyes. He hated
to see her so unsure.

"It was my pleasure. Joshua deserves the
upbringing you'll give him. Right now, I have
to make good on my promise to escort Mrs.
Haverty to the airport for her flight home to
Pittsburgh."

Gwen smiled hesitantly as she looked at her
mother-in-law. Softly, she said, "Charlotte.
Thank you."

Charlotte stared coolly at Gwen a moment,
then said, "I did it for Joshua. He asked for my
help and I gave it. You can return my kindness
by insuring your son knows about what I did
today."

"Perhaps you should tell him yourself. He's
just outside the courtroom with my father. And
perhaps you'd like to visit with him, maybe
even stay at the house for a few days." Gwen
sounded sincere, but Aaron could tell she
dreaded that Charlotte might accept.

The cool stare turned disdainful. "I'm going
home. Aaron is escorting me to the airport.
He promised to have my house open and aired
before my arrival, so I assume that's been
done."

"Yes, ma'am," Aaron said.

Gwen nodded, but Charlotte had one more thing to say.

"However, I would like to visit another time to see for myself that you're doing a proper job. Perhaps in the spring. Don't make me regret what I've done here today, Gwendolyn."

To her credit, Gwen didn't seem to take offense. Instead, she smiled and said, "We'd love to have you." Then, to Aaron's surprise, she hugged her mother-in-law. It was awkward, but also touching when Charlotte lifted her hand tentatively to Gwen's shoulder and patted gently.

When the two women stepped apart, Charlotte raised her palm to ward off the others waiting to thank her—Gwen's mother, Misha, other friends. "Get me to the airport, young man," she said to Aaron.

He took her elbow and played bodyguard, gently making a path through the crowd so he could get her out of there.

"You did that quite well," she said to him when they were in the hallway. "You should—"

But whatever she'd been about to say was cut off when Josh crashed into her and hugged her around the waist. "Gramma Char!"

"Joshua Clayton Haverty, mind your manners," she admonished as she just about peeled the child from her.

Josh seemed immune to her disdain. "Misha came out and told me what happened. Thank you for what you did."

"Now you'd best keep up your end of the bargain, young man."

"I will," he said. Then he saw his mother exiting to the hallway and he ran to her.

"I haven't had the chance to add my own words of gratitude for all this," Aaron said. "Thank you, Charlotte. We're all grateful."

She sniffed slightly, as if his comment deserved no reply. But then she added, "Joshua had best keep the promise I extracted from him when I agreed to come back—he must improve his marks in school. I assume you will make sure that happens. Now go fetch your car. My plane leaves in two hours and there's all that fuss getting through security."

Aaron grinned and did what the lady demanded. But before he left the building, he glanced over his shoulder for a glimpse of Gwen. He wanted to see her happy and relieved of the fears that had dogged her all these months. He got his wish. She was laughing with Misha, one arm draped over Joshua's shoulders.

How long should he wait before he called

her? Could he give her a few weeks, maybe a month? That wasn't very long, but it seemed like forever. He'd have to stay in close contact with Melody so he'd know how she was doing while he waited for the right moment. Otherwise, he'd be knocking on her door as soon as he'd dropped Charlotte off at the airport. With a growl of frustration, he forced himself to turn away to go fetch the car.

CHAPTER TWENTY

IT SEEMED LIKE FOREVER since Gwen had seen Aaron. And to add insult to injury, he no longer represented Release Initiative, so she was up against younger and less experienced attorneys. There was little challenge in that. Gwen missed him. Despite all the things about him she'd told herself she couldn't bear, she longed to see him again.

In the two weeks that had passed since Clay had capitulated and Judge Landau had decreed full custody of Joshua would remain with Gwen, she hadn't heard a whisper from Aaron. She recalled him telling her he understood she needed time. Maybe he'd been right about that, but two weeks seemed like enough time. She'd nearly finished her treatment with her psychiatrist and hadn't had any more bouts of rage or nightmares or confusion between past and present. She felt as free of Clayton Haverty as she ever would.

Joshua saw Ben at karate class, but Phyllis had served as Ben's chauffeur instead of

Aaron. Gwen had asked a few times if he wanted to have his friend over on the weekend. Josh had quietly declined her offers. And there had been no invitations for Josh to go to Ben's house.

She really missed Aaron—his smile, his serenity, his concern for others. During the day, she was too busy with her job and her son to focus much on this longing. But at night, lying in her bed alone, she had time to remember his kiss and his touch and his passion. She remembered he wanted her to be full partner in their lovemaking. And how her acceptance of that responsibility had made the experience all the more memorable.

When her cell phone rang, she jumped. And realized she'd been sitting at her desk at work, daydreaming. A file and several law books sat open before her, but she couldn't remember what she'd been researching. The cell kept ringing, and a tingle of excitement ran through her, from scalp to toes, as she irrationally thought maybe Aaron was finally calling her. She answered a little breathlessly.

"What is your problem?" Melody asked.

Gwen fought off disappointment. "What?"

"You've got custody of your son and your idiot boss had the sense not to fire you. So what are you waiting for?"

"I don't understand," Gwen said.

Melody sighed loudly into the phone. "I just got another call from Aaron. You remember him? Aaron Zimmerman? Used to make you crazy in court and most likely in bed, too?"

"Melody!" Gwen looked around the room to see if anyone had heard that. She remembered too late that she was alone in her office and talking to her friend on the phone. No one could hear. But it felt as if Melody had taken the thoughts right out of her head. Gwen's cheeks went hot.

"Don't you 'Melody' me. You know full well—"

Gwen cut her off as the words all came to her at once. "Why did Aaron call you? Is everyone okay? Is something wrong with Ben? Is Phyllis all right? Did you say 'another' phone call from Aaron?"

Melody didn't respond right away and Gwen had time to realize what her rush of questions meant. She needed Aaron and his family, needed to be with them. She loved them all— Phyllis and Ben and Aaron. Especially Aaron. It was her turn to sigh.

"Everyone is fine. Aaron called me to see how you and Josh are doing. He's called me just about every day since the trial with the same questions. I'm not your answering service, Gwen. Call him, for God's sake. Better yet, go see him."

"I didn't know he was calling you. Why would he do that? Why not just call me directly?" Oh, how she'd wanted him to call.

"I asked him that, of course. Something stupid about you not wanting to see him and also that you need time to get in touch with your feelings and how that's okay, but he wanted to make sure you and Josh are doing fine."

"I didn't say I don't want to see him," Gwen shouted.

"Harrumph."

"Okay, maybe I did. But that was before. I only meant that while I was fighting for custody."

"Then what the hell, Gwen? Why haven't *you* called *him*?"

Now that was a stumper. Gwen had no idea why she hadn't called him. No, wait, she did have an idea—she didn't like to take responsibility for her love life. For her whole adult existence, interactions with men had been initiated by them, never by her. She'd been pursued and then somewhere along the way, she decided she'd allow herself to be conquered. That was her pattern. But it hadn't worked out so well for her.

"Damn," she whispered to herself. Melody heard her.

"What does that mean?"

"It means I'm an idiot."

"You sure are," Melody agreed. She sounded happier than when the conversation had begun. "Okay, then, my work here is done. Call me after you've gotten laid." And she clicked off the phone.

Gwen sat very still and contemplated phoning Aaron herself. What would she say? She sighed again. For a kick-ass attorney, she was a complete wimp when it came to men. Especially Aaron. Because there was this little doubt dancing in the back of her mind that Aaron was really calling Melody to check on Josh and only incidentally to ask about her. What if he rejected her? That would be crushing. And as strong as she pretended to be, she really had a very vulnerable heart. Especially when it came to Aaron.

Much later, as she lay in bed with the covers pulled up to her chin, alone again, Gwen went over several ways she could approach a phone call to Aaron. She reviewed different strategies, talked through several possible speeches, imagined as many varieties of responses from him as she could. Then she realized she was planning her first contact with Aaron the same way she planned her questions to a witness. Frustrated, she turned on her side, determined to sleep.

TWO DAYS LATER, AS SHE walked to the coffee shop—the same one where she and Aaron had accidentally picked up each other's BlackBerries, she held her phone to her ear, listening to Logan.

"So the meeting with Ms. Smith-Calley was postponed," he said. "It'll be rescheduled for early next week. I'll take care of that for you."

"Thanks. You've been a big help, Logan. I'll be back in the office in an hour or so."

"Wait. There's one more thing," he said. There was a note of tension in his voice.

Gwen stopped in her tracks on the sidewalk, despite the cold wind whipping at the hem of her coat and skirt. She hoped he was not about to declare his barely concealed romantic interest in her. They'd been dancing around his attraction for weeks now, and Gwen just didn't have the reserves to deal with it today.

"I really have to get going," she said, but he started speaking before she'd finished the sentence.

"Melody Michaels left a crazy message for you on the office answering machine. Why didn't she call your cell, like she usually does?

Whatever. Here's the quote from her message. 'Tell Gwendolyn to call him soon or so help me I will bring him to her office in person.' That's the whole message. What is she talking about?"

Gwen had to laugh. "She's just being Melody. Don't worry about it."

"Okay, well, that's it," Logan said.

Gwen felt a pang for her long-suffering assistant. "Listen, Logan. There's this pretty young college woman I know. Very cute, very smart, unattached. You may have seen her at the custody hearing. Misha? I think you two would hit it off. Can I give her your number?"

Silence for a few beats. Then, "Sure. Why not? And if she calls me, you'll be forced to give me the time off from this crazy schedule you make me keep."

Gwen laughed outright, feeling really good about Logan for the first time in a while. "That's a deal. And I'm pretty sure she'll want to call if I put in a good word for you."

"Okay," he said. "Not certain I really want to date the boss's babysitter, but what the hell."

"Okay, then. I'll see you in an hour."

As she clicked off the connection, Gwen started walking again, desperate for a venti latte. The door to the coffee shop jingled merrily as she entered. The gas flame in a tiny fireplace embedded in the wall warmed the interior against the November chill. The aroma of coffee and cookies reminded her of her mother and father, who were already talking about coming for another visit, hoping for a less dramatic experience over the Christmas holiday.

The barista was the same one who'd been serving here for several months. Gwen smiled at her. "How are you today, Sandra?"

"It's a great day for coffee. What can I get for you?" she asked, as chipper as ever.

"Venti latte, no sweetener."

"Coming right up."

Gwen paid for her drink, then moved to the end of the counter to await her order. She glanced around the room, only half full at midmorning. Her gaze was drawn to the table where she and Aaron had begun their odyssey, and she froze. He was sitting there again, in the same seat.

He'd cut his hair. And he wore an actual suit that must have been recently purchased. It appeared to be tailored to fit him, for once. He looked a little tired. But he was smiling and that warmed her heart. She drank in the sight of him.

As she looked at him, he laughed lightly and she wanted to know what made him happy.

That's when she realized he sat across from a woman. A pretty woman, also in a suit, who wore her blond hair down around her shoulders and gestured with her hands when she spoke. Aaron's eyes danced with amusement as he listened to her.

Gwen's thoughts crashed together like dark clouds; she'd waited too long to contact him, but she would not let him go without a fight. She left the barista holding her steaming latte and marched toward Aaron's table. She had no idea what she would say or what the possible outcomes of a public confrontation might be. She acted on impulse. An impulse completely outside her comfort zone.

"Hello, Aaron," she said as she came to stand beside the table. She pointedly ignored the blonde, though she knew this was rude.

He got immediately to his feet. "Gwen," he said, almost a whisper.

"I've been meaning to call you," she began. "I should have done it a long time ago." The words started to flood out of her mouth and she had little control over what she was saying for the first time in her life. "I guess I was hoping you'd call *me,* because you know I'm not good at taking the lead in relationships. But then again, I suppose I should work on getting over that tendency. It hasn't done me a bit of good so far. And anyway, I just want to say that I've been thinking about you and that, well, to be honest, I've missed you. Because when I was with you, I felt better about everything. You just have this calmness and sureness about you that helps me focus and get past the unimportant things."

The woman was listening with interest, but Gwen went on before she lost her nerve. Looking once more into Aaron's warm gaze, she said, "And you're smart, smarter than I gave you credit for when we opposed each other in court. Plus, you're good with Josh—and I know I was upset at first when you thought you were the one who put the idea into the kids' heads to take matters into their own hands, but I talked to Josh and found out how desperate he'd been feeling for a long time, and that running away was something he'd been toying with for a while." She shook her head ever so slightly, knowing she was getting off track and trying to remember all the things she'd planned to say to him if she ever got the chance.

"Gwen," Aaron said again, very softly. He placed one of his hands on her upper arm, as if to stop her.

"No. Let me finish. This all needs to be said, even though I can see you've moved on.

It's important that I say the things I should have said long ago, even if they're too late. The thing is, I need you in my life and wish I hadn't been such a fool, waiting for you to make it happen. I should have gone to you right after the custody hearing and celebrated with you the way I wanted to. You're the reason I have my son with me and I should have thanked you for your awesome legal work and told you how much I appreciate all you've done for Josh and me. You're a wonderful man and an amazing attorney. We would have made such a great team, with me bringing the stability and you bringing the adventure. The boys would have done well with us as their parents. I would have done well, too." She glanced again at the woman Aaron had been talking to. The blonde seemed stunned.

But Gwen figured she was in pretty deep now and there was no reason to stop. "I just want you to know, well, you're an amazing person and I will always love you."

She stopped, hardly believing she'd said those last words out loud. Had she ever said them to any other man? Not that she could recall. And now she'd spoken them in public in a humiliating display. Embarrassing to the max, for Aaron and for her. "I'm sorry," she whispered.

"Don't be," he said. "I fell in love with you a long time ago. I'm damned relieved you've come around to doing the same." And he drew her into his arms and kissed her, right there in the coffee shop.

As surprise and relief and happiness suffused her, she thought she heard some whoops and cheers and clapping all around her. But then she was lost in Aaron's tender kiss and the realization that he wanted her still, that she was *not* too late. By the time Aaron pulled away from her, she felt weak-kneed and breathless.

"Okay, you're hired," said Aaron's companion.

"What?" Gwen didn't understand.

"I was interviewing Mr. Zimmerman for a position with my nonprofit legal service. After hearing all his qualities, legal and otherwise, I'd be a fool not to hire him." She got to her feet and slung her purse strap over her shoulder. "What do you say, Mr. Zimmerman? Do you want the job?"

"I do," Aaron said to her. "Thank you, Ms. Walker." He held out his hand to shake.

Gwen felt fresh embarrassment creep over her. "I'm so sorry for intruding."

Ms. Walker remained focused on her newest employee. "How about we see you in the office a week from Monday. Does that work for you?"

"Yes, it works very well." Aaron said.

The woman turned to Gwen. "Way to get your man, Ms. Haverty. Gutsy. So don't be sorry. I doubt I could have done the same."

"Desperation sometimes makes us do crazy things," Gwen said.

The woman laughed. "I hope you and I will be getting to know each other in the near future. For now, enjoy what you fought for."

Gwen smiled at her. "I will," she said as she watched Aaron's new boss head for the door. That's when Gwen realized everyone in the coffee shop stared at them, smiling. She wanted to crawl under a table and hide, she was so horrified by her public emotional nakedness. It was one thing to be center stage in a courtroom and another thing entirely to be stared at for baring her soul.

But Aaron saved the day again. "Refills for everyone on me!" he shouted.

The crowd cheered and headed for the smiling barista. At last Gwen could breathe again.

"I have to show you something," Aaron said to her. He didn't wait for her to agree, but just took out his BlackBerry and thumbed through the menu until he found what he wanted. "Look at this and know you are loved."

She took his phone and looked at the text message from Ben. Did u get job? I no u did. Now pls call Gwen so me & Josh don't hve 2 do r plan. Luv, B.

Gwen looked up into Aaron's eyes. "Is he joking or threatening?"

"Don't know yet," Aaron said with a grin.

"What was their plan?" she asked, feeling a little afraid of the scheming these two kids were so good at.

"I have no idea," Aaron said. "But together, I'm sure we can cope with all the plans our boys have in store for us."

* * * * *